S

ON THE LEVELS

An addictive crime thriller full of twists

DAVID HODGES

Detective Kate Hamblin Mysteries Book 12

Joffe Books, London
www.joffebooks.com

First published in Great Britain in 2023

Cover art by Nick Castle

ISBN: 978-1-83526-149-1

This book is dedicated to my darling wife, Elizabeth, for all her love, patience and support over so many wonderful years and to my late mother and father, whose faith in me to one day achieve my ambition as a writer remained steadfast throughout their lifetime and whose tragic passing has left a hole in my life that will never be filled.

AUTHOR'S NOTE

Although the action of this novel takes place in the Avon & Somerset Police area, the story itself and all the characters in it are entirely fictitious. At the time of writing, there is *no* police station in Highbridge. This has been drawn entirely from the author's imagination to ensure no connection is made between any existing police station or personnel in the force. Some poetic licence has been adopted in relation to the local police structure and specific operational police procedures to meet the requirements of the plot. But the novel is primarily a crime thriller and does not profess to be a detailed police procedural, even though the policing background, as depicted, is broadly in accord with the national picture. I trust that these small departures from fact will not spoil the reading enjoyment of serving or retired police officers for whom I have the utmost respect.

David Hodges

BEFORE THE FACT

The party was in full swing. The wayside hostelry just minutes from the university campus was shaking under the blast of two fifty-watt ultrasonic speakers strategically placed in opposite corners of the large function room. Among the array of flashing, multi-coloured lights shadowy figures jerked and twisted in a grotesque parody of modern dance to the cacophonous challenge of electronic synthesizers. In the midst of the dissonance a caterwauling female singer did her best to rupture her larynx as she tried futilely to compete with the overwhelming power of the instrumental backing.

After three years of hard graft in the various disciplines they had undertaken, graduation had finally been achieved and the youthful strivers were determined to let their hair down and celebrate in style before receiving their awards at the following day's degree ceremony. But not everyone was on the floor giving it their all. In a private room next door a small clique less enthused by the deafening music lounged in worn, upholstered chairs behind the tightly closed door, either drinking from cans of lager or bottles of vodka and taking it in turns to snort from the lines of cocaine that were deposited on the long coffee table in front of them. Having all shared the eight-room house on the outskirts of the small provincial town for the past two years, following their first twelve months as freshers living in rooms on the campus, it had seemed only right that they should have a last hurrah together before going their separate ways.

But rather than a hurrah, the gathering was about to develop into something of a conspiracy centred on the empty pint glass at one end of the coffee table. The "owner" of the glass, one Francis Templeton, had unwisely left it unattended while he went to find a toilet — and that had not gone unnoticed by the rest of his housemates.

The heavyset man with the shoulder-length black hair who had been bending over the coffee table straightened up and wiped some of the white powder from his nostrils. The twenty-five-year-old son of a wealthy investment banker in the city, Ronnie Brewer was the undisputed darling of the ladies with his craggy film star looks and muscular frame and he liked to see himself as the leader of the pack. But on this occasion, heady with a mixture of alcohol and coke, he was showing a very different side to his personality.

'Where's that tosser, Francis, gone?' he demanded, throwing a sour glance at the empty chair by the door. 'It's his round.'

On the other side of the coffee table, twenty-three-year-old Jeffrey Cartwright lit a cigarette and chuckled through the smoke, the dark, restless eyes in the pale, consumptive looking face glinting maliciously and the slightly crooked mouth affecting a lopsided smirk.

'That's the best time to go for a pee, Ronnie — when it's your round,' he sneered to general laughter.

The blonde-haired young woman in the tight, white trousers and seriously cropped top, who was sitting on the windowsill behind Brewer, looked up from studying the silver pendant dangling from her exposed navel. 'Exactly right, Jeff,' Abbey Granger agreed. 'That way your glass will be refilled by someone else while you're away.'

Brewer wasn't amused. Particularly as he didn't like Francis Templeton anyway and along with the rest of the group, was intensely jealous of the first-class BA Honours their unpopular, studious housemate was due to receive at the ceremony the next day. No one else in the room had managed more than a 2:2.

'Well, it's not going to work,' he said. 'It's that little jerk's turn and he's going to put his hand in his pocket like everyone else.'

There was sudden movement close to the vacant chair as tubby, ginger-haired teacher's son, George Lane, held up Templeton's empty beer glass in one podgy, freckled hand as if he were still at school. 'Tell you what,' he said, 'why don't we just order double vodkas when he gets back? That would teach him a lesson.'

'And what if he refuses to pay, man?' another deep voice chimed in. 'We could be saddled with the bill.' At twenty-six, bearded and totally bald, former chef and fitness fanatic, Lenny Welch, was the oldest one there. Born in Birmingham, but of Jamaican heritage, he had a quiet, reasoned approach to everything and was generally listened to by the others.

'Yeah,' Jimmy Caulfield piped up next to him. 'We'd look pretty stupid then, wouldn't we?' With his wispy beard, which he picked at constantly, and the palest of blue eyes, Caulfield was not the sort of twenty-three-year-old ex-grammar school boy to stand out in a crowd or to endear himself to anyone. In fact, he was a bit of an oddball. But as someone who ran with the hares and hunted with the hounds, he was an excellent social survivor and for that reason he had fitted well into the group, something Francis Templeton had never managed to do.

'I've got a much better idea,' Brewer said suddenly, his scowl replaced by a malicious grin. 'Let's *all* buy him another drink and fill his glass with the lot.'

The ginger-haired young woman sitting a little way back from the coffee table who had not yet contributed to the conversation, shook her head quickly. Tammy Morrison was a former hospital casualty nurse, who had resigned her job after conflict with the management and was keen to pursue a new career in psychiatry. 'Spike his drink, you mean?' she said, her eyes widening behind the slightly tinted lenses of her blue, plastic-framed spectacles. 'That's not nice. I don't believe in doing things like that to anyone. It could be dangerous.'

'Oh, Tam,' Brewer responded. 'We wouldn't give him anything really nasty. Just a little mix to teach him a lesson for being such a prick.'

She smiled uncertainly. 'As long as it's not too heavy,' she said. 'I don't want him to end up in the ICU.'

Brewer slapped his thigh. 'Then we're all agreed? We can call it the Francis Cocktail.'

* * *

Francis Templeton left the pub a lot earlier than he had originally intended. After that last drink, he'd come over strangely ill. His head felt numb and he was having difficulty maintaining his balance and focusing his eyes. He'd been sick twice, but it hadn't made much difference. If anything, he was feeling a lot worse. He realised now that his drink had been spiked. He ought to have realised there was something wrong when he'd got back from the toilet to find a fresh pint waiting for him, despite it being his turn to buy the next round. But at the time he hadn't thought anything of it, assuming that whoever had bought it was just being generous. Now all he wanted to do was get back to the shared house and doss down for his last night. Shut out the world of spinning lights and whispering voices in the comfort of total blackout, in the hope he would be recovered early enough to attend his graduation in the morning.

He had always been the odd one out. He knew his other housemates laughed at him behind his back because he liked to drink milk and wasn't keen on boozy nights out, preferring to stay in his room listening to classical music while he studied. He was also aware of the fact that they had him down as a weirdo and called him a "tosser" behind his back. But he had never been any good at mixing and he'd been determined to get the highest grade he could on his graduation. He'd owed that much to his late parents who had sacrificed everything to put him through private school and then university. The old man had died in a car accident just three years after Francis' mother's death from a stroke, but he wasn't about to let them down just to fit in with a load of "Hooray Henrys" and "Henriettas".

Anyway, in a few hours it would all be over and he could head home with his prized parchment. All he had to do now was get himself back to the house tonight, though he sensed that in the state he was in that was going to be something of a challenge. Funny how the rest of his housemates had not come after him to make sure he was okay, but he wasn't surprised. Seeing him reeling about in the corridor outside the private room had clearly given them the entertainment they were looking for and they weren't interested in what he did after that. So much for so-called camaraderie, which he could certainly have done with at that precise moment.

He should have stuck to the top road back to Bridge House, of course, but it was a distance of at least a couple of miles and he wasn't sure he was capable of managing such a lengthy walk unaided, so he plumped for the shorter route via the riverside track he'd used before. Getting from the front door of the pub to the footpath without assistance had turned out to be even more of an effort of will than he'd anticipated and the foaming rush of the river bordering it all the way to the bridge now sounded like the roar of a furnace as he finally began to edge his way along the muddy track. There was a full moon, which should have been welcome, but its light seemed over-bright, dazzling him when it penetrated the overhanging branches of the trees lining the way and causing him to stop briefly to grab at a convenient branch or trunk to steady himself. Still, he mused, he was nearly there. Just twenty to thirty more yards to go.

In fact, he was about halfway to the bridge and the safety of the house when he slipped. Before he realised what was happening, he had pitched sideways off the path, his arms flailing the air in panic. Then the roar of the fast-running river was suddenly muted as the icy black water closed over his head and he was whirled round and round in the grip of the powerful current and propelled at breakneck speed towards the underground quarry workings beyond the weir . . .

* * *

'I bet Templeton is flat out in there,' Ronnie Brewer chuckled when he and the others got back to the house at just after midnight and trooped upstairs to their rooms. 'Shall we take a look?'

'Can't you leave the poor guy alone?' Tammy Morrison said wearily. 'We've had our fun. It's time for bed.'

But Brewer wasn't listening and he paused by Templeton's bedroom on the first landing and pressed his ear against the door. 'Not a sound,' he said. 'Obviously sleeping like a baby. Boy, will he have a head when he collects his certificate this morning.'

Raising a finger to his lips, he carefully eased the door open and peered inside. Moonlight flooded the room, revealing that Templeton's bed was empty and was still neatly made up, suggesting it hadn't been slept in.

Frowning, Brewer snapped on the light and stared around the room. 'Not in here,' he said, stepping back in surprise.

'What do you mean?' Morrison said as they all crowded the doorway to stare past him. 'He must have left the pub a couple of hours before us.'

Brewer shrugged. 'Well, unless he was so pissed he dossed in the wrong room, I don't know where he's got to.'

A search of the house soon kicked that theory to touch.

Morrison looked very worried now. 'But we saw him leave the pub,' she exclaimed, 'and it's only a short walk back here along the road.' She stared quickly at the other frowning faces. 'We-we would have spotted him just now if he had passed out enroute.'

'Maybe he didn't use the road like us,' Cartwright said, staring at her and holding her gaze. 'Could be he took the shorter route.'

'What? The riverside walk?' Abbey Granger put in. 'Only an idiot would use that muddy path in the dark. It's dangerous.'

'He was pissed,' Lenny Welch reminded them, as if that answered the question. 'He may not have been thinking straight.'

'We'd better go and look for him,' Morrison exclaimed. 'It's our fault if he's fallen down somewhere.'

Moments later their torches were waving wildly among the trees lining the footpath as they called out Templeton's name repeatedly. But the only answer they got was the angry roar of the river.

'This is pointless,' Brewer said finally after they had returned to the pub, found it locked up for the night, and retraced their steps. 'We're wasting our time.'

'So where is he?' Morrison shouted, her panic infecting the rest. 'What if-if he slipped and fell in the river?'

'If he did, he'll be in the old quarry workings by now, the speed of that current,' Jimmy Caulfield said helpfully.

'We ought to call the police,' George Lane suggested. 'They'll get a search going.'

'And what good would that do, in the dark this time of night?' Brewer snapped, 'especially if he reappeared in the morning, making us look like fools. No, we're best leaving things until daylight before we do anything. See if he turns up.'

'And what if he *has* fallen in the river?' Morrison demanded. 'Are we just going to walk away and do nothing?'

Brewer was plainly rattled by the suggestion and he snapped right back at her more brutally than he had intended. 'If he went in there then he'll be a goner anyway. Nothing we can do about it now.'

'I agree with Ronnie,' Cartwright commented. 'Best we wait until daylight.' He forced a short laugh. 'I can't see Templeton missing his own graduation ceremony.'

There was a ripple of half-hearted, uneasy laughter.

'Exactly,' Brewer said. 'Now I'm going to bed. We'll probably have a good laugh about all this after the graduation ceremony.'

* * *

But they didn't. Francis Templeton was nowhere to be seen in the big, packed hall on the campus where the graduation ceremony was held in the morning. As all the other students began to drift away with their parents and partners after the certificates had been presented and the customary photographs had been taken, the seven of them temporarily shed their relatives, ostensibly for final goodbyes, and met up in the deserted common room.

'I've re-checked Francis' room,' Tammy Morrison said. 'There's no sign of him, his bed hasn't been slept in and he hasn't even packed up his stuff.'

'Was anyone coming to collect him after graduation?' Brewer asked.

She shook her head. 'Parents dead, and no other family as far as I know. He told me he was going to catch a train home to wherever that was after the presentation. But what's that got to do with anything? I thought we were going to report his disappearance to the police this morning.'

Brewer snorted. 'And what would we tell them? That we think one of our housemates must have fallen into the river and drowned last night after we spiked his drink? Look good that, wouldn't it? We might even end up on a potential manslaughter charge.'

'But-but what are we going to do then?' George Lane said, his face pale and registering a tic in his right cheek.

'Nothing. We let the whole thing run its course. It's all very tragic, but we have to keep things in perspective. No one suggested Templeton should walk back along the river bank when he was pissed. It was his own fault.'

'Yeah,' Cartwright agreed. 'Why should we ruin the rest of our lives by getting the police involved over an unfortunate accident?'

'But we did it to him. We-we killed him,' Lane persisted. 'We'll end up just like the crowd in that-that old Columbia film we all watched. Remember? *I Know What You Did Last Summer*. That guy those kids ran over, he came back from the dead and went after them.' His voice had risen to a higher falsetto and he was visibly trembling, obviously very near the edge. 'It'll be the same with us. We'll never be allowed to get away with it.'

'Don't talk crap, George,' Lenny Welch said angrily. 'Get a grip on yourself, man. That was just a bloody film. Anyway, no one killed Francis. *If* he is dead then he did it all by himself. End of.'

Morrison stared at each of them in turn, horrified by some of the things that had been said. 'So what happens when questions start being asked as to why a dedicated student like him didn't turn up to receive his top grade degree certificate? Or come the new term, another student moves into his room and finds all his stuff still there?'

'Yes,' Abbey Granger put in dramatically, her eyes widening, 'or if-if his, you know what, is later found in the river?'

'Okay,' Brewer acknowledged reluctantly, 'so there'll be a police inquiry. Standard practice. But what's that to do with us? If the police get in touch and ask us about it later, all we say is that the eight of us were drinking at the pub and he must have wandered off on his own somewhere.'

'Exactly,' Lenny Welch finished for him. 'We just keep schtum about everything else. They can't expect us to be our brother's keeper.'

Morrison shook her head several times. Feeling her legs starting to give way, she sat down heavily on a convenient chair. 'I can't believe this is happening. It's all so wrong.'

'Wrong or not,' Jimmy Caulfield pointed out, 'it's the only solution, it really is.'

Brewer nodded. 'Dead right. So we've just got to put it behind us and move on.' He stared at each of them in turn. 'And don't forget, we were all responsible for spiking Templeton's drink, so we're all equally guilty.'

That sobering truth settled on the shoulders of them all like a cold, dead hand.

CHAPTER 1

Early afternoon on a bleak winter's day. It had been a long drive from London and the couple in the black Volvo XC90 could never have been more relieved to spot the finger post pointing down a track leading off the winding lane they were negotiating. They had been following it for the best part of an hour across the desolate snow-carpeted countryside of the Somerset Levels and both were desperate for a warm fire and a strong drink to restore their flagging spirits.

'Warneford Hall Hotel,' the young woman in the front passenger seat said triumphantly. 'At last.'

The heavyset man with the collar-length black hair who was behind the wheel swung hard right and eased the big four-by-four through the narrow opening between high banks surmounted by skeletal hedges. The heavy car slithered in the deepening snow, then righted itself and trundled on.

'Sat nav says another mile and a half,' he said, and pointed towards a cluster of tall chimneys rising above a patch of woodland in the distance. 'Looks like the place there, in the dip.'

She cast dubious glances through wide gaps in the hedges. Empty fields dissected by bare, thorny hedgerows practically buried in the snow and lines of coppiced willow trees stretched away in every direction. Here and there her gaze caught the glint of water where the deep irrigation ditches, or rhynes as they were called in this part of the world, cut through the overall whiteout, but for the most part it was a monotonous, unwelcoming landscape which held little invitation to explore.

She frowned. 'Pretty remote spot, though, isn't it? Sort of *banshee* country, don't you think?'

Ronnie Brewer chuckled. 'From what I hear, you're more likely to encounter the dreaded *hinky-punks* — what they call will-o'-the-wisps, in this part of the world — than banshees. Just don't go chasing any eerie blue lights in the middle of the night, that's all.'

His attractive girlfriend of two months shivered. 'You can bet on that,' Victoria Adams murmured with a slight shiver. Then she broke off as just after they had crossed a decrepit looking wooden bridge, which seemed to shake under the weight of the heavy vehicle, they slid to a halt before a pair of open, wrought-iron gates set in a six- to seven-foot high wall. To one side of the gates a tired wooden sign read *Warneford Hall Hotel*, but the sign itself was partly obscured by a banner stuck across it diagonally, bearing the words *FOR SALE* in bold red letters.

'For sale?' Brewer exclaimed. 'That's a surprise. Looks like our stay here might be shorter than we expected.'

'Suits me,' Adams murmured. 'Shall we turn around now?'

He chuckled again. 'Where's your spirit of adventure, Vicky? We'll only be here for a couple of days. Then it'll be back to your favourite partying set in the Smoke.'

She grimaced. 'Can't wait,' she retorted. 'I've got bad vibes about this place.'

'Rubbish,' he countered. 'How could you have? You haven't even seen it yet.'

But his incredulous whistle seemed at direct variance to that dismissive retort when he eased the car through the gateway and the hotel came into view at the end of a long tree-lined driveway.

Built of grey stone, its walls visibly scaling from the insidious creeping damp to which the marshy climate of the Levels had subjected it for so many years, Warneford Hall was a gloomy looking two-storey property. It had a pitched slate roof, triple-pot chimney stacks at each end and an ugly clocktower, with a crenelated top to it, rising from the centre of the building. There was a single-storey, wooden outhouse to one side of the hotel and beyond it the skeletal remains of what seemed to have once been a formal garden backing on to a lake with a small island in the middle.

'Bit creepy, I have to admit,' he acknowledged, throwing a sidelong glance at her as he swung the car in a half circle before reversing back against a snow-covered hedge facing the front of the house next to a rough-looking BMW saloon.

'I rest my case,' she said. 'Still want to stay?'

Switching off, he sat there for a few moments listening to the ticking of the hot engine and staring through the side windows at the snow-carpeted forecourt and encompassing grounds.

'Of course I do. I was with these guys living in the same house at uni for two years. I could hardly turn down an invitation to meet up with them all again after such a long time, could I? It'll be great to see them and reminisce over the old days. Anyway, you know what they say, "never judge a book by its cover".'

'Yes,' she agreed with a wry smile, 'that's very true and anyway, maybe Count Dracula isn't at home just now.' Then she added mischievously, 'When is it you last saw any of these housemates of yours? Must have been a while ago — when you were young.'

'What do you mean, when I was young?' he retorted. 'It was only five years ago and I'm still only a youngster.'

He peered at himself in the rear view mirror, sucking his cheeks in and out and frowning. Five years of the executive highlife as an investment banker in his father's firm had certainly taken its toll on him. The muscular body with its barrel chest, which he had once been so proud of, had turned to fat and the one-time shoulder-length black hair, now cut back to a more respectable collar length to suit his executive status, was already starting to thin in places. No doubt due to his previous use of cocaine as well as the frequent after-dinner cocktails with his moneyed clients, he mused regretfully. But there was some consolation. The sharp blue eyes, craggy features and generous credit card still pulled the "birds" and Victoria was his fourth or fifth girlfriend in twelve months.

Allowing his gaze to slide sideways, he studied the latest love of his life almost with a kind of reverence. The long, raven black hair framing the delicate, ivory skin. The high, well moulded cheekbones. The almond-shaped hazel eyes and full red lips. She was, he always thought, like a reincarnation of the ancient Egyptian queen, Cleopatra. She certainly turned heads when she went anywhere and he could hardly wait for the others to see her. They would be in awe, and who wouldn't be? She was his best one yet. He'd met her at a party at Claridges, when she had more or less introduced herself, and they had subsequently spent a fantastic fortnight together on the ski slopes of St Anton in Austria as well as in a very large bed. A sharp-minded twenty-six-year-old who apparently held a senior position in corporate finance, she was certainly not just a pretty face, but at the same time was probably the best lay he had had in his life, and he was looking forward to what her inventive spirit might have in store for him that night.

'So how many of these characters might turn up?' she asked, treating him to a secret smile when she caught his gaze on her.

He cleared his throat. 'Hopefully all seven of them,' he said, then quickly corrected himself, conscious of a sudden spurt of acid in his stomach as his thoughts flashed back to another old house near a bridge spanning a fast-running river. 'Well, there were originally eight of us, but there was an, er, accident and—' he shook his head quickly to try and erase the memory of Francis Templeton's face from his mind — 'one of our housemates fell in a river and drowned.'

She looked horrified. 'How awful. How on earth did that happen?'

'Slipped on a muddy path, we think,' he said tersely, anxious to get off the subject. 'Probably had too much to drink.'

'How old was he?'

He grimaced. 'Does it matter? Poor devil died, that's all. In the past now. Best forgotten.'

'Did you see him fall in?'

He shook his head, his irritation growing. 'None of us did. We weren't there at the time.'

'Then how do you know he drowned?'

'Er, we don't. We sort of assumed he had. He disappeared and as far as I know, his body was never found.'

'What a dreadful thing. So, in a way, this celebration here could equally be regarded as a sort of wake?'

'A what?'

'You know, remembering the housemate who passed?'

He clenched his teeth tightly in a sudden spasm. Why on earth did she have to stir up the memory of that bloody awful business? He had almost wiped it from his mind over the years.

'Can we just forget the whole thing?' he said. 'Bit painful for me. Now let's get inside the house. More snowflakes are already falling.'

Her eyes widened as she looked out of the window. 'How lovely. Just think, we could be snowed in here if it continues at this rate.'

He threw open his door and made his way round to the back of the car to open the boot and pull out their suitcases. 'I bloody well hope not. I don't want to miss the forthcoming parties back in the Smoke by being stuck in some back of beyond place like this.'

'As I said just now, you wanted to come.'

'I know I did and I'm sure it'll be fun.'

He set down the cases and opened her door to help her out, then jumped as her hand slid under his coat and gave him an intimate squeeze. 'Of course it will be,' she agreed. 'After all, what could be nicer than a roaring log fire, lots of wine and a big, soft bed?'

'Hey, you two, none of that out here.'

Brewer whirled round at the sound of the voice and saw a familiar looking figure walking towards them from the hotel's open front door, flicking the stub of a lighted cigarette into the snow as he did so.

Brewer embraced him in a brief bearhug. 'Shit, Ronnie,' Jeffrey Cartwright responded, expelling a cloud of cigarette smoke, then sniffing as if he had a bad cold. 'You're a sight for sore eyes after all these years.'

Cartwright was dressed in a brown suede jacket over brown corduroy trousers and Brewer was surprised to see how much he had aged in just five years. The restless dark eyes and shoulder-length, black hair were just as he remembered and the slightly crooked mouth affected the same lopsided smirk. But the pale features were drawn and lined, with the cheeks hollowed out and skeletal, almost certainly through the tell-tale ravages of cocaine. So Jeff was still "using" then, and it was obviously destroying him. Brewer couldn't help wondering how his former friend and housemate was still managing to hold down a job and whether he was still following the career in accountancy he had worked for in his degree. Seeing how Cartwright looked, he felt a real sense of relief that he had finally kicked the habit himself after those wild days at uni.

'So, who's the lovely lady?' Cartwright asked, unashamedly undressing Adams with envious eyes.

Brewer introduced her to his old housemate and Cartwright bowed theatrically and kissed her hand. 'What on earth does a gorgeous woman like you see in a fat old fart like him?' he joked.

'Ignore him,' Brewer said. 'He's always like this. A regular dipstick. Let's get these cases inside. I could do with a drink.'

Cartwright led the way, showing them into a black-and-white tiled hall with a large brass dinner gong at the far end standing beside an ornate oak staircase rising to the next floor. Doors opened off on both sides and a passageway disappeared down the left-hand side of the staircase, perhaps to the kitchen or staff quarters, and a further one to the right, possibly to guest rooms.

'How very *Downton Abbey*ish,' Brewer commented drily. 'I should have brought my jodhpurs. So where's that welcome drink?'

Dumping the suitcases down in the hall, he and his girlfriend followed Cartwright through a doorway on their left.

There was a large, oak-beamed room beyond, furnished with a pair of fully upholstered three-piece suites and several part-upholstered chairs. Logs blazed in an inglenook fireplace with an iron cage beside it stuffed with logs, and the dancing flames were reflected in the pair of transom windows, which overlooked the snow-covered forecourt. To one side of the room there was a long table laden with plates of sandwiches, coffee pots and fancy crockery.

'What, no booze?' Brewer exclaimed.

Cartwright made a face. 'Seems not,' he said. 'Just coffee and tea.'

'Sod it, I was looking forward to a scotch or a glass of wine.'

'Well, you're out of luck, my man.'

'But is this all for us?' Adams asked.

Cartwright shrugged. 'Presumably. Haven't seen anyone else yet, but there's a notice pinned to the wall over there explaining what's what.'

They wandered over to it and studied the message typed neatly on an A4 sheet of paper.

It read:

Welcome to the Warneford Hall Hotel. Please help yourself to the buffet provided. Your rooms are ready for you to occupy and the keys are in the doors. Meals will be served daily in the dining room at the following times:

Self-service continental breakfast 8.30–10 a.m.

Self-service buffet lunch 12.00–2.00 p.m.
Dinner 7.00–9.00 p.m.
The management regrets that as the hotel is now in the
process of being sold, only a skeleton staff can be provided,
hence the self-service meals at breakfast and lunch, and bed-
rooms will not be serviced each day. We hope you will bear
with us for the weekend and nevertheless enjoy your stay.
Should you require any further assistance, please ring one
of the wall bells provided in all public rooms.

There was no signature, but beneath the notice was a guest list, together with the relevant bedroom allocations.

'Well, that's short, but not so sweet,' Brewer remarked and returned to the table where Adams was pouring coffees. 'I wonder just how much of a skeleton crew they're actually talking about. Bit of a poor show all round. No hot meals at breakfast and lunch in weather like this, no room-servicing, hardly any staff? What sort of a hotel is it?'

'It was your choice,' Cartwright retorted.

Brewer frowned. '*My* choice? How do you make that one out?'

'Well, you're the one who seems to have arranged this little get-together for us all.'

'Me?' Brewer glanced quickly at his girlfriend. 'Like hell I did.'

Cartwright grinned. 'Very generous of you to stand the cost of everything too, I must say.'

'You're talking bollocks.'

Cartwright rummaged in his coat pocket and produced a crumpled sheet of paper.

'Then you must be getting Alzheimer's, old son, if you can't even remember sending the invite.'

'Give me that,' Brewer snapped and grabbed the sheet of paper from him.

It was an email attachment embellished like a party invitation, with a coloured frieze of balloons and bubbling bottles of champagne around the edge. The sender was shown as Ronnie Brewer and it read:

Hi, Housemates,
It's 5 years since we shared that horrible old house at Uni. Time we got together for a much needed reunion, methinks. Join me at the Warneford Hall Hotel on the Somerset Levels for a weekend of fun, frivolity and loads of booze — if you dare!
Ronnie.

The "from" and "to" dates were printed directly beneath, together with the full postal address of the hotel and the sat nav link. There was also an RSVP, which directed replies to a printed email address, and carried a bracketed note: "New Email. Old one hacked".

Brewer's face wore an angry frown now. 'But I didn't send this. That isn't even an email address of mine at the bottom. Yeah, I have a new email since uni, but that isn't it.'

'Well, your name's on the invitation?'

'Maybe it is, but you know very well I didn't send it.'

'So how would I know anything of the sort?'

Brewer stared at him fixedly, his eyes gleaming. 'Because the invite came from you, you arsehole.'

Cartwright's grin vanished. 'What, poor, old, impoverished Jeffrey Cartwright? You have to be joking. I had no idea this place even existed until I got here.'

Brewer checked his own coat pocket and produced the copy of another email and handed it to him. It was an identical party invitation, except for the fact that the name of the sender was shown as "Jeff Cartwright".

Cartwright's eyes widened and he fumbled for another cigarette. 'Someone must be having a laugh and it isn't me,' he said, lighting up between loud sniffs.

'You shouldn't be smoking in here,' Adams interjected. 'It's illegal in public places now.'

'Tough,' Cartwright replied, continuing to smoke. Then he added, 'And this isn't *my* email address either.'

'So who *did* send it?' Brewer challenged.

'How the bloody hell should I know? I did try and contact you on your old mobile number when I got the message, as no mobile number was given on the email, but I got "unobtainable", so guessed you must have changed it and gave up.'

'I did. New provider. But someone must have fixed up the bookings at this hotel, so it should be relatively easy for the management to tell us who that was.'

Striding back to the notice on the wall, Brewer pressed a small brass button set in a silver coloured pad beneath it.

As he returned to the table for his coffee, the door opened and a thin, elderly woman with a sallow, hatchet face and grey hair tied back in an unbecoming ponytail materialised.

'Yes?' she said severely, casting a disapproving glance at the smoking cigarette in Cartwright's hand.

'And you are?' Brewer asked.

'Daphne Parsons. I works here. What can I do fer you?'

He held the invitation he had received up in front of her. 'My friend and I both received invites here for the weekend, but we have no idea who they came from. We didn't send them ourselves. Can you enlighten us as to who arranged this booking?'

She glanced briefly at the email without making any real attempt to read it, then shook her head and ran both hands down the sides of the grey apron she was wearing. 'No idea, sir.'

'But if you work here, you must have some inkling as to who made the booking?'

'Weren't me. I be just the general cook and bottle-washer, that's all.'

'Then what about the terms of our stay? According to the notice on the wall over there, we and our other friends who will be arriving shortly, are staying here on a full board basis, so someone must have at least put down a deposit to secure the rooms?'

'Dunno nothin' 'bout that. Far as I knows, everythin's been took care of.'

19

'What?' Cartwright exclaimed. 'You mean someone has paid for the entire bill in advance?'

She shrugged. 'So we was told. Me and me hubby was kept on just to look after last few guests still on hotel's books. We got rooms out back till we finish up. Rest of regular staff got fired month back when, all of a sudden like, it were decided to close hotel and sell up, though t'ain't actually on the market yet. We had nothin' to do with no bookin's.'

'So who hired you? They must know the score.'

'S'pose they do, but all I knows is that Mr Hapgood, last hotel manager, asked me and Tom — that's me hubby — to do this last job a'fore he left. Paid us a nice bonus, too, as we been workin' here so long.' She nodded respectfully. 'Real gen'leman, Mr Hapgood.'

'Was Mr Hapgood the owner then?'

She shook her head. 'Not him. Never know'd who owners was. Always answered to Mr Hapgood.'

'And there are no other staff, like on reception or administration or anything?'

'No need for any. Bein' as last guests booked in be yourselves. All I got to do is cookin', layin' up tables and servin', while Tom keeps fires goin' in rooms an' does any maintainin' needed, just as Mr Hapgood asked.'

'And where is this Mr Hapgood now?'

'Dunno. Just went. Ain't seen him since. Not 'spectin' him back neither on account of hotel closin' down.'

Brewer shook his head in disbelief and ran a hand through his hair in a gesture of frustration. 'Incredible.' He sighed. 'Absolutely incredible.'

Mrs Parsons made no further comment. But it was plain that she really couldn't care less about it all and was just anxious to get on. 'Will that be all then, sir?' she said finally. 'Dinner be at seven, mind.'

At which point, she turned on her heel and left the room.

* * *

'I just don't get this,' Brewer muttered after the elderly woman had closed the door behind her. 'None of it makes any sense. Why would someone invite everyone here just for the fun of it and, on top of that, shell out for the cost of it all?'

'Well, it could only be one of our crowd,' Cartwright pointed out. 'No one else would know or care that we all shared the house at uni.'

Adams sighed heavily, plainly bored with the whole discussion. 'Does it really matter who sent it?' she interjected. 'Our weekend is all paid for, so let's just have the fun that's been promised. Now, I need to pee.'

At which point, she headed for the door.

'She's right, you know,' Cartwright said, staring after her. 'Let's just accept the situation. Maybe someone came into money or something and just wanted to spring a surprise on his or her old mates?'

Brewer snorted. 'Can you see any of our lot doing that?' he said. '*I* can't — only if it was done as a sick joke. You know, book the place, then saddle the rest of us with the bill?'

'That can't be it. The old girl's already said everything's been settled.'

'Well, some bugger's playing games and I intend finding out who it is.'

Cartwright started at the sound of a car engine and, dumping his coffee cup back on the table, he crossed to one of the transom windows and ducked his head to peer out.

'Well, you should get your chance now,' he remarked, glimpsing the flash of headlights in the midst of what were now quite heavy flurries of snow whipped up by a wind that was already rattling the window panes. 'Looks like the whole gang have arrived — and they've brought more soddin' snow with them!'

CHAPTER 2

Moments later the front door burst open and half a dozen figures smothered in snow stumbled into the hallway, laughing and chattering excitedly.

'Bloody hell, man,' Jimmy Caulfield exclaimed from the depths of his hoodie. 'I didn't expect this. Never thought we'd ever get here.'

'It's called snow, Jimmy,' Brewer retorted with a grin, gripping his hand.

'Tell me about it,' Caulfield threw back. 'Some of the roads in were already impassable and I saw even a couple of gritters had got stuck. Weather reports are saying it's unprecedented for the Southwest and they're promising freak blizzards tonight.'

'Ruined my hair too,' Abbey Granger moaned, as ever focusing on the things that really mattered and shaking her blonde hair to rid herself of her unwanted snow cap. Then abruptly she spotted Brewer and gave a shriek. Throwing her arms around him, she crushed him to her wet fur coat in a characteristic hug. 'Ronnie, love. I can't believe it. This is wonderful.'

Brewer kissed her perfunctorily on the cheek, then turned away to greet the others as she transferred her attention to

Cartwright with equal enthusiasm. Clapping Lenny Welch on the shoulder as he materialised wearing a reindeer mask over the hood of his anorak, he grabbed the front door to let Tammy Morrison in behind him.

'Hi, Tam,' he said, squeezing her arm. 'Didn't come all the way down here in that old crock you used to have, did you?'

She gave him a faint smile and rested the holdall she was carrying on the floor in front of her. 'Died on me last year, Ronnie,' she replied. 'I haven't got a car at the moment. Fortunately I already had Abbey's mobile number, so I rang her a week ago and she kindly offered to pick me up from Taunton railway station.' She tapped the holdall. 'But don't expect any flashy outfits for the weekend. I had to travel light. Only just got here too. They closed the lines just after I arrived due to the worsening weather.'

He frowned. 'Not surprised. They say a nasty storm's heading our way.' He brightened. 'Still, you're here now and it's great to see you again.'

'You too, Ronnie,' she said quietly. 'It's been a while. Really good of you to arrange this celebration.'

Brewer's grin faded and he grimaced. 'Thing is, I didn't,' he replied brusquely. 'I'll tell all of you about it shortly.'

Turning back towards the others milling about behind him, he shouted, 'Okay, people, coffee and sarnies in the room over there. Help yourselves.'

But as Cartwright led them all into the lounge past their temporarily abandoned cases, he stared about him in puzzlement. 'Hey, just a minute. Where's George Lane? Has he chickened out on us?'

Only Tammy Morrison seemed to hear the question above the general chatter and laughter, and she pushed back through the others, her face grave. 'You haven't heard then?'

'Heard what?'

'George won't be coming, Ronnie. He's . . . he's dead, I'm afraid.'

Brewer gaped. 'Dead? George dead? What are you saying?'

She shrugged and there were suddenly tears in her eyes. 'Drowned, Ronnie.'

'Good grief! How?'

'You know he loved fishing?'

He nodded, trying to process the information he'd just received.

'It seems he must have fallen into a lake near his home. The police found his body wedged under the ice about two weeks ago.'

'But he was a strong swimmer.'

'Would have made no difference in those conditions, Ronnie.'

'But how do you know about this?'

'If you remember, I live — lived — just around the corner from George. I know his mum and dad well. I know the lake too. Have often walked around it. I went with his dad to ID the body.'

He took a deep breath. 'This is bloody awful.'

'I know it is. Tragic.' She bit her lip and just for a moment held his gaze. 'Ironic, though, isn't it? Him drowning like that. Just like poor Francis Templeton.'

Acid reflux welled up in Brewer's throat again. 'Just coincidence,' he said gruffly, desperate to avoid any further discussion of something that had been haunting him for so long.

'Do the rest know?' he added.

She shook her head. 'Not yet. I haven't even told Abbey. I thought it best to tell everyone when we're all together.'

He grimaced, thinking again of the question he was about to broach and putting it to one side for the moment. 'Brilliant start to the party, isn't it?' he said sarcastically. 'Trust old George to put the mockers on everything.'

* * *

There was a stunned silence in the room after Tammy Morrison had delivered her news. For what must have been at least half a minute, no one moved. Those who had been helping themselves to coffee or sandwiches seemed to freeze where they stood or sat. Cups poised unmoving. Sandwiches stationary before open mouths. It was as if they had been turned to stone at the flick of an invisible magician's wand.

Finally, Abbey Granger broke the spell. 'You never told me about this in the car, Tam.'

Morrison nodded. 'No, I know. Sorry, but I wanted everyone to hear at the same time.'

Before Granger could say anything else, Caulfield followed up with an unhelpful comment of his own. 'Same as Francis,' he said.

Brewer threw him a daggers look from the fireplace where he had been loading more logs on to the dwindling flames. 'It's nothing like Francis,' he snapped.

Caulfield was undeterred. 'Funny, though, isn't it?'

'I don't see anything funny about it,' Lenny Welch said. 'Poor guy's dead. That isn't funny.'

Caulfield shook his head. 'No, not that sort of funny, Len. I mean, it's sort of, er—'

'Ironic?' Morrison suggested, using her own earlier description.

'Yeah, that's it. Ironic. That he died in the same way as Francis . . .'

'Ironic then,' Brewer cut in hastily, returning to the chair he had been occupying. 'So, shall we leave it at that? When's the funeral, Tam?'

'Not yet. There's got to be an inquest. You know, official cause of death, that sort of thing. It's just a formality. Police say it's likely to be put down to accident.'

'We should go. Pay our respects.'

Morrison nodded. 'I'll let you all know when it is.'

'Poor old George,' Abbey Granger said in a low voice. 'Who'd have thought such a thing would happen to him? Mind you, he was always a bit paranoid about things, wasn't he? Sort of weird at times. Remember how he reacted the morning after Francis disappeared? Talking about that horror film, *I Know What You Did Last Summer*. Saying we could end up like the kids in that. Enough to frighten the knickers off you.'

'I'd like to see that,' Cartwright remarked through more sniffs as he tried futilely to inject a bit of humour into the dismal atmosphere. 'You know, your knickers getting frightened off.'

But his comments met with a stony silence and a contemptuous toss of the head from Granger.

'He rang me, you know,' Tammy put in again.

Welch frowned. 'Rang you?'

She nodded. 'Yes, about a month before he died. Said he'd received one of the invitations to this get-together, but that there was no way he was going to come and he had already sent his apologies. He was in a terrible state and said he'd been unable to sleep ever since and was on anti-depressants.' She hesitated, as if unsure how to continue. Then she added, 'Something about him being haunted by a ghost.'

'A *ghost*?' Welch echoed. 'Oh come on!'

She shrugged. 'That's what he said. Apparently he was convinced Francis had come back and was stalking him.'

Caulfield laughed uproariously. 'Well, spooky wooky wooky!' he mocked. 'Maybe he should have got hold of *Ghostbusters*.'

'Just shut it, Jimmy,' Brewer rapped, nevertheless feeling his skin crawl. 'We can do without that sort of crap. So let's change the subject, shall we?'

There was a general murmur of agreement, though things had gone very quiet in the room now and no one else was laughing.

Brewer took the silence as his cue and reaching into his back pocket, he held up the email invitation he had received. 'Okay, so moving on. I assume you all got one of these invitations for this long weekend and I'd like to know whose name is at the bottom of each.'

Welch glanced at his own email and shrugged. 'Bit of a daft question seeing as you sent them yourself.'

Brewer scowled. 'Thing is I didn't. So could you all please check to see whose name is at the bottom of the invite you have? Sort of like now.'

There was a flurry of movement, followed by a chorus of, 'Yours, Ronnie.'

Morrison stared at him. 'I don't understand. What's going on?'

He took a deep breath. 'Fact is, I don't know whether it was done as a joke, but someone sent the invitations out under my name, without my knowledge.'

There was a loud guffaw from Caulfield. 'Bollocks, Ronnie. You're just trying to renege on payment for the weekend.'

'No, I'm not,' Brewer snapped back, and he showed his invitation to Morrison sitting next to him.

She stared at it and raised her eyebrows. 'This one has Jeff's name on it.'

'Precisely.'

Abbey Granger looked confused. 'But why would Jeff's name be on Ronnie's and Ronnie's on everyone else's?'

Morrison smiled faintly. Abbey had never been the sharpest knife in the drawer. 'Because Ronnie would hardly have sent an invitation to himself, would he, Ab? So to make his own invitation seem credible, they signed it off with Jeff's name.'

'But why not use Jeff's name on all the other invitations as well?'

A groan went round the room and Morrison took a deep breath. 'Because . . .' she began. Then she broke off and waved a hand dismissively. 'Forget it, Ab,' she finished. 'It's not important.'

'And you're saying all this was a con by one of us?' Caulfield exclaimed.

Brewer stared at him grimly. 'That's exactly what I'm saying,' he said, 'Whoever did it has to be someone in this room.'

'And why would any of us do something like that just to land you with a stupid bill?'

'That's just it. There seems no point to it. I've already confirmed that whoever sent the invitations also paid for the whole full-board booking in advance, so there's nothing at all *to* be paid.' Brewer's gaze roved around the room, settling on each face in turn. 'Okay, fun's over. Which of you dingbats is behind this?'

But his accusation was met with five blank expressions and before he could say anything else, the door opened and Victoria Adams breezed into the room.

'Well, are you going to introduce me to everyone, Ronnie?' she said, smiling innocently at the gaping expressions on the faces in front of her. 'Especially as I have just found the bar.'

* * *

As the domestic drama was being played out in the lounge of the Warneford Hall Hotel, unbeknown to Brewer and his friends, another drama was unfolding on the top lane just a mile and a half away in the midst of the developing blizzard.

The little Mazda MX5 had been struggling gamely through the snow for miles since setting out from just outside Chard what seemed like an age before and it was now starting to flag. Built more for speed, cornering ability and the open road, the sports car was well outside its comfort zone in the horrendous conditions it was facing. With hindsight, the couple peering through the narrow windscreen along the twin beams of the headlights would have been the first to admit that their bargain break in Devon, against the advice of the weather-forecasters who had predicted the freak conditions, had perhaps been a bad idea.

The loud "bang" and the torrent of steam that suddenly erupted from under the bonnet only served to reinforce that fact, and as the engine died and the car slid into the side of the road, the woman in the anorak and bobble hat who was crouched behind the wheel made her feelings abundantly plain.

'Bloody shit!' Detective Sergeant Kate Lewis exclaimed. 'Now what?'

Her detective constable husband, Hayden, grimaced at her outburst and opening the passenger door, climbed out into the snow with his torch to check on what sounded to him like a terminal problem.

It didn't take him long to have his misgivings confirmed. 'Head gasket, I suspect,' he shouted back to her, sticking his head out briefly from under the bonnet.

'What can we do?' she asked when he climbed back into the car.

'Nothing. It's a major repair job.'

Kate came out with an even choicer expletive and he snapped, 'Helps, does it? Using foul language like that?'

'What do you want me to do? We're stuck in the snow miles from anywhere with a blown head gasket and a bloody blizzard on the way.'

'And a mouthful of abuse will solve all those problems, will it?'

She snorted her exasperation. 'Don't be a muppet, Hayd. Just for once in your life forget your trivial hang-up about my swearing and concentrate on getting someone out to us PDQ.'

'I don't know who that would be. You heard the radio broadcast earlier. This freak storm has hit most of the Southwest, from Devon and Cornwall right through to Bristol and, as we've already discovered, many of the roads are already impassable.'

'Okay, so with foresight, we should have stayed at home this week, but we had to use up our annual leave and we deserved a break anyway. Now are you going to ring someone or do I have to do it like I do everything else?'

Hayden scowled and, switching on the interior light, he jerked his mobile from his pocket to call the emergency breakdown number printed on the card affixed to the dashboard. But after stabbing at the keys irritably for several seconds, he slumped back in his seat with a resigned shrug.

'It's dead,' he said. 'No signal.'

'But there has to be.'

She tried her own phone but got the same result.

'Probably the weather,' he suggested. 'Or maybe we're in a poor reception area.'

She opened her mouth to say something, but with the oath on the tip of her tongue thought better of it and said instead, 'Well, we can't stay here all night. We'll both freeze to death.'

'So what do you suggest we do?' he asked drily. 'Walk home? It can only be about twenty odd miles to Burtle — if only we knew where on earth we were in the first place.'

'You and your bloody shortcuts,' she said, rounding on him. 'We should have stuck to the route the diversion sign gave us, but you had to go off-piste and do your own thing, didn't you? Now look where we are.'

'That sign would have sent us back the way we had come. I had to take a calculated risk . . .'

'Calculated risk, bollocks.'

'There you go again. Back to foul language!'

Kate threw her door open, ignoring him, and stumbled out into the snow. The falling flakes seemed even more dense than before, whipped up by a strengthening wind that moaned around her like a live thing, and in the gradually fading half-light she saw that the wheels of the car were already part buried in the snow. She felt a sudden sense of panic. They had to find some shelter before it was too late and they became virtually entombed in the car. But where? As far as she could see, there was not a human habitation in sight.

She heard the crack of Hayden's door being forced open against the snow piling up against it through gaps in the adjacent hedgerow and shouted at him as he climbed out again.

'We've got to make a move — now.'

'What, you mean walk?' he shouted back. 'In this? We only have shoes on and these anoraks. Going on foot would be total madness.'

'It would be even madder to stay here.'

'But if we waited long enough, another car could come by and pick us up.'

Kate controlled herself with an effort, well aware of her overweight husband's hatred of walking — or any form of exercise, for that matter. 'Hayden, we're not on a main road, but in a wiggly lane few people are likely to know about. No one is going to come by . . .'

Then abruptly she broke off and stared hard through the falling snow. Lights. She could have sworn she'd seen them flickering in the murk on the other side of the hedge adjacent to the car. Some distance away and lower down as if in a dip, but there anyway. She wiped the snowflakes from her eyes and looked again. The snow parted briefly under a stronger blast of wind and yes, there they were again. Five or six glittering lights. A house or farm of some sort.

'Hayden!' she shouted as he opened the passenger door of the car again, obviously with the intention of stubbornly climbing back inside. 'Look. There's a house or a farm down there. There must be an entrance further along the lane.'

'A what?'

Turning, he shielded his eyes with both hands and stared over the hedge to where she was now pointing. At first nothing and then he shouted back,

'So, what are we waiting for? Let's get our bags out of the boot.'

They found the opening in the hedge about fifty yards away. It was now almost dark, but Hayden's torch revealed a narrow track on the other side and best of all, a finger post beside it bearing the most welcome of all signs: *Warneford Hall Hotel*.

CHAPTER 3

The bar was a reasonably sized square room on the other side of the hallway. It boasted a long counter at one end, which was modestly equipped with a couple of taps, one for beer and the other for lager, plus an ice bucket and a tray piled high with packets of crisps. There was a row of shelves on the wall behind the counter displaying a variety of alcoholic drinks, including a range of spirits, and a cupboard beneath equipped with two sliding doors. One of these was open, revealing bottles of red wine, and there was a fridge next door to the cupboard with a glass door containing white wine held horizontally in a rack. There was no till, just a neatly labelled *Honesty Box*, containing small change and some lower denomination notes, and a printed A4 sheet of paper in a plastic holder beside it listing the price of each drink.

'Honesty box?' Jimmy Caulfield exclaimed with a throaty guffaw. 'Someone has a trusting nature.'

Victoria Adams nodded. 'Cheaper than retaining bar staff, I suppose.'

'And we will all pay for what we use,' Tammy Morrison said pointedly, glancing round at the others crowding into the room. 'The hotel has gone to a lot of trouble to make sure the bar is well stocked for us.'

''Course we will,' Caulfield agreed with a big grin. He was already behind the counter working one of the taps over a pint glass. 'What's everyone having?'

Moments later, Jeffrey Cartwright raised his glass of vodka and said loudly, 'A toast . . .'

Hesitantly at first, everyone followed suit. Only to abruptly lower their glasses in embarrassment when Cartwright added with a smirk, 'To Francis Templeton. May he rest in pieces.'

'Not funny, Jeff!' Morrison snapped after a pause. 'Not funny at all. He died because of us.'

'Tammy's right,' Brewer practically snarled and downing his whisky, he slammed his glass on the counter and stormed from the room. 'Just drop the bloody subject.'

Adams caught up with him in the hallway, looking tense. 'Francis, was he the lad you told me about who drowned?' she asked.

Brewer picked up their suitcases and nodded curtly, turning towards the stairs.

'Why did Tammy say just now that he died because of all of you?' she said, following him.

He glanced at her quickly over his shoulder. 'Er, figure of speech,' he replied. 'We were all drinking together before it happened. I suppose it's natural to feel responsible for what happened to him in those circumstances.'

'But you told me earlier that none of you were with him when he died, so how can you blame yourselves for his death? It was an accident, surely?'

He stopped on the landing and swung round on her, his face savage. 'What's this? The bloody third degree? Of course it was an accident. What else would it have been?'

She flinched and held up both hands in front of her apologetically. 'Sorry, I was just curious, that's all. You were so angry with your friend over the toast.'

'Hardly surprising, is it? Now, as I said before, let's drop the subject. We came here for a fun weekend. I don't want to think any more about Francis bloody Templeton.'

They continued in silence to their room after that and they said very little to each other as they unpacked. Despite what he'd said about dropping the subject of Francis Templeton, Brewer still couldn't get his former housemate out of his mind or stop himself mentally reliving that last night at university when he and the others had taken it in turns to add all those different spirit shots, including whisky, vodka and — worst of all — absinthe, to the pint of lager they had bought for him.

The cheerless atmosphere of the bedroom didn't help his downbeat mood either. It was furnished with old, dark-wood furniture, ornate Victorian-style wall lights and loud, rose-patterned fabric wallpaper which refused to match the blue carpet. It did have a four-poster double bed, but it was minus its canopy and looked as though it might once have graced the bedroom of one of Shakespeare's cronies. Furthermore, the mattress sagged noticeably in the middle.

'No wonder the place is up for sale,' he shouted through the ensuite bathroom door where his girlfriend was now showering. 'I reckon we should repack and head back to London.'

There was a loud thud from inside the bathroom, as if Adams had dropped the soap, and the hammering of the shower died. The next moment the door opened and she emerged, dripping wet with a towel drawn around her slim body and her hair tucked up inside a nylon shower cap.

'You're not thinking of leaving?' she exclaimed. 'We've only just got here.'

He watched her pull the nylon cap off her head and shake her long black hair free. He was unable to take his eyes off her and his throat had suddenly dried up. 'But-but it's a dump,' he faltered. 'Even the bed's crap.'

She glanced across at the four poster and raised her eyebrows. 'Looks all right to me,' she said.

Smiling lasciviously, she slowly loosened the towel and allowed it to drop to the floor. Then she brazenly stood there, her slim, pale body wet and glistening in the light of the bedroom lamps.

'Do you really want to head straight back to London before dinner?' she asked.

* * *

The track was on a downward slope and the hedgerows on either side had been planted on high banks, so that the snow was now beginning to pile up in drifts between them. It was over Kate and Hayden's ankles before they had gone a hundred yards and the strength of the wind was increasing all the time, blowing the icy flakes into their faces, temporarily blinding them. But they had no option but to keep going, and they bent their heads into it, following the beams of their torches and forcing themselves on.

It hardly seemed credible to Kate that they were in England. The conditions were more like those she would have expected to face in somewhere like the Arctic. It was certainly unprecedented for the Southwest. She had never known such appalling weather in all the years she had lived in Somerset. Floods, yes, but not this. It was no doubt all down to climate change, or so the scientists would have everyone believe. Fortunately their bags were fairly light as they had packed only the minimum for their short break away and the bags themselves were adaptable and could be worn as haversacks, which made things much easier. But the going was still tough and they needed all their strength and willpower to continue. For Hayden, overweight and unused to any form of real physical activity, it was doubly hard and twice he fell over as he lost his balance. The signpost had said it was just one and a half miles to the hotel, but it seemed more like double that distance and they were both beginning to think they would never get there at all when they found themselves crossing a shaky wooden bridge over a part frozen river. Shortly afterwards they were stumbling through the open gates of the Warneford Hall Hotel, hardly noticing the *FOR SALE* sign. Exhausted, frozen stiff and with sodden feet that they could no longer feel.

They didn't bother to ring the bell on the front door. But the door was unlocked anyway, so they went straight in, expecting to be confronted by the usual reception desk. Instead, they found themselves in a bare hallway with black and white floor tiles and an elderly, grey-haired woman with her hair tied back in a ponytail who was in the process of striking a large gong standing in one corner.

She turned as the booming of the gong died away, alerted no doubt by the intensely cold draught from the front door and the scrape of shoes on the floor. For a moment she studied the snow-caked visitors with raised eyebrows, then approached them with folded arms.

'Sorry,' she said. 'Hotel be full.'

Kate pulled back the hood of her coat and treated her to a grim smile. 'Is it?' she replied. 'Well, I'm afraid you'll have to find us a bed somewhere, even if it is just a couch in a corridor. There's no way we're going back out there tonight.'

'Our car broke down in the top lane,' Hayden explained quickly, his nose crinkling as the smell of cooking wafted out into the hallway. 'We're happy to pay the going rate. Only we're exhausted.'

Daphne Parsons looked them both over and frowned. 'Hotel be closed fer good when guests we got now leave,' she said. 'Can't book no more in. No idea what goin' rate would be. No one to take no money now neither.'

'All we want is a place to rest,' Kate snapped. 'Surely you have somewhere?'

Mrs Parsons looked them over again, then seemed to come to a reluctant decision. 'S'pose two extra won't make no difference. Whose to know anyways? One guest I were 'spectin' didn't turn up, so I got a vacant room. But you'll have to make it up yourselves.'

Hayden breathed a sigh of relief. 'That'll be fine. Thank you.'

Mrs Parsons gave a thin smile. 'Welcome, I'm sure. Now I got to get folks' dinners out.'

She half-turned, then gave them both another searching glance, adding, 'Might as well join other guests in dinin' room. I done a pot stew. Plenty of that to go round.'

'That's most kind of you,' Kate put in with an appreciative smile. 'We're very grateful. But one other thing. Could we use your phone so we can call a breakdown?'

The woman gave a short laugh. 'Breakdown? Won't get one o' them out here. Most roads be blocked. Anyways, phone's broke. Line must be down.'

Kate watched her cross the hall and disappear into a passageway to the left of an ornate staircase.

'At least we'll get a decent night's sleep,' she said, throwing Hayden a quick glance.

He nodded slowly. 'That's if the ghosts let us,' he said drily, peering around the hallway, 'and the stew isn't laced with arsenic.'

* * *

The bedroom was on the upper floor halfway along the main corridor. It was quite dark and smelled slightly of damp. But as Kate observed, "beggars can't be choosers". Furthermore, the bed was comfortable, with extra pillows and some clean linen in the antiquated wardrobe, and there was a well-appointed ensuite bathroom with a shower over the old-fashioned bath. The small colour television attached to one wall actually worked too and though it didn't have Sky, it did have all the main channels, much to Hayden's relief.

'At least we can keep our eyes on the weather forecast,' he called across to Kate from his familiar reclining position on the bed as she made them both a mug of hot coffee from the makings provided on an old-fashioned walnut dressing table. 'Maybe I'll even be able to catch up on the sport.'

She groaned. 'I can't wait,' she said with heavy sarcasm. 'Shut in here for the weekend with you glued to the football couldn't be a more exciting prospect. I think I'll just stick to the forecast.'

In fact, a news bulletin about the weather was broadcast while they were drinking their coffee, and it didn't look good. There were alarming pictures showing banks of thick white snow, buried street signs, stranded cars and overturned lorries, together with shots of a howling blizzard alleged to be on its way up country from Cornwall. The reporter could hardly contain his excitement as he piled on the gloom, repeating Met Office warnings to stay indoors, and to avoid driving anywhere in the Southwest before coming out with Armageddon-like promises of worse to come over the weekend.

'Seems like we'll be stuck in this place for a bit,' Hayden observed. 'Ironic when you think that we abandoned the remaining two days of our break at Chard simply because the weather was getting bad, and now we're marooned here.'

Kate grimaced. 'Charlie Woo at Highbridge nick could soon be tearing his hair out. We should be back on duty on Monday and we've no way of letting him know what's happened.'

Hayden looked less than bothered by the fact. 'Can't be helped. Nothing we can do about it.'

He brightened. 'Could be we won't be able to get back to work for another week yet,' he added optimistically. 'It wouldn't be our fault if that were to happen either. Just one of those things.'

She shot him a critical glance. 'As usual, your attitude adds a whole new dimension to the term workshy,' she said gravely. 'You couldn't be lazier if you tried.'

He grinned. 'I've always adopted a unique approach to things, old girl,' he said. 'I'm a free spirit. A one-off.'

'Oh you're a one-off all right,' she retorted. 'There could never be another one like you. Nature's learned her lesson!'

Finishing their coffee, they showered, changed into fresh, dry clothes and made their way back downstairs to the dining room, where they found a table already set for two by the door. The only other guests in evidence was a group of seven occupying a long table under the window opposite, which appeared to comprise several small tables like theirs pushed together.

There were three women and four men in the group and a couple of them nodded in their direction as they entered the room. Kate surmised that they were probably walkers, or delegates attending a business conference who had also been caught out by the snow. Whatever the truth of the matter, it seemed they had something to celebrate, going by the number of bottles of wine and glasses of beer or lager already on their table even before the main course had been delivered, and their voices were raised in excited, raucous conversation.

'Bad form to behave like that at the dinner table,' Hayden commented haughtily, just loud enough for Kate to hear. 'Obviously a load of plebs.'

She shook her head. 'Don't be such an arrogant snob,' she replied. 'They're not hurting anyone and they're plainly having fun.'

'Maybe,' he acknowledged grumpily, 'but they're still a rabble.'

He would have said more, but at that moment a young, ginger-haired woman wriggled out of her seat and came across to them with a smile and a half-full bottle of red wine.

'Tammy Morrison,' she said. 'You must be frozen after wading through all that snow. Mrs Parsons said your car broke down.'

'You could say that,' Kate answered with a short laugh. 'Head gasket. We're beginning to warm up now, though.'

The woman poured some wine into each of their glasses. 'Hope that helps,' she said. 'Enjoy.'

Then with another smile, she left them to it and went back to her table.

'Uncommonly decent of her,' Hayden remarked, taking a sip of his wine.

'Even though she's with the plebeian rabble?' Kate said with a mischievous glint in her eyes.

He grunted but made no reply.

The evening meal turned out to be excellent. The pot roast Mrs Parsons had mentioned was particularly tasty and proved to be "laced" with nothing more sinister than cinnamon. It was followed by apple pie and custard, and Hayden had the bare-faced effrontery to do his best Oliver Twist impression and ask Mrs Parsons for a second helping. Only to receive a hostile glare in response, and no extra pie.

Before they could get up to leave after the meal, Tammy Morrison came over to them again and said, 'We're going to the room next door. As you're on your own, would you like to join us?'

'We'd love to,' Kate replied with a smile and dug a reluctant Hayden in the ribs, murmuring, 'Come on, misery guts,' as they followed them all out into the hall.

The small number of seats in the so-called lounge were soon filled — not that there appeared to be any other guests likely to contest the fact — and fuelled by an excess of alcohol, the lively conversation of Tammy and her friends got even more so. Privately, Kate couldn't help wondering where they'd got all their bottles of wine from and who was paying for it, but it was shared so generously with Hayden and herself that she decided that it would be indelicate to ask — and it really was excellent wine!

On top of that, alcohol tended to loosen tongues and as a police officer trained to observe people, she found the interplay between all the different characters fascinating as she sat in the background, listening to the reminiscences about their time at university and what they had done with their lives since graduation. In stark contrast to her intense interest in them, they displayed a remarkable incuriosity about Hayden and herself and Kate was quite surprised that none of them, not even the convivial Tammy, made any attempt to quiz them as to who they were and where they had come from. The ex-grads appeared to be totally wrapped up in themselves and their own little world. Almost as if they had overlooked the fact that they were sharing their reunion celebrations with two perfect strangers.

That suited Kate anyway. The last thing she wanted — and she knew Hayden would be of a similar mind — was for the other guests to learn that they were police officers. From past experience she knew that such a revelation was likely to give rise at the very least to suspicion and at the very worst open hostility. So she was content just to sit there quietly with her drink and simply take it all in, relieved to escape having to contribute to the general conversation herself, apart from giving an occasional nod or an encouraging smile at an appropriate moment to fit in.

By the time she decided to call it a night and extricate her husband from the clutches of a sexy blonde called Abbey Granger, whose daring cropped top and bare midriff with its glittering navel piercing appeared to be holding him spell-bound, there wasn't a great deal she didn't know about their fellow guests and why they were celebrating. Had the name of Francis Templeton come up, she would have known a lot more, but unsurprisingly, he received no mention at all.

CHAPTER 4

The blizzard hit the hotel at just before midnight, the temperature in the room dropping appreciably and the mournful moans of the earlier snowstorm rising rapidly in volume to a demonic howling. It shook the old building with the violence of a terrier with a rat in its jaws and threatened to stave in the rattling windows against which sharp icy particles, instead of feathery snowflakes, now hammered with relentless force. Hayden, who much to Kate's irritation always slept the sleep of the dead, remained on his back with his mouth open, snoring his head off. Completely unaffected by the din. But for Kate it was an entirely different story. After two hours trying to get to sleep with all that was going on around her, she finally gave up. Throwing off the sheets and blankets, she swung her legs over the edge of the bed and stood there for a moment, wriggling her toes and shivering in her thin nightdress. Then grabbing her dressing gown from the foot of the bed, she padded to the window and peered through the misted glass. But she could see nothing but a frenzy of twisting, plunging tree branches within a swirling maelstrom of hail whipped up by the wind and backlit by an unnatural bar of flickering moonlight.

Casting a venomous glance at her "sleeping beauty" of a husband, she crossed the room to the small table in the corner and turned on one of the wall lights to make herself a black coffee from the makings provided by the hotel. Then she sat down on the chair drawn up at the dressing table and sipped her drink slowly while she reflected on the previous evening's gathering and the other guests she had met.

They were certainly a disparate bunch. Overweight investment banker Ronnie Brewer, she decided, was the dominant "alpha male". It was apparently five years since the six graduates had been at university together, but it was plain that he still held sway over them.

Interestingly, though, the stunning girlfriend he had brought along with him was a different story. Victoria Adams may have come across as an unassuming, compliant sort of young woman, but Kate sensed an independence and inner strength in her that was hidden only just beneath the surface. Without a doubt, she was the one who called the shots where Brewer was concerned, even if she chose to let him think it was the other way round, and Kate couldn't help asking herself what someone like her could possibly see in a pompous, overweight specimen like Brewer. At which point, she glanced across at her other half now spread out on the bed like a beached porpoise and smiled ruefully, deciding not to go there.

Then, feeling guilty for her disloyal thoughts, she quickly returned to her reflections on the other members of the group and immediately the face of a sly looking man with a pasty complexion and crooked mouth who had been introduced to Hayden and herself as Jeffrey Cartwright, thrust itself before her mind's eye. From the run of the conversation, she had surmised that Cartwright had been Brewer's sidekick and close confidant on campus. But it seemed that despite the passage of time, he had happily slipped back into the very same role since their arrival at the hotel. A clever cunning man, she thought, but one who from his gaunt physical appearance and dilated pupils, had to be well into cocaine or heroin addiction, which made him wholly unpredictable.

The remaining two men in the group were total opposites. With pale blue eyes that seemed to be perpetually on the move and a straggly beard he constantly picked at nervously with his finger and thumb, Jimmy Caulfield struck her as a rather weak, creepy character, who was just along for the ride. She put him down as the sort of person who always went with the crowd, keeping a low profile and running with the hare and hunting with the hounds. Not a man to be relied upon, she thought, but a survivor and someone who was likely to turn quite nasty if he was in a corner.

Conversely, Lenny Welch, apparently a one-time body-builder whose family had originally hailed from Jamaica before they emigrated to Birmingham where he was born, was the strong, silent type. A man with a mind of his own and the sort of muscular physique that could only have been achieved through dedication to personal fitness. To an extent, he reminded her of the fictional character, Mr T in the eighties film series, *The A Team*, which she had recently watched on DVD. But he was a lot more personable and though similarly bearded like Mr T, there the resemblance ended, because he was totally bald.

As for the two women, they were also total opposites. Abbey Granger was easy to categorise. Kate had met her ilk many times in the past. Of average intelligence, but shallow, self-interested and over-sexed, her main focus would always be on her hair and personal appearance, and Kate thought it more likely she would have gone to university not to improve herself, but to meet boys and to party.

Tammy Morrison on the other hand was the unknown quantity. She came across as a gentle, caring person, and the revelation during the conversations in the lounge that she had previously worked as a casualty nurse in a hospital ICU seemed to bear this out. Yet Kate was not sure what to make of her. Intelligent she certainly appeared to be, with a warm pleasant manner, but there was a shadow behind those bespectacled eyes that Kate found impossible to read. For some reason it bothered her.

Something bothered her about the gathering itself too. Despite the exhibition of lively bonhomie, she had sensed an underlying tension in the room. It was as if the partying was just a front. A desperate attempt by the group of friends to rid themselves of a spectre that was lurking somewhere in the background. A spectre they were reluctant to name but which threatened them all equally. She may have imagined it, of course, but if that was the case, why had the feeling of unease remained with her?

Finishing her coffee, she set the cup back on the little table and tried to give the issue some thought. But she hadn't realised just how tired she was and within seconds her head had drooped and she had plunged into a deep sleep. She awoke later with a stiff neck and an immediate awareness that the noise of the storm had subsided, reducing its cacophony to its former low moan. There was still a wind of sorts, but the blizzard had thankfully blown itself out.

Focusing her gaze on the double bed, she smiled to herself. The big mound in the middle was still there, tangled up in the blankets, and in common with the storm, the loud snores that had earlier emanated from it had reduced to a low rumble. Hayden was still dead to the world. She stretched her cramped limbs in the padded chair and glanced at her watch, surprised to see that it was just after half four. She must have been out for the count for around four hours.

She climbed to her feet, intending to join Hayden back in bed, but then suddenly stopped short. The loud cracking and creaking of loose floorboards from just outside the room had been quite distinct. She frowned. Who on earth could be wandering about the hotel at such an early hour?

Quickly changing direction, she crossed to the bedroom door instead. Opening it as quietly as she could, she peered through the gap. The corridor outside was lit by a number of flickering wall lamps spaced a few feet apart. Their light faded into shadow at each end, but nevertheless, she could see that the corridor was deserted in both directions. There was no sign of anyone, just some dark marks in the pile of the fawn, threadbare carpet, which looked like dirty, wet footprints. Someone with wet shoes or feet had obviously just walked past. But where had they gone? She hadn't heard another bedroom door close. Also, where had they been to leave such a distinctive trail? Surely not outside the hotel in such awful weather? As all rooms were apparently ensuite, they wouldn't have needed to leave their own to take a shower elsewhere, wetting the carpet on the way back. Most strange.

She was about to close the door again, when there was a loud crash which seemed to come from downstairs, followed by another crash a few seconds later. It sounded like a door banging in the wind, but where it was and why it had suddenly come open was a mystery. Nevertheless, she felt bound to take a look, if only to satisfy her natural curiosity.

Ducking back inside her room, she tugged her trousers off the hangar in the wardrobe and hurriedly pulled them on over her nightdress. Then slipping her bare feet into a spare pair of shoes, she grabbed her coat from the back of the door and snatched the bedroom door key from the lock before leaving the room in a rush.

She didn't bother to check the corridor to the left. She had already done that shortly after their arrival. There was just another narrow staircase in an alcove at the end, leading up to what was obviously the room in the clocktower. Heading the other way, she heard the crash of the door twice more before she reached the top of the main staircase, which dropped away into the gloom of the hall.

Another crash as she felt her way down and she was astonished when a light suddenly came on to see a figure dressed in an anorak, corduroy trousers and trainers fumbling with the front door in the hallway below, trying to pull it shut. It was Tammy Morrison.

Morrison turned quickly, seemingly startled by her approach. Her ginger hair looked wet and windblown and there were traces of snow on the toes of her trainers. She was not wearing her glasses and for a second she squinted at Kate as if she had trouble recognising her. Then she smiled as recognition finally dawned.

'Oh hi, Kate,' she said. 'I heard the loud banging and came down to see what it was. Someone must have left the door open and I can't seem to be able to close it.'

Kate smiled in return. 'You look as though you've been out for a stroll,' she said.

Morrison laughed and smoothed her hair back with both hands. 'What, in this weather? You must be joking. Anyway, not without my glasses. Can't see much at a distance without them. Quite short-sighted, I'm afraid. But the door was slamming back against the wall outside and I had to pop out over the step to reach it and pull it back.'

'Funny anyone would want to go out on a night like this,' Kate replied and bent down to peer at the lock. 'No key either. Mrs Parsons mustn't lock the place up at night.'

'No need,' another voice said coldly and that very person wearing a dressing gown, pushed between them. 'Nobody bother us round here. Too far out, see, an' village still be six mile away when you gets to top lane.'

The older woman took hold of the door and pulled it shut with some force before twisting the handle sharply to the right.

'Difficult lock till you gets to know it,' she went on, eyeing them both suspiciously. 'What you be doin' down here this time anyways? Ought to be in bed like other folks.'

She spoke like the governess of a private boarding school and Kate raised an eyebrow. 'The door should be locked at night, Mrs Parsons,' she said tightly. 'We were both awakened by it banging and came down to check.'

Parsons nodded and waved an arm towards the passageway beside the staircase. 'Heard it too. Come to fix it 'afore it woke up whole place. Tom and me, we has couple of rooms at back just down there, see. But he sleeps real sound like. Wouldn't have heard a thing.'

She peered at the tiled floor and looked down at Kate's shoes with a scowl. 'Dirty my floor there then, did you?' she asked. 'Only just cleaned up after folk arrived yesterday. Now I be doin' same thing again today.'

Kate glanced at the trail of dirty wet marks on the tiles between the front door and the foot of the stairs and shook her head. 'Nothing to do with me, Mrs Parsons,' she replied. 'You'll find marks like that on the carpet upstairs too. It looks like someone went for a walk outside a little while ago and didn't wipe their feet on the door mat or shut up shop properly when they came back.'

Parsons frowned. 'Can't see who would want to go out there at this hour. Blizzard's left snow piled up two feet at least. No way anyone could go anywhere till it clears.'

Kate forced another smile and turned towards the stairs. 'At least no harm's been done. I'm back off to bed.'

'Don't fancy a nightcap, do you?' Morrison blurted, then laughed. 'Well, more of a "daycap" actually.'

Kate hesitated and glanced at her watch. It was getting on for five. 'Might just as well, I suppose,' she said with a shrug, thinking of Hayden's snores. 'I won't get to sleep again now anyway.'

Mrs Parsons grunted sourly. 'Please yourselves. You knows where bar is.'

The bar room was cold, so they both took their glasses of vodka back into the lounge where the open fire was still just smoking.

'That was a funny business about the door,' Morrison said, dropping into a chair as close to the inglenook as possible. 'Maybe it blew open of its own accord. I mean, who would want to go out there in a howling blizzard?'

Kate dragged another chair over to her. 'Bit weird, I agree,' she replied. 'Though the actual blizzard seems to have died down now.'

'Snow is still falling though,' Morrison continued. She gave a short laugh. 'Maybe the culprit was Jimmy and he went out there to get some night shots with his camera.'

'Jimmy?'

'Yes, Jimmy Caulfield. He's a teacher, but his real love is amateur photography. He's pretty good at it too, though he's a bit of a fanatic. Used to go out in all weathers when we were at uni, just to get that special shot. Right headcase, he is.'

Kate nodded. 'Have to be a headcase to wade into all that snow out there.' She threw a glance at the window where she could see that the flakes were falling heavily, backlit by the strange moon that had materialised in the midst of the blizzard. 'Hasn't stopped either.'

'No, I know, and I hope we don't end up being stranded here. I want to get home straight after this weekend. There are some big parties I've been invited to.'

'But what made you come here in the first place? You must have heard the weather forecast.'

'I did, but I never thought it would be as bad as this. Anyway, I had already confirmed that I was coming, so I couldn't very well let everyone down.' She hesitated. 'Though, I have to say, exactly who arranged it all *is* a bit of a mystery.'

Kate looked puzzled. 'But I assumed it was what's his name? The big guy, Ronnie Brewer?'

'The rest of us did too, but he says he had nothing to do with it and his own invite claims to have come from Jeff Cartwright, something Jeff hotly denies.'

'But who's paying for it all then?'

Morrison shrugged. 'Don't know. According to Mrs Parsons, the weekend was booked and paid for in advance by some unknown person.'

'Yet you said just now that you confirmed you would be attending. So who did you send the confirmation back to?'

'To the email address printed on the bottom of the invite, which all of us thought to be Ronnie's and Ronnie thought to be Jeff's.'

Kate shook her head several times. 'Talk about confusing.'

'You're confused? Think how all of us feel. After all, why would anyone bother to invite us all here for a bogus get-together, paying for it all in advance, then simply walk away from it once we'd arrived without revealing the reason? What did they get out of it, except a big bill?'

Kate laughed. 'It's like a plot from an Agatha Christie novel.'

Morrison gave a little snort. 'I just hope it won't end like one.'

Before Kate could give the matter any further thought, they both heard heavy footsteps in the hallway and a tall, slightly stooped elderly man in jeans and an old grey sweater appeared in the doorway.

'Mornin',' he said cheerfully. 'Thought I hear voices in here. Mind if I sees to fire, ladies?'

They both stood up and moved out the way while he bent down and started clearing out the remains of the logs from the grate with a small shovel and tipping them into a metal bucket he was carrying.

'You must be Tom,' Kate said.

'That be me,' he replied, half-turning his head. 'Good, old, reliable Tom. Hear from Daphne you had bother with front door.'

'It apparently blew open or was left open by someone and it got caught by the wind,' Morrison said.

Parsons rubbed his nose on the sleeve of his sweater, leaving a black mark. 'Dunno how that could have happened, less it were old woman up to her tricks again. She be a pesky nuisance right enough.'

'What old woman?'

He swivelled round on his haunches to face her. 'Mawgana Keegan,' he replied. 'Said to haunt Warneford Hall. Always walkin' up and down place, frightenin' folk half to death.'

Morrison's eyes widened. 'You mean a-a ghost?'

He nodded, his expression serious as he turned back to his fire. 'Must be, I s'pose. Seein' as she died 'bout hundred and fifty year ago. Thing is, Warneford Hall were a manor house at start. Built by sea-farin' fella called Rupert Keegan for his young wife, Mawgana. Story goes he caught her in bed with another man an' in his rage threw acid in her face as punishment, then locked her up in clocktower. But she broke out an' chucked herself off roof. They do say as acid burned her face right off an' to this day she walks 'bout Warneford Hall with no face inside her hood.'

Morrison stared suspiciously at the back of his head. 'Are you pulling our legs?'

'Me? Now why would I be doin' that?' He turned again, still serious. 'Place were built where it shouldn't ha' been, see. On what they calls Ghost Marsh. Lot of funny things happens on that there marsh. Don't do to go wanderin' 'bout place.'

Kate treated him to an old-fashioned look. 'I think it's time we went back upstairs, Tammy,' she said drily. 'Leave Mr Parsons with his fire and his faceless apparitions.'

'But a ghost!' Tammy exclaimed, pulling at Kate's sleeve as they returned to the hallway. 'I'll never be able to sleep properly again.'

Kate paused at the bottom of the staircase. 'For pity's sake, Tammy,' she said wearily, 'it was a wind up.'

'You sure?'

'Absolutely positive. He was spinning us a yarn.'

But staring up at the gloom of the landing as they climbed the stairs, she felt a sudden chill run down her back.

Reaching the top of the stairs, thankfully without encountering any apparitions, Kate checked out the footprint trail on the carpet, walking slowly along the corridor in the hope of seeing if it ended by a particular door. But she soon realised she should have carried out the check when she'd first seen the trail, not left it until after she had spent so long chatting with Tammy Morrison in the bar. As it was, the trail seemed to fade progressively as she advanced and the marks petered out altogether halfway along the corridor. Just after her own bedroom door. There were six other rooms beyond, three on each side of the corridor. Whoever had returned from their night "hike" could have gone back to any of them.

Then, driven by a sudden thought, she got down on her hands and knees and crept slowly on for a few yards beyond the point where the trail ended and it was then that she noticed the disturbed carpet pile. Someone had taken the trouble to wipe the carpet clean, possibly with a dry cloth, after she had seen the marks, and the rubbing motion of the cloth had left its own signature. But the "evidence" had faded completely within two to three feet as the pile had settled back as before.

Straightening up, she returned to her room and closed the door quietly behind her, gnawing at her lip thoughtfully as she headed past her still sleeping husband to the bathroom for a shower. Okay, so there was no reason why someone shouldn't be able to brave the weather and head outside for some fresh air in the middle of the night. It was certainly eccentric in her view, but it was up to them and nothing to do with her or anyone else. Furthermore, they hadn't committed a criminal offence, either by failing to shut the front door properly afterwards, or by leaving a dirty trail on the tiled hall floor and the corridor carpet because they hadn't wiped their feet as they should have done.

These were just simple mistakes anyone could have made. Yet for some unaccountable reason she had become hung up on them. On the face of it, that was ridiculous and Hayden would have really gone to town on her with what he would have described as nothing more than a bonkers obsession. But there was more to it than that and the burning question in her mind was why would someone go to the extent of trying to obliterate part of the dirty trail they had left behind just to prevent it being traced back to their room? Mrs Parsons was quite a formidable person, but even her wrath was unlikely to have been the motivation for someone to take so much trouble to cover their tracks. There had to be another more significant reason, and it was then that another thought dawned on Kate. For them to have only carried out such remedial action once she had spotted the marks and gone downstairs to investigate the banging door suggested that they knew she had spotted them. That meant she was being watched, but by whom and for what earthly reason? As she turned on the shower the initial blast of cold water brought with it an unsettling feeling. A premonition of something that she couldn't name. An invisible shadow that peered at her covertly from the intricate labyrinth of her mind, and the chill remained deep inside her even when the hot water was finally streaming down her body.

CHAPTER 5

Breakfast was poorly attended. But Kate was not surprised after all the heavy drinking that had taken place the previous night and she felt more than a little pleased with herself for restricting her own intake for a change. In fact, apart from Kate and Hayden, whose iron-clad stomach seemed unaffected by the amount of alcohol he had consumed, only Tammy Morrison and Victoria Adams put in an appearance, nodding to them with a smile as they walked into the room.

'Bit of a rough night, wasn't it?' Adams called across after helping herself to the cold buffet laid out on a separate long table at the side of the room.

Hayden nodded, but he was too engrossed shovelling his way through the mountain of cold meats, cheese and rolls on his plate to respond with anything more intelligible than a grunt.

'Pretty wild,' Kate agreed. Then adding, with just the hint of a self-satisfied smirk, 'How's the boyfriend this morning?'

Adams made a face. 'Paralytic. I had to put him to bed and spent the night in our room with earplugs in, while he lay there and snored.'

'Not going to turn up for breakfast then?'

Adams gave an unamused laugh. 'Be lucky if we see him before evening dinner the way he is, and I suspect the others will be the same.'

Kate shrugged, staring across at the window and the mounds of snow covering what she could see of the forecourt, which extended down the side of the hotel between it and a wooden outhouse. As she looked, she caught sight of the figure of Tom Parsons in a thick coat, gumboots and a woolly cap with earflaps bent over a spade at the corner of the building.

'Seems Tom is out there already trying to clear a way through at the front of the hotel,' she said, 'but at least the snow seems to have stopped falling.'

'He's been out there for a couple of hours now,' Adams replied, following the direction of her gaze. 'I came down earlier to check on the breakfast and popped my head out the door. He was already at it then. Can't see him making much of an impression on it all, though. It seemed pretty thick to me. Even the cars seem to be buried to halfway up their doors and you can hardly see the lake.'

'Lake?'

'There's one on the other side of the forecourt, just beyond the garden,' Morrison answered for her. 'Poor old fish won't be happy. They're effectively sealed up there under the ice.'

'Lake don't freeze right over,' another voice put in. 'It be fed by underground springs from Ghost Marsh.'

Mrs Parsons had entered quietly and now stood just inside the doorway, a sour look on her face. 'T'others comin' down for breakfast then?' she went on. 'It be close on ten now and I got to clear away.'

Morrison shook her head. 'I should forget them,' she replied. 'I don't think they'll be wanting breakfast.'

Parsons nodded. 'Fancied as much,' she said, her obvious disapproval giving a sharp edge to the tone of her voice. 'I'll clear away when you be finished then.'

She made to leave, but Morrison suddenly fired a question at her, bringing her to a stop. 'Mrs Parsons, is it true that Warneford Hall is, er, haunted?'

Parsons turned back from the door and stared at her. 'Tom been spinnin' you one of his yarns, has he?' she asked. 'You don't want to be listenin' to that silly old fool.'

'So what he said about a faceless ghost called Mawgana Keegan walking about the place is untrue?'

Parsons considered her question for a moment, then ran the palms of her hands down her apron as she'd done before, a faint contemptuous smile hovering over her thin lips. 'I ain't never seen no ghosts here,' she said without answering the question. 'But folk do tell of things happenin' out on Ghost Marsh at night. Flashin' lights, strange shapes an' all sorts, 'specially when mist comes down. But I just sticks to me business an' keeps meself to meself.'

Then she pulled open the door and left them all to it, Morrison's question still unanswered.

'So, I'm still none the wiser,' Morrison commented ruefully.

'Maybe it's best to stay that way,' Hayden spoke up for the first time, pushing his empty plate away. 'Ignorance is always bliss, and anyway, an ethereal apparition is infinitely better than a real-life corpse, believe me.'

Kate glared at him in an attempt to shut him up, but she was too late and the inevitable follow-up question came immediately. 'Why, have you seen a corpse?'

For a second Hayden gaped, realising he had put his foot in it. 'Oh, er, one or two, yes,' he said vaguely.

Adams seemed very interested now. 'So, what do you do, Hayden?' she asked. 'Not a mortician, are you?'

He gave an uneasy laugh, conscious of Kate's eyes burning into him across the table. 'Not likely,' he replied, his face reddening under her baleful gaze.

'Work in a hospital then, do you?'

He nodded. 'Something like that.'

'You too, Kate?'

Kate realised with a sense of resignation that she had been left with no option but to come clean. 'We're police officers,' she said quietly.

'Police?' Morrison exclaimed, her eyes widening. 'Good heavens.'

Kate waited for the usual inane questions to start. *Are you detectives? Do you work at Scotland Yard? What crimes have you solved? Have you arrested any murderers?* But instead an awkward silence followed. Morrison seemed to be quite taken aback and unsure what else to say, concentrating instead on the meat, cheese and croissants she had selected from the buffet. As for Adams, she just said wryly, 'Well, at least we can feel safe in our beds at night knowing you're here.'

Kate merely smiled a reply but conscious of the awkward atmosphere her disclosure seemed to have created, she was about to climb to her feet and escape to the comforting obscurity of her room, when her departure was halted by a dramatic unexpected intervention. The door suddenly burst open and Tom Parsons appeared, looking panicky and dishevelled.

'Need help,' he gasped. 'There be a body in lake!'

* * *

Ignoring the cold and in just the clothes they stood up in, Kate and Hayden followed Tom Parsons out the front door at a run, leaving Morrison and Adams standing hesitantly in the doorway, peering round the frame.

Parsons had dug out a dirty, now yellowish channel through the snow with his spade along the front of the hotel. But there was also evidence of another shallower track having been partially created by heavy feet, slipping and sliding, in a ragged, diagonal line across the buried garden. Presumably it had been made by Parsons' boots when he had spotted what was in the lake at the far end. But it was a struggle getting through and they were forced to wade up to their calves in the white stuff in order to reach their objective. At which point, Parsons threw out a restraining arm just in front of a partially buried lifebuoy suspended in an open-fronted box on a post, which projected above the snow.

'Don't go no closer,' he shouted. 'We be right on edge of lake. Snow covers ice for 'bout twenty feet out towards middle and won't hold no weight. There be several underground springs feedin' lake, see, so it don't never freeze over completely. Maybe feller didn't realise 'afore he fell in.'

He pointed and Kate stiffened. The lumpy object was clearly visible in front of them a few yards out into the lake and to the right of the lifebuoy, apparently floating in a patch of open, grey water, where the ice had no doubt given way and devoured the layer of snow that had covered it.

'Foller me,' Parsons directed, 'but tread where I treads.'

As he moved off to the right of the lifebuoy, Kate spotted the start of a jetty jutting out into the lake from the bank. Its wooden slats were partially visible through footprints left in the snow and she guessed Parsons had already been on it.

Both Kate and Hayden advanced very slowly along it to a point level with the body in the water, which was about two feet from them.

Parsons pointed to a rake lying by his feet. 'Hooked him closer to jetty with that,' he said, 'but he were too heavy fer me to haul out.'

Kate knelt down, wincing as the snow soaked through the trousers she was wearing. Leaning out from the jetty, she was able to pull the floating body closer, gripping a broad belt tied round its waist over a thick khaki coloured coat.

'Give me a hand,' she said.

Hayden and Parsons knelt down beside her and took hold of loose folds in the coat with both hands.

'Right. One, two, three, heave,' she instructed.

They managed to get the body halfway up the side of the jetty, but its sodden, partially frozen weight proved too heavy for them and they had to let go. It took four attempts before they succeeded in pulling it out of the water completely and setting it on the jetty face down, and they crouched there panting heavily for a few moments before they were even able to speak.

The dead man was as stiff as a board and although Kate went through the motions of checking for any vital signs, not surprisingly there were none. He had obviously been in the water for several hours. Somewhat incongruously, there was a 35mm digital camera with the brand name Canon on the side looped around the man's neck by a thin strap. Even before they had managed to turn the body over, Kate knew from the conversation she had had with Tammy Morrison who the man was.

'It's Jimmy Caulfield,' she said.

'Looks like the poor devil slipped and fell in,' Hayden added. 'Maybe he couldn't swim.'

Parsons frowned dubiously. 'Must have broke through ice as he fell,' he said, 'an' he wouldn't have lasted long in that icy water.'

'He looked to be young and fairly fit when I last saw him,' Kate went on. 'I'm surprised he couldn't have got himself out again even so . . .'

'Does that matter right now?' Hayden cut in, visibly shaking. 'My trousers are soaked and I'm freezing to death.'

Kate nodded and glanced behind her. The large wooden outhouse she had noticed at breakfast was just a few feet from the side of the house behind them, a wheeled skip beside it from which the necks of a forest of bottles, no doubt empties from the bar, poked up through the mantle of snow. 'I suggest we put him in there,' she said, waving a hand towards the building. 'No sense carrying him through the hotel for everyone to see, and we need to preserve the corpse as much as possible for the doctor anyway.'

'Doctor?' Parsons echoed. 'What you need one o' them fer? Dead, ain't he? Any fool can see that.'

'Yes, but there will have to be a proper medical examination to confirm cause of death.'

'What you know 'bout that? Get it from telly, did yer? *Midsomer Murders* like?'

Kate sighed and shivered at the same time. The secret was out now after Hayden's indiscretion, so there was no point holding things back. 'We're both police officers,' she said. 'Good enough for you?'

Parsons was obviously taken aback and his aggressive responses died on his lips.

'Police, eh? Well, I be a monkey's uncle! But how do you 'spect to get a doctor out here then? Ain't one in village, which be well over six mile from top lane, an' after that blizzard, track over old bridge right up to lane must be three feet deep in snow now on account of it bein' between high banks. I been to look, see.'

'What about the fields on either side of the lane? They're higher up and not as contained, so the snow is likely to be shallower. Maybe we could at least get out to the top lane that way?'

He shook his head. 'More'n likely top lane be almost as bad as track up to it. Couldn't even walk it all in this cold neither an' be daft to try an' cross them fields instead. They's all be deep marsh under snow. Easy to get sucked down. Even cattle gets trapped, 'specially after heavy rain. I heard tell of fella sucked down few years back. Never found his body neither. No way out of here till thaw as I sees it.'

Kate showed her irritation. 'There is such a thing as a telephone.'

Parsons laughed. 'Aye, so there be, girl, but our phone line be down an' ain't no mobile signal out here. That's why me and missus don't bother with likes of 'em.'

Hayden released an explosive snort. 'Can we end the chat and just cart him to the outhouse, Kate?' he exclaimed, visibly shaking. 'You and I aren't exactly dressed for this. We need to get back in the warm before we freeze to death.'

Parsons had the key to the outhouse on a ring with other keys in his coat pocket and the extra wide door opened easily on well-oiled hinges. The building appeared to be about fifteen feet long by ten feet wide, with a narrow, high-level window on each side. A large number of logs had been stacked up against the left-hand wall for half its length and a mini tractor with an unattached trailer behind it was housed alongside. Various other bits of light garden machinery and gardener's hand tools were stacked untidily against the end wall, and a number of propane gas cylinders, petrol cans and steel drums, probably containing oil, occupied other available spaces. Fortunately, despite all that had been crammed into the outhouse, a reasonable amount of room had been left uncluttered just inside the door, so they were able to carry the body between them and lay it on some sacks on the floor. As they did so, Kate was conscious of several figures standing in the front doorway of the hotel, gawking at them. It seemed that Tammy Morrison and Victoria Adams had been joined by some of their other friends.

Locking the outhouse afterwards and pocketing the key herself, despite Parson's protests, Kate led the way back to the hotel, ready for the inevitable questions that would be greeting them.

'Was that a body?' Morrison whispered.

Kate nodded. ''Fraid so. Looks like a nasty accident.'

'So who is it?' Ronnie Brewer demanded, looking pale and the worse for wear.

'Your friend, Jimmy Caulfield. He seems to have been taking photographs and fell in the lake.'

'Damn fool,' Brewer said with a complete lack of sympathy. 'I always knew he'd come a cropper one day with that camera.'

'It's still very tragic,' Kate said. She moved to one side as Hayden edged past to head for the fire in the lounge and Parsons made for the kitchen, no doubt to pass on what had happened to his wife.

Brewer shrugged. 'His choice,' he said.

Morrison was plainly very upset. 'But Ronnie,' she protested, 'he *drowned*. Think about it, drowned just like George Lane and-and Francis.'

Brewer gave her a hard stare. 'Shut it, Tam,' he said, and flicked his eyes towards Kate in what Kate interpreted as a warning gesture. 'No connection. Just a coincidence. End of.'

Cartwright poked his head round the door frame. 'You guys gonna stand there all morning? We've already lost breakfast, but there's still some coffee left.'

'Should get up on time then, shouldn't you?' Adams snapped. But it was plain the comment was directed at Brewer rather than Cartwright, and she threw a scathing glance at her boyfriend as she pushed past Cartwright and led the way back into the hotel, making for the stairs.

Kate was not far behind her and she had just reached them when she glimpsed Morrison catch up with Brewer and say something to him, which prompted him to turn round quickly to throw what looked like a startled glance over his shoulder in Kate's direction.

Kate smiled cynically to herself as she mounted the first tread. *So you've just told him Hayd and me are both police officers, have you, Tammy? Now why should that be so important? What are you worried about? And prior to that, why did Brewer tell you to 'shut it' when you seemed to attach so much significance to the fact that Jimmy Caulfield had died from drowning?*

Something very strange was going on with this little group of former university graduates, and she was determined to find out what it was.

* * *

Kate could not find her mobile phone. She knew she had brought it up with her to her room when she'd first arrived and she was sure she had put it in the top drawer of the little cabinet on her side of the bed, but it wasn't there anymore. A painstaking search of the room had also met with no success. To all intents and purposes, the phone had simply walked. Yet everything else appeared to be exactly as she had left it, including her purse containing around a hundred pounds in notes and several credit cards. All that was missing from her drawer was her phone. To make matters even worse, there was no sign of Hayden's phone either, and she was positive she had seen him slip it into the top drawer of the cabinet on his own side of the bed.

When he appeared half an hour later looking for her, he confirmed that he had in fact left his phone where she'd thought.

'Bit of a rum do, eh?' he said in his drawling, pompous voice. 'I was going to suggest we tried getting a signal again now we're at a higher elevation, so we can get a crew out here to deal with this drowning incident.'

She nodded. 'That's what I was going to do,' she replied, 'but now we can't even try that. The phones can only have been nicked.'

He raised his eyebrows. 'It's hard to believe we'd get any intruders out here, especially in all this snow.'

'Well then, it must be down to someone in the hotel.'

He looked uncomfortable. 'Well, we can't go around making allegations without some sort of evidence and where would we start? We can hardly demand to search everyone's rooms and cars. I doubt that any of the other guests or the Parsonses would agree to that and we have no power to insist.'

Kate frowned, knowing he was right. 'So what do we do then? Just accept the fact, bearing in mind we have no other means of contacting anyone in the outside world in the meantime.'

'You make it sound as if we've been marooned.'

'Well, haven't we? This bloody snow has effectively imprisoned us here. Unless you feel like trying to get some help by wading through several feet of snow for six or seven miles to the nearest village in just an anorak and a pair of ordinary walking shoes which still haven't dried out since our trek yesterday? And don't forget too we are supposed to be back on duty at Highbridge nick on Monday, which in case it has escaped your notice, is the day after tomorrow.'

He chose not to answer and she continued in a rush. 'So what about the stiff we've stuck in the outhouse? In normal circumstances we would have left him on the jetty for the police surgeon to examine. Okay, so we had to move him to where he is now because of the circumstances, but we can't just leave him there until the snow decides to thaw. On the face of it, his death was due to an accident or misadventure, but we need an expert opinion to confirm that.'

'Well, we can't get one here or any backup either, so we have no choice but to sit it out and hope for that thaw. You have to see, old girl, that we've absolutely no other choice.'

'But what if it wasn't an accident, but something else? Shit, Hayd, we could be sitting on a murder here.'

He groaned. 'Oh for goodness sake, Kate, don't start doing that again.'

'Doing what?'

'Jumping to conclusions, like you have a habit of doing. Seeing something suspicious in everything.'

Her mouth tightened. 'Well, I've usually been right in the past, haven't I? Furthermore, there's something funny going on with this uni crowd anyway.'

'What sort of funny?'

She quickly told him about what had happened the previous night while he was out to the world, then related the strange behaviour of Tammy Morrison and Ronnie Brewer just prior to her return to her room after Caulfield's body had been found.

'They're all hiding something, I'm convinced of it,' she said to his further groans, 'and I reckon someone has stolen our phones to stop us trying to contact anyone.'

He propped himself wearily on the edge of the bed. 'Okay, I give up,' he said. 'So what do you want to do about it all?'

'Well, first I want to take another look at that corpse. Now it's out of the cold and in a dry, slightly warmer environment, any marks or other signs of violence should soon start becoming apparent.'

He agreed. 'Fine, so let's do it. If only to satisfy your suspicions and give me some peace.'

'*Then*,' she added with emphasis, 'after we've checked the house phone to confirm it really is out of action, I want to ask one of the uni crowd if I can borrow their mobile to try for a signal.'

He raised both hands, palms uppermost in a deprecating gesture. 'Anything you say, detective sergeant. Then maybe I'll be able to look forward to actually enjoying my buffet lunch in a couple of hours.'

CHAPTER 6

The house telephone did prove to be dead, as Daphne Parsons had claimed, and the outhouse with its concrete floor seemed as cold as the grounds outside. Kate shivered as she stepped through the doorway and switched on the light provided by the solitary bulb dangling from the ceiling. Jimmy Caulfield looked somehow smaller now. As if he had magically shrunk. He lay in a gradually expanding pool of water. The wide open, pale blue eyes had already lost much of their unusual colour and stared glassily at her as she bent down beside the still frozen shell that had once been a young, vibrant human being.

Peering closely at the body and checking the fronts and backs of the hands as best she could, Kate sucked her teeth thoughtfully for a moment, then turned her attention to the head, examining the skull beneath the stiff matt of brown hair with careful probing fingers. Moments later she paused and frowned.

Behind her, Hayden yawned and stretched his arms. 'Told you it was just an unfortunate accident,' he said. 'Chap slipped in the snow and fell over the edge of the jetty. Nothing more than that.'

'You reckon?' she replied quietly. 'Help me to turn him over.'

'Your word is my command, oh mighty leader,' he replied with a grin.

'Just do it, will you, Hayd?' she snapped. She was in no mood for misplaced humour.

Taken aback by the sharp tone of her voice, he bent over the corpse and did as she asked.

'Did you bring your torch with you as I suggested?' she continued.

'Of course.'

Using the fingers of both hands, she gently parted the hair on the left side of Caulfield's scalp. 'Shine it there,' she said triumphantly.

He did so, but then stiffened as the beam picked out a large, discoloured lump exposed by the tips of Kate's fingers.

'What's that then?' she said. 'Looks to me very much like a head wound of some sort. It's not too obvious yet because of the effects of the freezing water on his tissues. It should become a lot more noticeable over the next few hours with the slight change in the ambient temperature. Nevertheless, it is still a head wound, which could have been caused by a blow. '

'So he banged his head on something as he fell,' he said dismissively.

She stood up. 'Or someone else banged it for him, which is *why* he fell. I'm no forensic expert by any means, but there is in my opinion a distinct likelihood he was struck with something, fell into the lake and may even have been held under the water until he drowned.'

'The bump on his head proves nothing and you know it.' he retorted irritably. 'There's absolutely no evidence of foul play here. As I've just said, that swelling could have been caused by contact with something like the edge of the jetty when he slipped and fell. Or it could have been sustained earlier before he even left the hotel to come out here.' He gave her a hard, searching stare. 'Did you find any defensive marks on his hands? I saw you look.'

She shook her head.

'Well, there you are then, no signs of a struggle. You've already acknowledged that we're not forensic experts and everything you've come up with so far is nothing more than hypothesis.'

'What about the business with the door and the marks on the corridor runner I told you about?'

He shrugged. 'So someone went out and left the door open after they'd came back in. Or maybe the door just blew open in the wind. There's nothing to say the open door or the marks in the carpet pile are linked to Caulfield's demise.'

He paused a second to take a deep breath. 'Kate, you're trying to read something into this man's death that just isn't there. Without any real evidence, forensic or otherwise, to back up your suspicions, you have nothing.'

'You're forgetting our missing mobiles. Why would someone go to the trouble of nicking those except to stop us getting help in case we were finally able to find a signal?'

'Now you really are stretching things too far. People steal mobiles because they are a saleable commodity. At this stage we don't even know that they *were* stolen.'

'You're saying they just walked?'

'I'm *saying* that the two things are not necessarily connected.'

She stood up, her frown developing into a scowl.

'This bloody snow. If it wasn't for that, we could have got the police surgeon, maybe also the forensic pathologist out here.'

'Well, we can't, so you'll just have to accept the fact. Now can we get back to the hotel before we both catch pneumonia?'

She nodded reluctantly. 'At least it will be a lot warmer in there and maybe if the house phone is still out I can get hold of that other mobile to try for a signal again.'

But Kate was out of luck with any phone. Another check on the hotel land line revealed that it was still completely dead. As for borrowing another mobile, that proved to be a non-starter. The first person she met on entering the tiled hallway was Tammy Morrison on her way to the lounge for the buffet lunch and before Kate could say anything, Morrison said, 'Ah Kate, I was looking for you.'

'For me?'

'Yes, you're a police officer, so you're just the person I should speak to.'

'Oh, why's that?'

'Well, it's most peculiar, but my mobile phone is missing from my room.'

'What? Are you sure?'

'Positive. I know I left it on my dressing table yesterday when I found I couldn't get a signal here, but it's gone. I've searched everywhere, but without success. I can only think that it's been stolen.'

'Maybe one of your friends took it for a laugh?'

She shook her head. 'But that's the whole point. I've checked with everybody and it seems their phones have all disappeared too.'

* * *

It was noisy in the dining room where everyone had gathered for the buffet lunch. All the other guests were there and everyone seemed to be standing around talking at once. The conversation slowly died when Kate and Hayden walked in behind Tammy Morrison.

Ronnie Brewer turned on the new arrivals belligerently, his fists clenched. 'What the hell's going on in this place?' he demanded. 'First, Caulfield ends up drowned in the lake and now there's a bloody tea leaf at large who's nicked all our mobile phones.'

His manner suggested that he thought Kate and Hayden were somehow to blame for it all.

'Yeah—' Jeffrey Cartwright sniffed through the usual smoke haze that surrounded him — 'and right under the noses of the Law too.'

'The Law?' Abbey Granger echoed, obviously having not yet been made aware of the identity of the other two guests. 'What, you mean, police?'

'Yeah, Old Bill.' Brewer almost spat the word. 'It turns out that these two are coppers.'

'Is that right?' Lenny Welch asked. 'You're actually police officers?'

Kate nodded and he laughed without humour. 'Well, you kept that quiet, didn't you?'

'Why shouldn't we?' Hayden said defensively. 'We're not on duty at the moment and therefore, what we do for a living is irrelevant.'

'You still might have told us,' Granger retorted. 'It was a bit sneaky not to.'

'Why sneaky?' Kate responded with feeling. 'What difference would it have made to the present situation if we had?'

'Whoever took our phones might not have done it if they had known the pair of you were police officers . . .'

'Our mobiles appear to have been stolen as well,' Hayden cut in sharply, 'so we're all in the same boat.'

'Well, that's rich,' Welch said, laughing again. 'Our finest done over as well.'

'So what are you going to do about it?' Brewer continued.

Kate shrugged. 'What would you suggest?' Then she added waspishly, 'Carry out strip searches of everyone?'

'This isn't a joke,' he snarled.

Kate nodded grimly. 'Oh, it's far from being a joke, Mr Brewer. We have a dead man lying in the outhouse out there, who seems to have drowned in circumstances that require proper investigation. Now with the line to the main house telephone down, the loss of our mobiles means that we have no way of communicating with anyone in the outside world, even were we able to get a signal.'

Brewer's eyes narrowed. 'What are you alleging? That Caulfield's death was not an accident?'

'I'm alleging nothing. But it does seem strange to me that someone has chosen this precise moment to steal all our mobiles, thus preventing any possible outside contact.'

'Well, as I said, you're the police. Do something about it.'

Kate smiled faintly. 'Police officers, yes, but not magicians, Mr Brewer. This is not an Agatha Christie scenario where we call in Hercule Poirot, then assemble in the lounge to announce the outcome.'

Brewer's anger took a nose-dive and he suddenly looked a bit sheepish, staring down at the floor.

'So, who could possibly have taken our phones?' Morrison put in, perhaps sensing the tension building up in the room. 'I can't see one of us doing it.'

'Maybe it was Mawgana?' Cartwright said, giving a half-hearted laugh. 'Tammy told us about the ghost that's supposed to wander about the hotel. Maybe she snaffled them.'

'Oh, don't,' Granger said with a shiver. 'This place is creepy enough without something like that.'

'Then we're left with just Mr and Mrs Parsons,' Welch said.

'Or the coppers themselves,' Cartwright sneered again. 'After all, they *say* they are police officers, but how do we actually know that? They could be con artists.'

Kate sighed and dipping into her pocket, she produced the wallet holding her warrant card showing her photograph and the force badge. Placing the wallet on the table, she nodded to Hayden and he did the same.

'Take a look,' she said. 'Both Hayden and myself are on CID at Highbridge police station.'

'And you're married?' Welch asked, looking surprised after peering at them both.

''Fraid so,' Kate replied. 'Police officers do sometimes get married like everyone else, you know. It may even surprise you all to learn that we also drink, go on holiday, have sex and sometimes even produce children.'

Cartwright scowled at the sarcasm, but he was the first to take hold of and closely scrutinise the warrant cards, leaving the rest to follow suit.

'You could have made the things yourself,' Brewer accused following his own scrutiny of them. 'After all, who knows what a police ID should look like? It could be anything.'

'Yeah,' Kate said. 'We went into our local badge maker and printers and got the whole thing done in readiness for when we had arranged to break down a mile and a half from this hotel, just so we could drop in and steal your mobile phones. Sounds eminently feasible, doesn't it?'

'Can we just cut this silly nonsense out?' Welch said angrily. 'I am quite satisfied with who Kate and Hayden say they are. What I want to know is how we are going to get out of this dump, and the sooner the better.'

'What about our phones?' Granger exclaimed. 'Mine was a designer mobile and it cost me a bomb.'

'Well, knowing you, it would have done, wouldn't it?' Cartwright retorted. 'But bollocks to the phones. We can claim those on insurance.'

'We should at least check to see if Mr and Mrs Parsons have any idea who could have taken them,' Victoria Adams put in for the first time.

'We don't know nothin' 'bout no mobile phones,' a familiar voice snapped from the open doorway. 'Tom and me don't use them things.'

Adams flinched and looked down at her feet in embarrassment as Kate turned to face Daphne Parsons with an attempt at a smile. 'No one is accusing you of anything, Mrs Parsons,' she said. 'But it *is* a bit of a mystery.'

'I ain't worried 'bout no mystery,' the other said, fastening her hostile gaze on Kate. 'What I be worried over be that-that thing you got my Tom to leave in outhouse. So poor devil drownded, which be a terrible business, but 'tain't no reason to leave his body like that. T'ain't decent.'

Kate nodded. 'No, it isn't decent, Mrs Parsons,' she agreed, 'but we haven't any choice in the matter. While the roads are impassable due to the snow and we have no way of contacting anyone, we are left with no alternative but to leave it there. Without wishing to sound indelicate, we need Mr Caulfield's remains to be kept in the coldest environment available because of degeneration, and the outhouse seems to be the only suitable place there is.'

Parsons grunted. 'Long as he be gone soon as there be a thaw. Tom and me got to make sure Warneford Hall be left all proper an' tidy like 'afore we go. That be what Mr Hapgood paid us fer.'

Then with a face as hard and grey as flint, she turned on her heel and left everyone to chew over the situation with the buffet lunch that nobody wanted now.

There was an awkward silence for a moment after she had gone and then Cartwright broke the spell with one of his caustic comments.

'Well, what a sweet old-fashioned thing,' he said. 'Nice to see how concerned she was about the death of one of her guests.'

'Problem is, what do we do now?' Brewer said, ignoring him. 'Her suggestion about waiting for the thaw doesn't work for me. We were only apparently booked in here until Monday morning and it's already Saturday. If this weather continues, we could be stuck in this place for days.'

'I can't have that,' Granger exclaimed. 'I've got things arranged.'

'You're not the only one,' Morrison said. 'We all need to get out.'

'So how do you suggest we do that?' Adams asked. 'We've no means of contacting anyone for help.'

'What about trying to drive out?' Brewer suggested. 'I've got a big four by four. Maybe I could have a go at it.'

Kate shook her head. 'Tom Parsons told me that the lane leading up to the main road is blocked by deep snow. You'll never be able to get through it, not even on four-wheel drive.'

'We'll see about that,' Brewer retorted. 'At least I can have a go. It's better than sitting on my arse in this place.'

'Don't be a fool, Ronnie,' Adams exclaimed. 'You'll destroy your car.'

He grinned. 'Not my car,' he said. 'Belongs to the firm.'

But he was denied the opportunity of trying out his reckless attempt. Watched from just outside the front door by everyone else, he managed to dig out one of the front wheels with a short-handled spade from the boot, but that was as far as he got.

'Shit!' he snarled. 'Bloody tyre is flat.'

'Well, we're not going to stand here and freeze while you change the wheel,' Adams called out to him. 'Just leave it, will you? It was a daft idea anyway.'

But Brewer was not listening. He had turned his attention to the other front wheel for some reason and was now hacking desperately at the snow in which it was partially buried, like a man who has lost his mind.

'What the hell are you doing?' Cartwright shouted, once again puffing on a cigarette. 'It's no good clearing that one until you've changed the flat.'

Brewer straightened up and turned to face them all, panting heavily. '*Both* tyres are flat,' he shouted back. 'Some bastard has slashed them with something.'

'What?' Kate exclaimed. Followed closely by Hayden, she stomped through the snow to join him by the car. Then after bending down to examine a tyre each, they exchanged glances.

'He's right,' Kate said grimly, straightening. 'Looks like a blade of some sort was used on this one.'

'Same with this one,' Hayden said, brushing the wet snow off his trousers as he stood up. 'Two cuts, each about a centimetre long. Someone meant business.'

Kate frowned as another thought occurred to her. Turning back towards the others gathered around the front door, she called out to them. 'The tyres have been deliberately slashed. You'd all better check your own motors.'

'I've only got light shoes on,' Abbey Granger protested, but she was pushed aside by everyone else. Heedless of what they had on their feet, they made a beeline for their own vehicles lined up against the hedge on either side of the big black Volvo.

The shouts of anger were not long in coming as wheels were cleared of snow with hands, sticks and anything else that was available. All four wheels on every car had received the same treatment.

'Now do you believe me?' Kate breathed into Hayden's ear. 'There's something very wrong here and someone wants to stop us leaving.'

* * *

Back in their room, Kate and Hayden sat on the edge of the bed and discussed what had just happened.

'The tyres must have been done last night,' Hayden said, 'while everyone was asleep. Most likely just after the blizzard had abated.'

'During the same time period that Jimmy Caulfield ended up in the lake,' Kate pointed out meaningfully, 'and also when that business with the front door occurred. Maybe Caulfield spotted the perp doing the tyres when he came out of the hotel on his way to take some pictures of the lake, or the perp *thought* he had clocked him. That would explain why Caulfield had to be silenced.'

He threw her a weary sideways glance. 'You never give up, do you?' he said, but she could tell that after the latest shock developments he was now wavering in his outright rejection of her views on Caulfield's demise.

'But you must see that there has to be a connection between all the things that have occurred since we arrived at Warneford Hall,' she insisted, pressing home her advantage. 'It's all too much of a coincidence.'

He grimaced. 'Okay, If I were to humour you for just a moment and accept your wild theory about Caulfield's death as being plausible, answer me this: why would your perp want to stop everyone leaving here? Why would they cut off all means of contact with the outside world and then slash everyone's car tyres?'

Her face was grim when she replied. 'Maybe because whoever the perp is, he or she has more targets in mind, and now, because of who we are, that could very well include us.'

* * *

The evening dinner was a fractious affair. The group of so-called friends on the long table were at each other's throats for most of the meal, and the tension in the room could have been cut with a knife. Plainly, panic was setting in after the latest shock over the slashed tyres on top of the theft of everyone's mobile phones. No sympathetic thought seemed to have been given to Jimmy Caulfield, who was lying stiff and cold in the outhouse next door. It was all about the threat to the social lives of each member of the group and the realisation that they could miss all their decadent fun by being stuck in the hotel — unless someone came up with some brilliant solution. Even when Daphne Parsons complained frostily while serving dinner that her own car had been immobilised in exactly the same way, they displayed a total lack of interest in her and her husband's predicament, and they certainly didn't care a jot about Kate and Hayden's situation. In fact, with the exception of Tammy Morrison who kept her own counsel throughout and almost seemed to retreat into herself, they seemed to regard the plight of the detectives with a kind of malicious satisfaction, as if what had happened on this ill-fated weekend could be laid at their door for somehow failing to get to grips with things.

In his usual laidback way, Hayden ignored the sniping he and Kate received, murmuring to her during the meal that they were all "lowbrow plebs" anyway. But it really got to Kate and she angrily abandoned her sweet halfway through to return to her room. Much to the annoyance of her other half who had to leave his behind as well.

'If I'd remained there any longer,' she blazed, as she closed the bedroom door behind her and wheeled round to face him, 'I'd have said something to those selfish, arrogant bastards that I really would not have regretted. The corpse of one of their so-called friends and former housemates is lying next door and all they can think about is the possible ruination of their bloody social arrangements.'

Still angry with her for the way she had torn him away from his meringue pie, it was on the tip of his tongue to give vent to his own feelings, but seeing how furious she was, he decided against it and went for the softer option.

'They're frightened,' he pointed out, and poured her a glass of wine from the bottle of red he had brought up from the bar the previous night. 'They feel trapped and confused by what's going on. It's a typical human response to look for someone to blame.'

She took a sip from her glass and nodded. 'Okay, okay, I get it,' she acknowledged. 'Sorry about your meringue.'

He tipped the remaining wine into another glass and drained it. 'Meringue's not important,' he lied. 'But what's happening here is.'

'Ah, then you're finally coming round to my way of thinking about Caulfield's death as suspicious?'

'I'm not saying that,' he said grudgingly, 'but I do agree that something is certainly going on at this place. The theft of the mobiles, the slashed tyres — you have to wonder what the purpose of it all is.'

'Some sort of vendetta, do you reckon?'

'What, against everyone?'

'Well, it certainly looks like it. From what Tammy Morrison told me in a chat I had with her this morning, the whole crowd seem to have been lured here by a bogus invitation.'

'Bogus? What do you mean by bogus?'

So she told him.

He emitted a low whistle when she had finished. 'But who could have done the luring and for what purpose?'

'No idea to both questions, but I can't see it being anyone other than one of our delightful fellow guests.'

'Maybe, but there's also Tom or Daphne Parsons, don't forget.'

She shook her head dubiously. 'I don't see the pair of them being involved in any way myself. I can't imagine Daphne Parsons wading through the snow to slash car tyres, for example. Or thumping someone over the head and pushing them into a lake.'

'No, but husband Tom looks pretty fit and from what you've told me, he was up and about pretty early this morning, ostensibly attending to the fire in the lounge.'

'But why would either or both of them have it in for their guests? As far as I know, they'd never met any of them before they turned up here on the mystery booking. So how would they know anything about them? The university the crowd attended was five years ago, way up north, and since they left uni, they've been living in different places all over the UK. How could there be any sort of a connection between them and the Parsonses who on their own say-so have worked at this hotel in Somerset for years?'

He shrugged. 'Unlikely, I agree, but we shouldn't discount them completely.'

'Maybe not, but my money's on one of the ex-grads.'

'Which one?'

'That's the million dollar question. From what I've seen of them, the field's wide open. I didn't take to any of them. I think they're all capable of anything if it suits, maybe with the exception of Tammy Morrison.'

'Why not her?'

'Just a gut impression. She strikes me as the odd one out. Not completely comfortable with their company.'

He smiled. 'That's because she was the only one who didn't harangue us just now.'

She shook her head again. 'Not at all. I just find the others a pretty disreputable bunch, that's all. There's definitely something going on between them that they're keeping schtum about. Some guilty secret, I reckon, which I suspect is the key to all this.'

'Then maybe you should try and get Tammy to tell you what it is?'

She nodded. 'First chance I get. There's something you can do, too. Check the house telephone line. After all that's been happening, I suspect that it isn't down but has actually been tampered with.'

CHAPTER 7

There was history between Lenny Welch and Abbey Granger. They had first met at university as freshers and their sexual chemistry was such that it had led to a carnal relationship that lasted for much of the three years that they were there. Their differences in personality and life experience should by rights have got in the way, but sometimes exact opposites attract to a greater extent and that was the case where they were concerned.

Welch was a tough, down-to-earth former street kid from a rough area of Birmingham, who had often been in trouble with the police, but had managed to shed his neighbourhood connections and move to the other side of the city. There he had got a job as a kitchen assistant in a big restaurant, studying hard in his spare time to improve his education. He then caught the owner's eye and in four years worked his way up the chain to resident chef. Two years after that, he won a university place to read economics, turned his back on the past and after getting his degree, got a job as a chef in a prestigious London hotel.

Granger, on the other hand, was from a well-to-do English family with a big country house near Newbury in Berkshire, whose parents bred racehorses. Their only daughter had been spoiled all through her childhood and although educated at a ladies' private academy, her life's ambitions had proved to be as shallow as her intelligence. She had left the academy for university with the aim of having fun and dating as many boys as possible, with her degree course in media studies very much secondary to that. She got her degree — just — but also earned an unenviable reputation for wild partying and sexual promiscuity. She had an insatiable sexual appetite and Welch had taken full advantage of this, particularly when the pair shared Bridge House with Brewer, Cartwright and the rest. They were seldom out of each other's beds. In the five years since, Granger had been through numerous relationships, with both sexes, but each one had failed. As a result, she was still single and living at home with her long-suffering parents, working at a local beauty parlour part-time as she pursued her key interests in jewellery, fashion and, of course, men.

For Welch, rebounding from his own disastrous relationship a year ago, meeting up with Granger was an opportunity to renew his carnal acquaintanceship. After slipping her the wink in the bar that night, he left his room at around eleven and paid her a visit two doors down the corridor. The room was unlocked and she was waiting for him in the big double bed, wearing nothing but a lascivious smile.

The night was theirs and Welch very reluctantly quit her bed at around one thirty a.m. to return to his room, leaving Granger to slip into a hot foaming bath to ease her strained muscles. Inevitably she soon found herself drifting off in the hot water and because of this, she didn't hear the outer door open and close shortly afterwards. But she heard the creak of the floorboards moments later as someone stepped into the bathroom behind her.

She smiled lazily and raised one foamy arm in a limp wave. 'Thought you'd come back, Lenny,' she said in a thick, weary voice. 'But I'm too tired right now.'

'Then you ought to get some sleep, shouldn't you, Abbey,' another voice replied. But it wasn't the voice of Lenny Welch . . .

* * *

Kate awoke suddenly, her heart racing. Noises again. This time more pronounced. A series of thuds. Like someone banging on the bedroom wall. Then what sounded like a sharp cry that was cut off. What on earth . . . ?

She glanced at her watch on the bedside cabinet. It was caught in a sliver of moonlight filtering through a chink in the curtains. It was one thirty a.m. As usual, Hayden was in a deep sleep beside her. She could hear him breathing steadily.

Folding back the bedclothes, she swung her feet over the edge of the bed and padded to the door, where she paused to listen. In stark contrast to the previous night, everything was deathly still. Tightly clenching her teeth, she very carefully opened her door to peer out.

The corridor wall lights were out this time, but a single small skylight above her door admitted a bar of moonlight, which grazed the carpet and weakly illuminated the corridor for part of the way in each direction before being consumed by the heavy gloom. She glanced quickly to her right in the direction of the staircase to the hall below. She was able to see that the corridor was deserted. Turning her head in the opposite direction, she detected movement at a point just before the moonlight faded into blackness. Straining her eyes, she glimpsed a figure dressed in a long hooded coat moving silently away from her past the other bedrooms, towards the end of the corridor. Whether the "marauder" was a man or a woman it was impossible to tell, but almost at the same moment it was swallowed up in the darkness as if it had never existed.

For a moment Kate just stood there staring into the gloom into which the figure had disappeared. As with the episode the night before, she was unsure exactly what to do next. So someone in a long hooded coat had been for a walk? So what? There was nothing illegal or unusual about that. One of the other hotel guests may have been unable to sleep and gone for some fresh air. It was nothing to do with her and it didn't follow that this would lead to another body in the lake. She was being presumptive and ridiculous. *Go back to bed, woman,* a voice in her brain urged. *You're turning into a neurotic.*

But she couldn't shake off the feeling that something was wrong. Finally her curiosity about the identity of the nocturnal wanderer won the day. Pulling on her dressing gown and slippers and grabbing her torch from the dressing table, she left the room again and headed off along the corridor in the direction taken by the mystery figure.

The line of bedroom doors on either side of the corridor were all closed and a couple of times she heard loud snoring coming from inside a room as she passed by. But there were no other sounds to attract her attention, not even the single bang of a door to indicate that perhaps her quarry had gone back to bed. Then after a few yards, the beam of her torch met the end wall of the corridor with its small, thickly curtained window, and she stopped dead and frowned. Not a sign of anyone and she knew full well that she couldn't have missed anyone in the last few yards. Not even in the heavy gloom. So where had the mystery man or woman gone? The only other exit from the corridor was via a small archway to her right, which she understood led up to the room in the clocktower. But who was likely to be going up there in the middle of the night?

Shrugging her shoulders, she ducked her head through the arch and started up the short staircase to a small landing at the top. In front of her was just a single wooden door equipped with an old-fashioned lock, but no key. She pressed her ear against it to listen for any movement inside. There was not a sound and even after trying the door several times, it didn't budge. It was obviously tightly fitted. She had no idea what was inside, except the back of the tower clock, of course, and she didn't care either. The only thing that concerned her was where the figure in the corridor had gone and how it could have disappeared so quickly and completely.

At which point she found herself remembering Tom Parsons' imaginative story about Mawgana Keegan, and she shivered. 'They do say as acid burned her face right off,' he'd said, 'and to this day she walks about Warneford Hall with no face inside her hood.'

She shook her head irritably, furious with herself for even thinking about what he had said. Fact! Ghosts only existed in folklore. As an experienced, no-nonsense police detective with her feet firmly on the ground, she was not about to pay attention to the ramblings of a superstitious old man.

With this in mind, she shone her torch slowly around the landing, looking for another door. There wasn't one, but almost immediately the beam picked out a big double cupboard with sliding doors, that was set against the wall on the opposite side of the landing to the clocktower door. Heart racing, she approached it cautiously. Then grasping the knob on the right hand slider, she gritted her teeth and pulled the door back.

To her relief, her gaze met nothing but brooms, a vacuum, an electric floor cleaner and an assortment of brushes, buckets and mops. Above her head there were several shelves packed with spare sheets, towels and tablecloths. All neatly folded but likely to be surplus to requirements with the proposed sale of the hotel, unless a future buyer intended staying with the hospitality trade.

Taking a deep breath, she reclosed the door and slid the other door back on its runners. Only to stagger backwards with a shocked cry as the figure in the long, hooded coat erupted from the blackness inside. Her last recollection was of the beam of the torch penetrating the hood and a pair of dark eyes glaring at her from a hideous, featureless face resembling nothing more than an artist's creased, blank canvas. Then her world dissolved into blackness.

* * *

Kate regained her floating senses with a thumping headache and feelings of nausea and disorientation. It was pitch dark and it took her a few minutes to work out where she was and why she was lying on the floor. Then her fumbling, out-stretched hand closed on her torch and switching it on, she climbed groggily to her feet with the support of a nearby wall. The torch's beam shook slightly in her hand as she swung it in a half circle around her, but everything came back to her when it picked out the gleaming hinges of the clocktower door. She was alone, thank goodness. Her attacker had disappeared. But as memory returned, she grimaced, condemning her weakness for fainting. She very rarely fainted and she was surprised that she had done so this time. Especially as she didn't believe in apparitions anyway. Then she frowned and sniffed the air a few times. She could smell something strange. Something with a strong, sweet odour to it. It was all around her like some kind of pervasive miasma and her face felt slightly wet. The truth dawned on her immediately, and she recalled feeling the blast of some sort of cold mist in her face just before she had passed out. Chloroform, it had to be. A spray device containing chloroform. She felt her way down the stairs to the corridor, then made her way slowly back to her room, fighting the urge to throw up at every step. So, the Warneford Hall ghost carried a chloroform spray, did it? Well, that had to be a first for a resident of the so-called spirit world, and maybe that same spray had been used to subdue Jimmy Caulfield before he was pushed in the lake . . .

* * *

'But was it something to do with what you'd eaten?'

Hayden's face was pale and anxious, and he handed Kate a second glass of water as she sat shivering on the edge of the bed. Surprisingly for Hayden, he had been woken by the sound of her being violently sick in their ensuite toilet and she still hadn't had a chance to tell him what had happened.

She shook her head and gave him the glass back. 'I just ran into a ghost, that's all,' she said. 'One carrying a chloroform spray.'

He gaped at her. 'A what? Have you got a fever?'

'No, Hayd, I haven't got anything,' she said grimly. 'But you're not going to like what I have to tell you.'

He didn't either and for several minutes he just sat there staring at the floor as he tried to take it all in, his face reddening more and more as the minutes past.

'Gordon Bennett!' he exclaimed at long last and, jumping to his feet, he began marching up and down the room like someone reacting to the claustrophobic confines of a prison cell. 'Don't you ever learn? This is the second time in two nights that you've left the room to go off on some daft expedition of your own. Now look what's happened to you.'

'It was hardly an expedition, Hayd,' she retorted. 'It was only just down the corridor.'

'Don't be so blessed pedantic,' he snapped. 'You know what I mean.'

She sighed and pulling the duvet back, slipped under it with her back up against the pillows.

'Whatever you say,' she said, 'but what just happened to me puts a different complexion on everything. I mean, why was that character wandering about the hotel in the middle of the night and who was inside that hooded coat? I don't believe in ghosts any more than you do, and I've never heard of one carrying a chloroform spray before.'

She frowned. 'Would you stop walking up and down like an idiot and get back into bed?'

He grunted and coming to a stop, climbed under the duvet beside her, looking a little sheepish after his outburst.

'Maybe you were mistaken about the spray? You saw a shadow or something and just fainted with the shock?'

She raised her eyes to the ceiling in a weary gesture. 'Have you ever known me to pass out like that before, except after a skinful?' she retorted. 'That apparition and the knock-out spray were real, Hayden, only there wasn't actually an apparition at all. It was someone in this hotel up to no good.'

'What sort of "someone"? Male or female?'

'I've no idea. They were wearing some kind of mask.'

'But why use the spray on you?'

'They must have sussed that I spotted them in the corridor and was following them. Could be it was a warning, or I was too close to something they didn't want me to find out about.'

'Then why not simply waste you as you think they did Jimmy Caulfield?'

'Wrong place and wrong time for that, I would suggest. They obviously weren't prepared for it. Also, perhaps they thought killing a copper was a step too far.'

'Or they hadn't killed anyone in the first place and this ghostly appearance was just a game that went a bit too far, making them panic when they found you on their tail.'

'If it was just a game, why carry a lethal chloroform spray around with them?'

'No idea.'

She studied him earnestly. 'Listen, I think maybe that spray was used on Jimmy Caulfield. That you were right about him not being hit over the head but suffering the injury when he fell. After what happened to me tonight, I reckon it's far more likely he was anaesthetised before being pushed in the lake.'

He tutted and cast her a critical look. 'The lake again, is it? Look, you still have no evidence that he *was* pushed. It's still possible he slipped and was overcome by the icy temperature of the water.'

She plumped up her pillows and, sinking down in the bed, turned over on her side to face him. 'Not a chance. Even you have finally had to admit that something is going on at this hotel. We need to get to the bottom of it before something even worse happens and I feel in my water that we're running out of time.'

He gave a horrendous yawn and ran a hand through his untidy thatch. 'Well, let's do that in the morning, shall we? Sorry if I lost my rag, but sometimes you get me so frustrated.'

Feeling much improved, she grinned mischievously and ran a bare foot down his leg. 'You don't have to feel frustrated, Hayd,' she said. 'I'm always here for you . . .'

'Eh, what?' In the act of lying down, he shot up again, as if he had been given an unexpected injection in the behind, throwing her a horrified, wide-eyed glance. 'No, no, not that sort of frustration,' he protested hastily. 'Don't forget, you must still be suffering from shock and anyway, we-we need to get some sleep.'

'Spoilsport,' she murmured as he dropped back down again, pulling the bedclothes securely around him. 'I thought it was always the woman who was supposed to have a headache.'

He seemed not to have heard her and minutes later to her chagrin, his ragged snores filled the room as he fell into a deep, untroubled sleep while she could only lie there and envy him. Tossing and turning in a futile attempt to follow his example, she couldn't help her gaze constantly straying to the end of the bed, half-expecting to see the head and shoulders of a hooded figure rising above it in the gloom, its extra-long arms and claw-like hands creeping up the duvet towards her. As a child, she had always feared the bogeyman she was convinced was hiding under her bed. Now, as a fully grown woman, despite the fact that she had always joined with Hayden in scoffing at the supernatural, the bogeyman had returned to haunt her dreams. But this one was not some ethereal entity of fantasy folklore. It was made up of flesh and blood. As such, it was far more deadly.

CHAPTER 8

Lenny Welch awoke early and grinned as he remembered the fun and games he had had the previous night with Abbey Granger. She hadn't changed since Bridge House at uni. The same insatiable sexual appetite. The same raw passion, and what a body! She had to be around thirty, but she still had the figure of the twenty-four-year-old he remembered all those years ago. He had left her room exhausted, which is probably why he had overslept. Thinking of her lying naked in that big double bed down the corridor, he couldn't help feeling horny all over again, and he was tempted to pay her another visit right there and then. But he thought better of it. His stomach had decided that breakfast was the priority. He could always continue where he had left off later in the day. So he headed for the shower instead.

Everyone, including the two coppers, seemed to be already in the dining room when he got there, with one exception.

'Abbey not down yet then?' he asked no one in particular as he loaded his plate from the buffet and poured himself a coffee.

There was a loud guffaw. 'What's up, Lenny?' Jeffrey Cartwright called out. 'Missing her already?'

Welch turned slowly towards the long table of grinning faces. 'Don't know what you're talking about,' he said. 'I just wondered why she was the only one not here.'

'Perhaps you wore her out,' Ronnie Brewer suggested, 'though knowing Abbey, I wouldn't have thought that was possible.'

'Come on, Lenny,' Cartwright persisted as Welch frowned with contrived puzzlement. 'I saw you sneak into her room last night. Heard a noise, you see, which I thought was a knock on my door. But when I opened it, there was good old Lenny Welch creeping into Abbey's room in his dressing gown just as the clock in the hall downstairs struck the witching hour. You always were a horny sod.'

'Yeah,' Brewer added, putting the boot in. 'You were never out of Abbey's bed at uni. I don't know why you two bothered to have separate rooms.'

More laughter followed and Welch treated his tormentors to a self-conscious grimace before sitting down with them. As he did so, he glanced across the room at the other smaller table where Kate and Hayden were sitting, but there was no returning smile from either of them, and he found Kate's penetrating stare quite unsettling.

'Think what you like,' Welch went on, munching on a crisp bread roll filled with ham, then gulping from his cup of coffee. 'All that's long over.'

'So you say,' Cartwright countered. 'But I bet Abbey will have a different story to tell — probably one full of disappointment.'

Welch stood up quickly. 'I don't have to stay here and listen to this,' he snarled. 'I'll finish my breakfast somewhere else.'

Then he stalked from the room, spilling some of his coffee down his trousers as he went.

As the laughter from the others followed him, Tammy Morrison stood up, dabbing her mouth with a napkin. 'I might take her up a coffee,' she said. 'She drank an awful lot again last night and I think we should make sure she's okay.'

'Suit yourself, *Mother Teresa*,' Brewer mocked. 'Maybe you should take her up a sausage too just to remind her how her night ended . . .'

'Don't be so damned crude, Ronnie,' Victoria Adams cut in, and she also stood up. 'I'll come with you, Tammy. Us girls must stick together.'

As the pair of them left the room, Morrison carrying a cup of black coffee in one hand, Kate looked across at Hayden with a tight-lipped smile. 'Interesting,' she said softly.

He raised an eyebrow. 'How so?'

She waited for Brewer and Cartwright to lapse into a conversation about other things before continuing. 'The fact that Cartwright saw Welch out of his room last night. I wonder if his visit to Abbey was a blind or that he was on his toes elsewhere afterwards. Also, it begs the question whether Cartwright was telling the truth about answering a knock on his door. Maybe he was out and about himself. You know, wearing a long, hooded coat and a face mask.'

'If that was the case, why would Cartwright admit to being up at all? If you're thinking he could be your nocturnal marauder, why would he want to draw attention to himself by saying what he said?'

Kate didn't get the chance to reply. The piercing scream from somewhere above their heads put paid to any further conversation. Pitching her chair backwards in her haste to get up, she raced for the door, leaving Hayden struggling to follow and the two on the other table sitting there with their mouths hanging open as if suddenly struck with some sort of paralysis.

There was a further scream even as Kate reached the hall and she almost bowled over Daphne Parsons emerging from the passageway to the kitchen as she raced for the stairs.

Tammy Morrison met her on the landing, her spectacles askew and her face chalk white. Her eyes were wide and staring and even as Kate got to her, her legs gave way and she collapsed in a heap at her feet, shaking and sobbing in the grip of hysteria.

Kate didn't wait for an explanation but turned towards Daphne Parsons who was only halfway up the staircase behind her, puffing and panting with the exertion. 'Look after her,' she threw back over her shoulder and ran on down the corridor to where she could see an open doorway.

Victoria Adams emerged from one of the bedrooms as she got there, looking grim and pale-faced. 'It's Abbey,' she said. 'There's been a dreadful accident.'

'Accident?' Kate queried, pushing past her into the room. 'What sort of accident?'

'A fatal one,' Adams replied. 'I'm afraid Abbey's dead.'

* * *

Abbey Granger was indeed dead. Very dead. She was lying on her back in her bath staring at the ceiling with glassy eyes through a much depleted layer of soapy bubbles. One arm hung over the side of the bath and beneath the limp hand a tumbler was lying on its side on the mat. A half-empty bottle of blended whisky stood on the corner of the bath, its screw top floating in the water.

Kate reached into the bath and released the plug, then slipped an arm under the apparently lifeless young woman's shoulders to haul her head clear of the water.

'Help me get her out,' she called to Adams who was still standing in the doorway.

'But she's dead,' Adams replied tersely.

'Just help me, will you,' Kate snapped. 'I need you to grab her legs.'

Adams seemed reluctant to touch the body, but at this point Hayden arrived, panting heavily, and bent down beside Kate to do the job for her.

With Hayden's assistance, Granger was lifted out of the bath and laid gently on the mat spread out on the floor beside it.

As with Caulfield, it was plain that she was already dead, just as Adams had pointed out. Kate knelt down beside her body and tested for vital signs, nevertheless. But there was no pulse in either her neck or in her wrist. Kate stood up and shook her head in resignation.

'Silly girl should have left the scotch alone,' Adams remarked. 'Tragic waste of life. Really tragic.'

'Thank you, Victoria,' Kate said sharply, unimpressed by her reluctance to help. 'I think we can manage now. It might be a good idea if you went to see how Mrs Parsons is getting on with Tammy. Your friend was in a bit of a state just now.'

Kate expected Adams to argue. She had already decided that Brewer's polished, self-assured girlfriend was someone used to being in control of things and not the type to readily accept instructions from anyone. But on this occasion she was wrong. Adams simply shrugged her shoulders and flounced off back into the corridor, seemingly content to let the detectives get on with it.

Kate closed the bedroom door and turned to Hayden. 'So, another drowning?' she said in an acid tone. 'Seems even the bathtubs around here need to carry a "deep water" health warning for would-be bathers.'

Hayden's gaze roved around the bedroom through the open door, then back to the bathroom and the corpse they had just laid on the mat.

'Looks like she had a fun night before this, though,' he said. 'Bedclothes have been kicked or thrown off the bed, so that they are lying on the floor in a heap and a rather nice shorty nightie is draped neatly over the back of the chair there, which suggests she never bothered to put it on when she went to bed last night.'

Kate nodded. 'The bathwater was cold and coupled with the condition of her skin would suggest that death occurred several hours ago. Maybe Cartwright was telling the truth when he said he saw Welch paying her a late-night visit. It's likely the visit was prearranged and that she didn't bother to put on her nightdress because she knew it would soon be coming off when he joined her in her bed. Then after he had gone, she decided to take a hot bath, intending to return to bed following a relaxing soak.'

'Not a good plan if you're bent on knocking back half a bottle of scotch at the same time, though,' Hayden commented. 'Especially if you've already had a few.'

'So you think it's just another case of death by misadventure, then?' Kate snapped. 'She got drunk and slipped under the water while in a stupor. Simple. End of?'

'It *is* a plausible scenario.'

'As plausible as the one where a man accidentally falls into an iced-over lake and drowns, you mean?'

He sighed, seeing the antagonism in her expression. 'Okay, okay, it is a bit of a coincidence, two drownings on the same weekend, I'll give you that.'

'It's a lot more than a bit of a coincidence, mister. If you remember, I told you earlier that I was wakened at around one thirty a.m. by some noises. That's what made me check the corridor outside our room in the first place. Well, the noises amounted to a series of quite loud thumps accompanied by a sharp cry—'

'Maybe the headboard of Granger's bed striking the wall when the two of them were . . . er, enjoying themselves?' he interrupted.

'Couldn't have been. The bedhead in this room faces the outer wall of the hotel, so it's too far away. The noises I heard were much closer, as if something was actually hitting the other side of our bedroom wall. And what abuts that wall but the ensuite bathroom we are now standing in.'

He pursed his lips thoughtfully. 'Okay, so let's say Welch and Granger finished up in the bath. He got carried away and she ended up being drowned as a result. Don't forget, he's a big, fit lad and quite strong with it, I would have thought. Drowning her would have been quite within his capabilities.'

His continued scepticism angered her, but she felt some relief that he was now at least starting to consider the possibility of "foul play".

'That doesn't work for me. To start with, the bath is not big enough for two people. Secondly, why would he want to kill her anyway? By all accounts, the pair of them hadn't seen each other for five years and had once been lovers. No, horrible though the thought is, I think it more likely that the noises I heard were made by Granger fighting for her life against an intruder who entered her room sometime after Welch had left, and I am pretty sure that defensive bruising will ultimately become evident on her body to bear this out.'

'Fat lot of good any marks will be to us while we're stuck here. We need forensic support and a PM now to establish anything for certain, and the way things are going it looks like that might not be for another week.'

'Then in the meantime, I suggest we carry out any inquiries we can and see where that leads us.'

'What inquiries would those be?' His tone was cynical.

'To start with, there's the house telephone line that you have still to check and while you're doing that, I think I'll have a chat with Tammy Morrison. I suspect there's a lot more going on in that pretty little head of hers than we appreciate, and after what she witnessed here today, I think that, with a bit of encouragement, she might be prepared to tell me what guilty secret everyone has been hiding, which Ronnie Brewer seems so desperate to keep quiet.'

But Kate's plans were rudely interrupted.

They had just carefully laid Granger's corpse back in the bath where it was cooler and were on their way to the door, keys in hand, when Lenny Welch stumbled into the room. His eyes were wide and staring and he had the look of a man in shock.

'Is it true?' he said in a throaty, hesitant voice. 'They say Abbey's dead.'

Kate nodded. 'Yes, I'm afraid it's true.'

'But-but how? I mean . . .'

Kate saw no reason to withhold the information as she would have done in a normal inquiry, since everyone would be aware by now of the cause of death.

'She drowned, Lenny. In her bath.'

He gulped. 'But she can't have . . . I need to see her.'

'That's not possible,' she said firmly.

She saw his fists clench into balls as he glared at her. 'You can't stop me.'

Kate didn't back down one iota and she felt Hayden tense behind her. 'Oh, but I can, Lenny,' she replied. 'The deaths of Jimmy Caulfield and Abbey Granger are now the subject of a police investigation and if you obstruct it in any way, you commit a serious offence.'

Just for a second, there was an ugly sneer on his face. 'So what are you going to do marooned out here in the snow? Arrest me and stick me in the cells?'

'Don't be a fool, Lenny,' Hayden's quiet voice put in and he stepped in front of Kate to face him. 'You're already in a dodgy position having been with her last night. If you do anything stupid now, you'll only make things worse for yourself.'

For a moment it was touch and go. But then abruptly Welch's shoulders sagged, his hands relaxed and he suddenly burst into tears.

Kate took a chance and stepping past Hayden, took Welch by the elbow and led him across the room to the bed, where he sat trembling and sobbing on the edge of the mattress. Turning briefly, she indicated to Hayden with a nod of her head that he should leave.

He frowned back, looking doubtful. 'You sure?' he mouthed.

Her lips tightened and her look said it all. With a shrug he left.

As soon as he had reluctantly closed the door behind him, Kate sat down beside Welch and forced a small smile. 'What exactly happened last night, Lenny?' she asked gently. 'I know you slept with Abbey.'

He dried his eyes on his sleeve and sniffed. 'Yeah, I was with her, but not the whole night.'

'When did you leave?'

'Must've been about one. She said she was going to take a bath, so I went.'

'Did you see anyone in the corridor on your way back to your room?'

He shook his head. 'No, the place was dead quiet and it's only a few feet away besides.'

Then he hesitated and stared straight at her, understanding suddenly dawning. 'You don't think I killed her, do you? Your guy said something about me being in a dodgy position. Are you saying she was-was murdered?'

'We're not saying anything at the moment, but you have to agree, two drownings in two days, it's a bit unusual.'

'Yeah, but Abbey was in her own bath, whereas Jimmy was obviously out in the storm. No wonder he slipped and fell in the lake. He was just being stupid . . .' Again he hesitated. 'So you think someone killed him too?'

'Maybe. We don't know.'

'But why?'

'We don't know that either. Is there anything you can tell me that might throw some light on why someone might have wanted to kill either Jimmy or Abbey? I get the impression that you are all hiding something from the past. Something that could explain a lot.'

He looked away from her and she saw his jaw tighten. Then after a long pause he faced her again and shook his head. 'Nothing I know of, and Abbey was just a lovely person who wouldn't have done anything to anyone.'

'How long have you known her?'

'Since uni. We all stayed in a place called Bridge House after our fresher's year and Abs and me found we got on well together.'

'Had you seen her since leaving uni five years ago and arriving here?'

More hesitation, then he nodded again. 'Yeah, we met up several times after leaving uni. She lived just a few miles away from me, so we made some trips together, you know, evenings out and that, and we had two or three weekends away.'

'So you knew she would be coming here for this weekend?'

'We both knew about it. Thing is . . .' He paused again. 'I had decided I was going to ask her to marry me this weekend.'

'And did you?'

He nodded. 'Last night. She was thrilled to bits and we were going to announce it to the others today.'

Kate's face hardened and quite deliberately she changed her tactics to test his reaction. 'You sure she didn't turn you down? You haven't actually said she gave you a "yes". Maybe she said "no" and that maddened you enough to want to kill her. Maybe you came back into her room after leaving, found her in the bath half cut and held her under the water until she drowned?'

Kate got her reaction immediately and it was a lot more violent than she had anticipated. His eruption from the bed almost knocked her flying and the next instant he was towering over her with both fists raised threateningly and his face contorted in fury. 'You stupid bitch,' he shouted, 'I didn't do anything to her. I would never have hurt her. I loved her, don't you understand?'

But then Hayden was there, striding across the room to step in between the two of them for the second time, his own fists clenched and his jaw thrust out aggressively as he faced Welch down.

'That'll be enough of that,' he snapped in a masterful voice Kate never knew he possessed. 'Just control yourself.'

As before, Welch abruptly dissolved into a sobbing wreck, slumping into a chair in a corner of the room with his head in his hands.

Kate recovered her composure and leaned towards him while Hayden looked on with obvious disapproval. 'Sorry about that, Lenny,' she said, 'I had to put that to you and I'm satisfied you were telling the truth. Just two more questions. First, was Abbey a big drinker? The others seemed to think she was.'

He kept his hands cupped round his head, staring at the floor, then shook his head miserably. 'She-she only drank white wine and sometimes a little vodka. She-she couldn't handle alcohol, so half the time she just pretended to drink a lot to get on with the others.'

Kate's eyes narrowed. 'What about scotch? Did she like to drink whisky?'

Welch raised his head and peered at her through his tears. 'Whisky? She never touched the stuff. Hated the taste. Why?'

'A half-bottle was left on the side of the bath where she was found.'

His stare hardened. 'Then some bastard must have put it there.'

CHAPTER 9

'Well now, you *have* been my knight in shining armour today, Hayden,' Kate said mischievously after Welch had stumbled on his way. 'Twice in the past hour, too.'

He grunted. 'Don't let it go to your head, old girl, I was just stepping in as any man would where a woman's safety is involved.'

She pouted. 'Now you've gone and spoiled it all,' she said.

'And you were an idiot to wind up a man like that,' he reprimanded. 'Heaven knows what he would have done if I hadn't intervened.'

The glint left her eyes and was replaced by a troubled look. 'I had to test him,' she said, 'and it worked too. From the way he behaved and the answers he gave, I can't see him as being responsible for Granger's death. But after what he said about the whisky, I believe someone had to have been responsible for it, which means the theory I've held all along looks like being correct.'

To her surprise he didn't argue this time. 'I think you're right,' he said. 'Both deaths have to be suspicious.'

'Oh?' She raised her eyebrows. 'What brought about such a massive change of heart?'

'This,' he said, and reaching into his pocket, he held out a palm full of tiny lengths of what looked like coloured electrical wiring. 'Someone had some fun with the wires in the telephone junction box which connects the house phone to the external service in the hall. It was hidden behind a heavy cabinet on which the telephone was sitting and I had a job shifting the thing. I was able to undo the screws with a little screwdriver I've got attached to my keyring and found it pretty messed up inside.'

'So the phone *was* deliberately cut off?' she breathed.

He nodded grimly. 'And whoever did it wasn't taking any chances on it being reconnected any time soon. They didn't just rip out the wires. They vandalised the whole thing inside, so there's absolutely no way it can be repaired except by a qualified telecom engineer with all the right bits. When the phone stopped working, the Parsonses must have just assumed it was an outside breakdown in the service and they wouldn't have been too bothered anyway, as they were leaving here after the weekend. BT, or whoever installed the line, wouldn't have known it was out of action at the hotel either, and although any callers to Warneford would have heard the phone ringing from their end and would have assumed it was ringing here too, nothing would have been happening. A permanent open line situation would have been created.'

'And how on earth do you know so much about telephones?'

'I set up the phones in our cottage at Burtle when I first bought the place. It was sort of trial and error, but you can soon pick up the knowhow.'

'Well, clever old you.'

He shrugged. 'All part of life's learning curve,' he said modestly.

But once again she wasn't listening. 'So, taking the vandalised phone connection into consideration on top of the missing mobiles and the slashed car tyres, we must, without any further doubt, be looking at a double murder case. Someone lured all these people to Warneford Hall for the express purpose of killing each of them and that same individual made sure that once their potential victims had arrived they were effectively trapped here and were unable to summon help from anyone. Our killer must have really rejoiced when the freak snow storm added to their isolation.'

'You know the old saying: "the devil looks after his own".'

She treated him to a grim, almost triumphant smile. 'So do I get an apology?'

'For what? I've always been suspicious about things. Especially after all the other things that happened. I intimated as much to you.'

'Oh? When was that? In your dreams.' She stared at him fixedly. 'Hayden Lewis, you are an unprincipled lying hound.'

* * *

Kate found Tammy Morrison in her room. She'd guessed she would be there but had to knock three times before a tearful voice responded with a sharp, 'Go away.'

Turning the handle, she poked her head round the door and said, 'I wanted to see if you were all right.'

Morrison was lying on her bed with her shoes off and her head resting against a couple of pillows. It was plain that she had been crying and her dark eyes, no longer part shielded by her tinted spectacles, were red and puffy.

'I want to be alone,' she said. 'I can't handle conversation just now.'

Kate took no notice of the rebuff but closed the door behind her and went over to the bed, settling on the edge of the mattress at an angle facing the young woman. As with Welch, she gave her a reassuring smile. To her surprise Morrison scrambled up on to her knees and literally threw her arms around her neck, sobbing and hugging her tightly.

'It's Francis,' she choked, 'I knew he'd come back. First George, then Jimmy and now . . . and now . . .' She lapsed into incoherence.

Very gently Kate pulled her arms free and pushed her away so that the young woman sank back on to the bed in a kneeling position with her legs tucked under her.

'I think you had better explain, Tammy,' she said.

Morrison shook her head several times. 'I-I can't. The others would never forgive me.'

Kate took a deep breath. 'If you don't, I can't help you.'

Morrison wiped her eyes on the back of her hands and, leaning over to one side of Kate, she pulled a tissue from a box on the bedside cabinet and blew her nose.

'But it's so awful what we did,' she said a few seconds later.

Kate felt a familiar spurt of acid in her stomach and her eyes narrowed. She could see that Morrison was right on the edge of sensible reasoning and needed careful handling. If she was too overt, she could well put her off completely, but if she didn't encourage further dialogue Tammy could overthink things that were on her mind and clam up.

'Just take it easy,' she said. 'Would you like me to get you a drink of water?'

Morrison nodded and Kate went to the bathroom and filled a glass standing on the edge of the basin.

When she got back, Morrison looked a lot calmer and was sitting on the edge of the bed, wriggling her toes.

She took the glass with a muttered 'thank you' and drained it. Kate took it from her and set it on the bedside table. Then she sat down beside Morrison and smiled again but said nothing. She'd learned from experience that sometimes silence was the best motivator. After a long couple of minutes, Morrison glanced quickly at Kate and blurted out, 'We all killed Francis.'

Kate could barely conceal her shock. That was one thing she hadn't expected. 'Why don't you tell me what happened? First, who was Francis?'

'One of our housemates at uni. We were all living in a rundown place called Bridge House, you see, and we all got on pretty well. But Francis was sort of odd. He didn't mix much with the rest of us at all really.'

'Bit of a swot, was he?'

'A what?'

'You know, keen on studying.'

'Oh, I see. Well, yes, and because of that he wasn't popular with the rest of us. Especially Ronnie and Jeff. He never went out with us, you see, never bought a drink, never partied.'

She swallowed hard. 'The night before we graduated he came along to the pub with us to celebrate and we decided to teach him a lesson . . .'

'And you all spiked his drink?'

Morrison stared at her. 'How on earth did you know that?'

'Pretty obvious what you were going to say, Tammy. It happens all the time at uni. I was caught by it when I went there.'

'You did?' Morrison looked a bit more reassured. 'So that's what everyone did. I didn't agree with it, so I didn't take part in it. But I went along with the thing, which means I was equally guilty.' She grabbed Kate's wrist. 'That's why Francis has come back, you see. Why he's taking his revenge.'

'What do you mean, he's come back?'

She released a deep, trembling breath. 'That night he left the pub before us to walk home, but he never got there. There's this-this river close to the road with a footpath alongside it. We think he must have tried to walk home along the path, but he never made it. He must have slipped and fallen into the river and we never saw him again.'

'Surely the local police . . . ?'

'But that's it. We never told them about it. We searched for him, but when we couldn't find him, we just gave up and left for home after graduation the following morning.'

'Was his body ever found?'

'We don't know. The university is way up north and it would hardly be national news, would it? Accidents like that are pretty common at universities.'

'So presumably none of you were ever questioned about his disappearance?'

She shrugged. 'We never heard another thing.' Her eyes widened. 'Poor Francis must have drowned and we did it. That's why he's after us. Don't you see, he's picking us off one by one, making us drown like he did.'

'That's enough!' Kate snapped, seeing she was close to hysteria. 'Get a grip on yourself. There is no coming back when you are dead. Ghosts only exist in books and films. That's if he *is* dead, of course. You have no way of knowing one way or the other. He might have got himself out of the river or been rescued by someone and has chosen to keep quiet because he doesn't want anything more to do with any of you.'

Morrison swallowed hard again, hope in her eyes. 'You think?' Then the light died. 'But if that's the case, what about George, Jimmy and Abbey? All three of them died from drowning. How can that be coincidental?'

Kate frowned. 'George? Who was George?'

'Oh, er, George Lane. He was another student who shared Bridge House with us. He-he should have been with us here on this weekend too, but he ducked out of it and shortly afterwards he was found dead in a lake near his home. Presumed accident or suicide. He was also involved in spiking Francis' drink and he's been punished in exactly the same way as the others. Don't you see?'

'I certainly hear what you're saying and it does seem rather strange that all three of your friends should die from drowning. But if someone was behind their deaths, it will be a living, breathing human agency that was responsible, not some vengeful, ethereal spirit from beyond the grave.'

'And what about what we've done? If Francis *is* dead, we could be put in prison for murder.'

Kate tutted irritably. 'What you did was reckless and stupid, but it wouldn't be murder, and it would be hard to make a case for anything else either. Francis was presumably an adult, so he is responsible for his own actions. Drunk or not, he chose to leave you all and walk along that path on his own. But you should have reported what happened at the time and you will all come in for quite a bit of stick over that I must admit.'

Morrison lapsed into her former misery once more. 'That's if any of us are still here after this weekend.'

Kate patted her on the thigh. 'It's the job of Hayden and myself to make sure you are,' she said.

But she was nowhere near as confident as she tried to sound.

* * *

After Kate had passed on to Hayden what Tammy Morrison had told her about Francis Templeton, they made their way downstairs to join the other guests in the dining room. It was only just after midday, but Hayden's stomach was like an alarm clock set precisely for every mealtime and for him, being late was not an option.

The moment they walked into the room, however, Kate sensed lunch was going to be a bumpy ride. She was immediately confronted by a very aggressive Ronnie Brewer who made a point of breaking away from an intense low-voiced discussion he was having by the buffet table with Jeffrey Cartwright to have another go at her.

'So Abbey has snuffed it in the bath, has she?' he said, and Kate stiffened when she picked up the sneer in his tone.

'Yes, Abbey has passed, I'm afraid,' she replied coldly and made to turn away from him to join Hayden at the buffet table, only to find Brewer now virtually blocking her way.

'Pissed again, was she?' he said. 'Or was it dope?'

'Neither, from what I have been able to establish so far,' she replied. 'Now, I would like to get some lunch if you don't mind.'

He scowled as she pushed past him. 'So what was it then, if neither of those?'

'That's what we're trying to find out,' she threw back over her shoulder. 'And it would be nice if you could show a bit of sympathy for people when they lose their lives.'

He was behind her now as she put some food on a plate. He was almost breathing down her neck and his whole manner was threatening. She glimpsed Hayden watching him narrowly from a few feet away and she made a face at her other half, warning him not to do anything.

'That's enough, Ronnie,' Victoria Adams snapped from her seat at the dining table. 'Just leave it alone.'

'I don't like coppers,' Brewer continued. 'Especially coppers who try and put words into people's mouths. Lenny told me you gave him a grilling. Almost accused him of being involved in Abbey's death.'

Kate turned to face him. 'Did he now? Well, what I said to Lenny and what he said to me is between Lenny and myself.'

The sneer was back. 'Cocky little bitch, aren't you?'

Kate's jaw tightened. 'And you, Mr Brewer, are a total arsehole, so shall we leave it at that?'

'You can't talk to me that way. I pay your wages. You're a public servant.'

'I can talk to you how I please and I am not officially on duty at present anyway.'

'Then why are you poking your nose where it's not wanted?'

'To gather information and evidence for a suspected murder investigation that will eventually follow.'

'Murder?' Kate heard Adams exclaim. 'You're saying you think Abbey was murdered?'

'*And* Jimmy Caulfield, yes.'

'Bollocks!' Brewer snarled. 'You're trying to make something out of nothing. Who would want to murder Jimmy and Abs? You're talking a load of old crap.'

Kate sighed. 'As to who, Mr Brewer, that has yet to be established.'

Brewer glanced around him. 'There are only four of our uni crowd left. Are you saying it's one of us?'

'Well, is it?'

''Course not. Why would we want to kill one another?'

'Then who? The only other people here are Mr and Mrs Parsons.'

'I don't know. Could be someone hiding somewhere.'

'Out in the snow? An Eskimo perhaps?'

'Could be like that American movie, *Hider In The House*,' Cartwright chipped in, half joking.

Treated to blank looks, he grinned. 'Guy hides himself in someone's attic and lives there undetected in a little den he's constructed, while he starts knocking off the residents,' he explained crudely.

'Thanks for that, Jeff,' Adams said sarcastically. 'Just what we needed.'

Kate put her plate back on the buffet table, suddenly no longer hungry. 'I think we need to have a meeting,' she said. 'All of us. To discuss the situation properly. I suggest three o'clock this afternoon in the lounge.'

'Why not now?' Brewer demanded.

'Because we're not all here,' she replied, thinking of Lenny Welch and Tammy Morrison.

'That's their lookout,' Brewer sneered back.

She stared him out. 'See you all at three in the lounge,' she said without answering him and walked out.

CHAPTER 10

Kate's next port of call was the kitchen, and she found the Parsonses both there. Daphne was busying herself at the double sink in front of the window with a pile of dishes. Tom was lounging in one of two padded wooden chairs drawn up on each side of an alcove set back between a range of fitted kitchen units hosting a big Aga cooker. He was munching through a sandwich and had a mug of tea on the arm beside him. Kate's gaze quickly took in the rest of the room, noting a couple of large chest freezers and a tall refrigerator standing against the wall to her right, just inside, and an old-looking wooden door, perhaps accessing another room, between shelves laden with kitchen utensils directly opposite. There was another door with a glass panel in the far corner, which obviously accessed the rear of the property, and it stood ajar despite the chill of the room.

Daphne must have heard her approaching footsteps on the tiled floor of the passageway, for she turned quickly as she entered the room, a scowl on her face.

'Terrible thing,' she said before Kate could open her mouth. 'Young woman like that. Drownded was she, like the lad?'

Kate nodded. 'Apparently so. We've had to leave her in her room until we can get someone out here and I've taken the liberty of hanging on to her door key for now.'

'Seem to be collectin' 'em,' Tom said. 'Corpses, I mean. That's two already.'

'Can we have a chat for a moment?' Kate asked without answering him.

''Bout what?' Daphne answered. 'Ain't nothin' to talk on far as I knows. She was drownded on account of too much liquor, way I sees it. They all drinks too much. Wouldn't mind if they put money in honesty box to pay for it neither.'

Kate grimaced. 'The thing is, my colleague and I consider that she may have been deliberately held under the water by someone.'

'Murdered, you mean?'

'*And* Jimmy Caulfield, the lad you mentioned.'

The other blew out her cheeks in a gesture of shock. 'Well, that be somethin' else, that be. Ain't never thought somethin' like that would happen at Warneford Hall. 'Spectacle place, as was. Who would have done such awful thing?'

'We don't know and until we can find out, I think it would be wise to take precautions at night. Like locking your door when you go to bed and always staying together. I've arranged a meeting at three with everyone to discuss the situation and you'd be welcome to attend.'

Kate hesitated, then said. 'In the meantime, would it be possible for me to have a look inside the clocktower?'

'Why?'

'I want to check something out, that's all.'

'Answer has to be "no" to that,' Tom said, 'on account of there bein' no key. Never was in ten years we've worked here. Clock don't work no more anyhow, so no need to go up there.'

Kate's frustration showed, but she didn't press the point, seeing that it would be futile.

'So what can you tell me about this place?' she continued, leaning against the cooker and eyeing them both in turn curiously. 'You told me, Mr Parsons, that it was built as a manor house by a seafaring man called Rupert Keegan and that his young wife, Mawgana, committed suicide . . .'

'And haunts the place—' he began, but she cut him off.

'Aside from the ghost story, Mr Parsons, what happened to the property afterwards?'

Parsons shook his head slowly and drank some of his tea. 'Dunno much 'bout that,' he replied. 'History, see. But they do say as he sold up an' went back to sea an' house become a farm. Lasted 'bout 'undred thirty odd years, right up till recent like. Sort of handed down from father to son. Then business went bankrupt an' it were sold to some rich gent who turned it into hotel ten years back when Daphne an' me was took on.' He shook his head again. 'Never met new owner. Never knew his name neither. Always dealt with Mr Hapgood, the manager. But fella had a lot of rebuilding done inside to make extra bedrooms an' that. Hotel never did much good, though. As I said 'afore, it be in wrong spot out here on Ghost Marsh. Land floods regular like in winter an' it be too far out fer folk to want to come here anyhow. That's why they be sellin' up now, I s'pose.'

Kate pursed her lips thoughtfully for a moment, then pushing herself off the edge of the cooker, she walked towards the back door. 'Mind if I take a look outside?'

Daphne merely shrugged and turned back to her sink and Tom returned to his sandwich as if she wasn't there.

There was another hardstanding deep in snow outside and at the far end Kate saw a couple of barns, which looked to be derelict. Some yards to one side and beyond the barns was a fenced area with a notice on it that Kate couldn't read at that distance.

'Barns no longer used then?' she asked without turning round.

Tom Parsons spoke through a mouthful of sandwich. 'Not since we been here,' he said. 'Nothin' in 'em but stuff from old farm days. Al'ays said they should've been pulled down long ago. Right eyesore they be for guests wanderin' 'bout.'

'And what's inside the fenced enclosure?'

'Ah, that be the hotel pool in there.'

Kate turned back into the room. 'What, a swimming pool?'

He laughed uproariously. 'Aye, you could take a swim in it if you'd a mind to, but it be last swim you ever 'ad.'

'Stop your nonsense, Tom Parsons,' Daphne said sternly. Then to Kate, she explained, 'It be the old farm slurry pit, lass. Should've been filled in years ago but were just left there instead. Wouldn't be legal like today. Just a dirty old pond really. Fenced off for safety like. But fair stinks in hot weather, I can tell you.'

Tom was still chuckling and Kate threw him an old-fashioned look. 'And what's in there?' she asked, pointing to the old wooden door she had noticed on first entering the room.

'Old wine cellar,' Daphne said. 'But no good for that. Place floods in heavy rain. That's why all our drink be kept in the bar. Nothin' in cellar now, 'cept spiders.'

Kate shivered at the thought of the little hairy monsters. Her mind flashed back to a previous case she had dealt with involving a dangerous tropical version, which had escaped from a laboratory. That had really stoked up her arachnophobia in a big way.

'Take a look, if you like.'

Crossing to the small wooden door, she pulled it open and stared down into a pitch-black shaft. Fumbling round just inside, she found a switch and a naked light bulb flickered on from a cord dangling from the ceiling. It revealed a narrow wooden staircase dropping away into more darkness where the light failed to reach.

'Better take this,' Daphne said and pressed a torch into her hand.

Gritting her teeth, Kate ducked her head and began to feel her way down, switching on the torch as the darkness closed in around her. Something tickled her cheek and she shuddered, clawing whatever it was off her face and flicking it away into the gloom. One of the steps seemed to stir with a loud cracking sound. Then her torch caught a yellow glint. She stopped dead. The staircase went on, but she couldn't.

The small chamber she found herself in was full of still black water. How deep it was, she had no idea and she had no intention of trying to find out. Flashing the torch around the thick cobwebs with which the place was festooned, she carefully turned round and retreated back to the kitchen.

'What did I say?' Daphne Parsons said as she handed the torch back. 'Flooded again, I 'spect?'

Kate gave a quick smile of confirmation.

'You ought to keep that door locked in case someone falls down there,' she said.

The other shrugged. 'We knows 'bout it and ain't no one else s'posed to be in kitchen anyhow.'

Kate didn't pursue the point, but asked instead, 'Does this building have a loft?'

Daphne nodded, a little irritably this time. 'You want to see that, too?' she exclaimed.

'Nothin' to see up there but old cold water cistern an' more spiders,' Tom Parsons called from his chair. He produced a cob pipe from his pocket and began filling it dexterously with tobacco from a pouch. 'Hatch be on landing of staircase. But you'll need a ladder.'

Kate smiled wickedly as Hayden chose that moment to materialise in the doorway from the hall. 'I won't be needing it, thank you,' she said, 'but my colleague will.'

'Husband will what?' Hayden queried, looking wary.

'Tom here will show you, Hayd,' she said, and left him to it.

* * *

Hayden was not a happy man when he emerged from the loft. He had cobwebs in his hair, dirt marks on his perspiring face and a couple of tears to his stained trousers.

Kate, who was standing with Tom Parsons anchoring the ladder he had provided, tried to repress the chuckle that arose in her throat at the sight of him, but she only partially succeeded and Hayden glared at her.

'You can laugh,' he snapped, handing his borrowed torch back to Parsons. 'I nearly did myself a mischief among all those beams up there.'

'Sorry, Hayd,' she said. 'I'm not really laughing at you. What did you find?'

'Not a thing,' he retorted. 'Mice or rat droppings and loads of very large spiders, but nothing else. The only other things that are up there, apart from a water and header tank, are a roll of old carpet and a few empty tea chests. No sign of anything else.'

'So, no hider in the house?' Jeffrey Cartwright mocked, sniffing loudly as usual as he stepped round the ladder and headed downstairs.

Hayden glared after him. 'That cocky little twerp needs to be taught a lesson,' he said with uncharacteristic venom.

'He probably will be one day,' Kate commented, not really appreciating what she had just said. 'For the present, though, let's get this meeting over.'

They were all there in the lounge, even Daphne Parsons, and her husband went and sat beside her when he followed Kate and Hayden into the room.

'Well, you'll all be aware now,' Kate began, 'that Abbey Granger was found dead in her bath earlier this morning. The reason I've called everyone together just now is to emphasise that Hayden and I do not think her death was accidental, any more than we think Jimmy Caulfield's death was an accident. The brutal truth seems to be that someone — and we don't know who or why — killed them, and there is the distinct possibility that they will not stop with just the two.'

'So you think we are up against a serial killer?' Lenny Welch said, his voice trembling with the emotion he obviously still felt after Granger's death.

Kate shrugged. 'That remains to be seen, but one thing is clear. None of us, particularly all of you, can afford to take chances from now on. I recommend you to lock your doors securely at night, admit no one after you have turned in, and during the day stay together as much as possible.'

'How do we know one of us is not the killer?' Brewer said. 'Staying together with someone could be the worst thing to do if we happen to choose the wrong person.'

'It isn't one of us,' a quiet voice said and everyone's gaze focused on Tammy Morrison. 'I told you Francis would come back—'

'Enough, Tammy,' Brewer cut in, again trying to silence her.

'It's okay, Ronnie,' she replied sadly, 'Kate knows.'

'What?' Cartwright exclaimed. 'You mean you told her?'

'Stupid cow,' Brewer snarled.

'She had to know,' Morrison replied. 'It was all bound to come out eventually. We must take the punishment we deserve.'

'Well, you can take it,' Welch exclaimed. 'I'm not going to wait around here to be slaughtered by some maniac. I'm leaving first thing in the morning.'

'You can't,' Kate warned. 'There's no way out of here in this snow and, anyway, I require you to remain until I can be sure you had nothing to do with these deaths.'

Welch gave a hollow laugh. 'You require me, do you, love? Well, I hate to remind you, but you're not in any position to require anything. How are you going to stop me? Produce some handcuffs and cuff me to my bed? Get real.'

Then, before she could say anything else, he stalked out of the room.

'So what are you going to do about that, detective?' Brewer taunted. 'Call for the heavy mob?'

Cartwright laughed inanely, but he was the only one.

'I think you're all behaving like stupid children,' Victoria Adams said. 'Kate is only trying to protect everyone and if we're all innocent, why should we object to that?'

'I agrees,' Daphne Parsons spoke for the first time. 'Somethin' nasty be goin' on here. I don't know nothin' 'bout it and I don't want to know, but we all got to look after each other an' listen to what police lady says.'

'Maybe that's because you and your old man are behind it all anyway,' Brewer put in again.

'You watch your mouth, mister,' Tom Parsons shouted, rising half out of his chair. 'We be fine here 'afore you lot come.'

Daphne grabbed his wrist to restrain him and he reluctantly sat down again. Kate could see that things were getting out of hand and she decided it was time to lower the temperature in the room before someone got hurt.

'Okay, people,' she said, 'I think it's time we all calmed down and stopped going for each other's throats. All I would ask is that you take on board what I have just said and if you become aware of anything suspicious that you tell myself or Hayden here straight away. In the meantime, stay safe and vigilant.'

Before any further questions could be asked, she got up and left the room in much the same way as Lenny Welch had done.

CHAPTER 11

'Do you think Welch will try and leave tomorrow as he threatened?' Hayden asked Kate when they were back upstairs in their room.

'He's so wound up about everything that I wouldn't put it past him,' she said falling on to the bed. 'The trouble is, there's nothing we can do to stop him and he knows it.' Then she gave him her sweetest smile. 'Make us a coffee, will you?'

'What did your last slave die of,' he muttered sourly.

'Malnutrition,' she threw back at him. 'He didn't get the chance to eat.'

He muttered an unintelligible reply but still crossed to the dressing table to turn on the kettle. Then tipping the instant powder into two mugs, he stood there, waiting for the kettle to boil.

'So, what's your latest theory about the present situation?' he said over his shoulder. 'From what Tammy told you it seems very likely that Francis Templeton is what these killings are all about. But why would one member of the group want to kill another over it? They were all equally involved in spiking his drink.'

'Except Tammy Morrison,' Kate reminded him. 'Don't forget, she told me she was against what they proposed and didn't actually participate in the business, even though in the end she went along with it. Maybe she hadn't the strength of personality to oppose them all at the time, but since then has developed a conscience and needs to assuage her guilt by killing each of them in turn.'

He poured the boiling water into the mugs and stirred them. 'But you said at the start that you didn't see her as a murderer.'

'I know, but I'm not so sure now. She could be a clever minx. Anyway aside from her, perhaps it's time we re-assessed all our potential suspects to see if anything of significance stands out among them.'

He handed her a mug of coffee and stood there sipping his own and studying her face.

'Well, to my mind, Lenny Welch is the most likely candidate. He's obviously very fit and strong, and by his own admission he was hooked on Granger. Regardless of what he told you, she may have rejected his proposal, which maddened him enough to bump her off. You know the old maxim, if I can't have her, no one else will.'

'Then how does Jimmy Caulfield fit into things? Why would Welch murder him to start with? On the face of it, he doesn't seem to have any plausible motive.'

'Maybe Caulfield made a play for Granger and she chose him instead of Welch, which would have certainly given a man like our Lenny, who was already head over heels in love with the woman, a reason to kill his rival. And don't forget, at the meeting just now Welch showed a very keen desire to get away from Warneford Hall as soon as possible. After what you said, maybe he thought his luck was running out.'

'A good point. But there's also Ronnie Brewer to consider. He's shown himself to be a ruthless brute of a man. A bully who likes to get his own way. Someone with all the traits of a psychopath who will always be prepared to sacrifice others to save his own skin. Maybe he saw Caulfield and Granger as weakening over the Francis affair and feared they would ultimately blow the whistle on what happened? He was hard enough on Tammy Morrison when she looked like caving in and did you see his face when he found out just now that she had actually spilled the beans? It was positively evil.'

Hayden looked doubtful. 'Bit of a drastic step even for him to take, though, don't you think, over what was essentially a bad behavioural issue? He and his housemates didn't physically kill anyone. They just did something stupid that may or may not have resulted in a tragic accident. It was irresponsible, but hardly serious enough to warrant the murder of two people to keep it quiet. Also, don't forget, both the deaths occurred at night and since Brewer is sleeping with his girlfriend he would have found it almost impossible to slip out for any length of time without her being aware of the fact.'

'She could have been on sleeping tablets and dead to the world, if you'll forgive the pun.'

'Possibly, but there's no guarantee that they will always work one hundred percent. You should know that yourself from the time you used to take them because you said my snoring kept you awake at night. You still managed to wake up on occasions, didn't you?'

Kate smiled wryly. 'Even the ear defenders they use on firearms ranges wouldn't cope with the decibel level your snores reach, Hayd,' she sniped. Then she became serious again and paused to take a sip of her coffee, warming her hands on the cup for a long thoughtful moment before continuing.

'Okay, so passing on from Brewer, what about Jeffrey Cartwright? He seems a particularly nasty piece of work and he's plainly an addict, so anything could happen when he's off his head. Perhaps as well as using, he had been supplying Granger and Caulfield with cocaine or some other form of dope and they refused to pay up when he tried to collect?'

Hayden shook his head. 'That's a bit thin. First off, from what we've heard so far, the crowd hadn't seen each other for five years, with the exception of Granger and Welch, so how would he have been supplying drugs to Caulfield or Granger? Second, he strikes me as a bit of a spineless individual who hangs on to other people's shirttails, as he has done with Brewer since everyone got back together again. I don't think he has the guts, if you can call it that, to kill anyone. He's a rabble-rouser, not a doer. Finally, why would he kill someone because they hadn't paid him his dues? Then he would never be able to get hold of the money he was owed, would he?'

Kate set down her half-empty mug on the bedside cabinet. 'So that leaves us with just Tom and Daphne Parsons once again and, of course, Ronnie Brewer's girlfriend, Victoria Adams, none of whom apparently knew the victims before their arrival at Warneford Hall, so would hardly have had a motive for killing them. Plus the fact that Adams is sharing a bed with Ronnie Brewer, which works in her defence in the same way as it does for Brewer. One couldn't leave without the other knowing.'

'Then we're back to Cartwright's so-called "hider in the house" theory. Some deranged psychopath killing for the sheer fun of it, who has concealed himself somewhere in or close to the house.'

She snorted. 'Which is about as plausible as the ghost of Mawgana Keegan wandering about the place or Francis Templeton returning from the dead on a revenge mission,' she replied drily. 'Anyway, between us we've checked out both the loft and the cellar. Furthermore, all the bedrooms were occupied when we first arrived, except ours, so where would anyone have been hiding all this time? There's only a couple of old barns I saw out back today, but according to Tom Parsons, they are not in use anymore and are just derelict ruins.'

'There is one other place we haven't yet checked.'

'The clocktower.'

'Yes, the clocktower.'

'Which we can't get into.'

He scratched his nose and flashed her a little smirk. 'Unless, of course, we use the old police "Ways and Means Act",' he said, referring to the practical, but somewhat unorthodox approach the older generation of police officers used to adopt in order to achieve their objectives.

She stared at him, surprised that he of all people would have come up with a suggestion like that. 'Break in, you mean?'

'Nothing quite so drastic or unsubtle. I was thinking more of trying to spring the lock.'

'And you can do that, can you?'

'Never really tried.'

'Exactly. Which means that for the present there's only the barns.' She raised herself off the bed and went to the wardrobe. 'And there's no time like the present.'

He groaned. 'What? But it'll be dark before long.'

She pulled out her pair of still damp walking shoes and sat down on the chair by the dressing table to pull them on. 'Then we'd better get going, hadn't we?'

* * *

There was no one in the kitchen when Kate and Hayden walked in ten minutes later, which suited Kate perfectly. She had no wish to be called upon to explain to anyone what they were doing there. With this thought uppermost in her mind, she quickly made for the back door in case the situation changed, borrowing Tom Parsons' torch from the windowsill on the way.

A few idle snowflakes were falling again as they both left the house and crunched their way towards a pair of old, ramshackle buildings with pitched, corrugated iron roofs on the far side of the hardstanding Kate had observed before. There seemed to be a light drizzle mixed in with the light snowflakes and for the first time it felt a lot warmer, suggesting that a thaw could be on the way. If only . . .

'Doesn't look like anyone's been out here recently,' Hayden commented, staring past Kate at the thick white carpet stretching away in front of them. 'No footprints at all.'

'Snow would have obliterated any that were there,' she threw back over her shoulder. 'Don't forget, it's been pretty heavy over the past two days.'

'Yeah,' he agreed, 'but if our killer has been using either of the barns since last night he can't have been back to them. This check seems like a waste of time to me.'

With a chuckle she bent in mid-stride and, scooping up a handful of snow, turned briefly to toss it at him. 'Where's your spirit of adventure, Hayd?' she mocked.

He snorted, brushing the flattened snowball off his chest. 'That's not the first time you've said that to me over the years,' he reminded her, 'and every time you've said it we've ended up in heaps of trouble.'

Kate stopped by the first of the barns and bent down to study the rusted padlock securing the big, sliding steel door, noting at the same time the warning painted in peeling red letters across it: *Danger. Keep Out. Unsafe Building.*

'Doesn't look as though that's likely to happen this time,' she said with sudden irritation. 'Bloody thing's locked up.'

He grinned. 'What did I tell you? No one's been here. So can we go back now?'

She didn't answer but moved away from him to the right of the door and turned down the side of the building.

With another of his groans, he trudged after her, only to hear her call out almost immediately, 'We can get in here.'

There was a small side door about fifteen feet away and she had already tugged it open by the time he got to her.

It was her turn to grin. 'What is it they say?' she mocked. 'Where there's a will and all that.'

Then she stepped through the opening, leaving him with no option but to do the same.

The interior of the building was enveloped in a patchy gloom, relieved only by the fading afternoon light creeping into the place through a row of small, high-level windows in the right-hand wall. Within the gloom, a confusion of grotesque shapes, glaring eyes and jagged teeth manifested themselves like disturbing creations from an Isaac Asimov novel, taking on a sort of malign, robotic life of their own. Kate switched on the torch, skimming under the vaulted roof with its gable trusses and homing in on an antiquated looking tractor with its engine removed, a baler short of a wheel, and various pieces of light machinery boasting either spikes, blades or other mechanical attachments. There was enough metal in the sorry collection to gladden the eye of any passing scrap-dealer had there been one. As to why it had all been simply left in situ to rust away instead of being sold on was a mystery known only to the farmer who had walked away from his business and the would-be hotelier who seemed to have failed just as miserably with his own ambitious project. But there was nothing relevant to Kate and Hayden's search. No blankets, no sleeping bag, no sign of any discarded food or drink containers. Nothing in fact to indicate a rough sleeper. Checking further they discovered an office and a small tool store in the far corner. One containing empty racks and the other just an empty metal filing cabinet, a desk and a broken swivel chair, but nothing else save mouse or rat droppings on the floor.

Disappointed Kate led the way to the second barn some four to five feet away, ignoring Hayden's muttered objections as he stomped along after her. Externally, the building seemed to be of a similar design and construction to its neighbour and this time they found the big sliding door at the front shut but with the padlock hanging open on its hasp. With a little joint muscle power they were able to haul it back under the groaning scraping protest of its distorted runners.

Like the previous barn, the interior was pervaded by a patchy gloom into which a weak, grey light seeped through the row of similar small, high-level windows. The torch caught the metallic gleam of a double row of metal-railed cattle stalls, separated by a concrete walkway, which stretched away from them to disappear into a deeper gloom at the far end where the beam failed to reach. Following the walkway as far as they could, they found that the stalls finished just before a wide hayloft which spanned the width of the building. Once again there was no evidence to suggest anyone was using the place. It occurred to Kate that not even the most determined rough sleeper would have chosen the cold, wet concrete floor among the open stalls as a suitable place in which to doss down for the night.

'Told you it would be a waste of time,' Hayden said. 'We ought to be getting back to the house to wash up. Mrs Parsons will be starting to prepare dinner soon.'

Kate waggled the torch so that the beam jerked up and down as if in a spasm. 'We need to check what's on the other side of those end doors first,' she said and leaving him to follow her sighing his displeasure, she plunged into the deeper gloom under the hayloft. But once again she met with disappointment. The doors simply opened out on to a walled yard with a metal gate closing off the other end. Beyond the yard lay nothing but fenced, snowbound fields.

'Doubtless a back door for driving the cattle from the fields into the barn and out again,' Hayden commented as they went back into the building. '*Now* are you satisfied?'

But before Kate could respond, they both stiffened to the sound of a heavy thud above their heads.

'Someone must have followed us in here,' Kate breathed, holding up one hand to tell him not to move. 'They're up there in the hayloft.'

For a few moments they both stood stock-still and listened. Almost immediately they heard another thud and a distinct creaking noise issuing from the underside of the loft, suggesting someone was walking across it. Then silence.

'I saw a ladder set against the edge of the loft to our right,' Kate whispered. 'Time, I think, to pop up and say hello.'

Hayden gripped her arm, halting her in her tracks. 'I don't like it,' he said close to her ear. 'They know we are here, so why draw so much attention to their position? Could be a trap.'

She tore his arm free. 'A trap to do what?' she retorted derisively. 'Machine-gun us?'

Then before he could try and stop her, she stepped out from under the loft and crept quietly across the barn to where she had seen the ladder. At which point, there was a loud scraping sound and a dark figure heaved something over the edge of the loft just above her head . . .

CHAPTER 12

Hayden Lewis rarely moved quickly. He was by nature a lumbering, tank of a man who seldom saw the sense in too much exertion. But there had been a few exceptions in his life to that philosophy and the attempted murder of his beloved wife in the barn at Warneford Hall was one of them. What strange sixth sense had alerted him to the imminent danger she faced would always remain a mystery. But triggered by the scraping sound and the warning voice in his head, he literally threw himself at her from behind in a desperate tackle that would have been applauded by rugby fans as one of the best tackles of the season, bearing her to the floor under him and knocking most of the breath from her body. At the same moment a large, heavy object hit the concrete floor with a resounding crash just inches from where they both lay, producing a strong smell of spilled petrol.

For a couple of seconds Kate was too dazed and winded to appreciate what had just happened. But then as Hayden helped her back on her feet, there was the sound of a door closing somewhere above them in the black vault of the roof space. She was about to make an angry protest to her husband about his behaviour when realisation dawned.

'Quick!' she gasped, fumbling around for her torch 'They're getting away.'

The ladder up to the loft was just paces from them. But by the time she had located the torch and they had both managed to clamber up the creaking rungs, they were too late. Her would-be assailant had gone and they found themselves staring at the gathering dusk through a five foot by seven foot opening in the gable end wall, where the pair of loft doors, once used for the loading or off-loading of hay, had been burst open. Despite the fading daylight and the overhanging "widow's peak", they were able to pick out another ladder attached to the wall just under the doors. It didn't look very safe and had partially come away from its fixings, but it had obviously served its purpose as far as the intruder was concerned. There was no sign of anyone in the fields beyond.

'Whoever it was, they must have already known about this old hayloft,' Hayden growled.

Kate nodded. 'Obviously followed us to the barn and made their way up here while we were in the back yard,' she said. 'But for your quick actions, I would be under whatever it was they pushed over the edge.'

'Something pretty lethal, you can guarantee it,' he said and went with her to peer at the barn floor in the torchlight.

'It's a machine of some sort,' she said. 'Smashed to buggery now.'

He grunted. 'Looks like one of those portable petrol generators to me,' he replied. 'You can smell the spilled petrol even from up here. Probably needed in an old barn like this, too. No electric lighting as far as I can see.' He half-turned and waved an arm towards the far corner. 'But there's something else of interest over there. Noticed it when we went up the ladder.'

Kate turned to look. Even without using the torch, the light provided by the open hayloft door was good enough for her to see that there were at least half a dozen bottles standing on a shabby wooden table in the corner, with a canvas style camping chair alongside.

Hayden left her to make a closer inspection and as she joined him with the torch, he checked the labels on the bottles. 'Scotch,' he said. 'Seems like someone has a serious drinking problem.'

'Our rough sleeper?' she suggested.

He shook his head. 'I wouldn't think so. This is expensive stuff. Some of it is single malt. Anyway, there's no sign of any sleeping bag, mattress or blankets here. Loft floor would be pretty hard to doss on. No, I reckon this lot belongs or belonged to someone staying or working at the hotel.'

He bent over the table and, pulling out a single drawer, gave a low whistle. 'Not just a drinking problem either,' he said and thrusting his hand into the drawer he pulled out a wad of magazines, which he dumped on the table top.

Kate stared at them and flicked open a couple of the coloured pages. She shook her head as the naked bodies depicted in all their glossy obscenity seemed to writhe in the light of the torch. 'Porno,' she commented tightly. 'Last place I'd expect to find this sort of sick crap in a derelict barn at the back of a rural hotel.'

He grinned and produced a pipe and a tobacco pouch from the drawer as well. 'Seems we've found some fellow's secret den,' he said. 'It's a variation on the theme of the old man's shed. You know, a secret hideaway away from prying eyes where a man can do what a man needs to do.'

She threw him a sideways glance. 'Good job we haven't got a shed at home then, isn't it?' she sniped. But she changed the subject before he could respond. 'So, what do you think? Is our killer and the character who owns this dodgy stash one and the same person?'

'Possibly, though there's no way it can belong to some nondescript rough sleeper.'

'It could have been left here by a member of the hotel staff who was given the push.'

'What makes you think he will have left? I can't see an alkie abandoning so much expensive liquor and simply waltzing off into the blue.'

'Then there's only one person we can be talking about. Good old Tom Parsons?'

'That's the logical conclusion to draw from the evidence we've got to hand, yes,' he agreed, wandering away from her to stare idly through a small window just above the loft ladder. 'He smokes a pipe too, doesn't he? Saw him filling it when I met up with you in the kitchen earlier. Maybe he likes to keep a second one here? But for all that, it doesn't necessarily mean he's also our killer.'

'But it *does* mean we need to have a meaningful chat with him pdq . . .'

He didn't answer and she saw him suddenly stiffen. Then without turning his head he said quietly, 'Before we do that, there's something a lot more important we have to do. Come and take a look.'

Puzzled by the instruction and the urgency in his tone, she joined him quickly at the window and peered out.

'Down there,' he said.

It was now almost dark, but still light enough for her to see the snowbound yard and the fields and scattered copses beyond.

'What should I be looking at?' she asked, still puzzled.

'Check out the slurry pit.'

She lowered her gaze. At first all she could see was the fenced-off area with the circular pit.

'So?'

'Look again.'

She did so, concentrating her gaze this time, and the next moment she started with a horrified gasp.

Projecting from the layer of snow covering the pit was a human arm, with the hand extended as if in a gruesome, frozen wave.

'Victim number three,' Hayden commented.

* * *

The gate to the slurry pit was padlocked, but like the shed padlocks, this one was old and rusted. The hasp came away with little resistance under the impact of Hayden's foot. The smell from the pit had been noticeable even on the approach to the compound, but once inside it was overpowering despite the coldness of the air and the layer of snow, which had partially covered it. Both Kate and Hayden were acutely aware of the hidden dangers posed by slurry, including the release of such lethal gasses as ammonia and methane, and they made sure they didn't waste any time in carrying out their grisly task. Fortunately, the body was quite close to the edge of the poisonous lagoon and the frozen arm projected around a foot above the snow. In a macabre way it provided them with an effective means of retrieving the cadaver and they gritted their teeth and tried to hold their breath as they gripped the ice-cold limb to haul the body out on to the bank.

It appeared to be an elderly man dressed in a suit and waistcoat and, though coated in a revolting slime, it was in a reasonable state of preservation, possibly helped by the bitterly cold weather. They didn't linger to examine it any further but carried it straight out of the compound. They were in the process of doing this when a voice brought them to a sudden halt.

'What on earth you got there then?'

Tom Parsons was kitted out in a long hooded coat and wellington boots and was gaping at them in astonishment. Where he had just come from was not apparent, but Kate noticed a new set of deep footprints close beside those she and Hayden had made earlier. They stretched in a line from the back door of the house to the barn they had just checked, where they joined the tracks they had made towards the slurry compound in a confusion of disturbed snow.

'What does it look like, Mr Parsons?' Kate said in a tone as cold as the weather. 'He was in the slurry pit where someone had obviously dumped him.'

'Any idea who he could be?' Hayden asked and, gritting his teeth again, he wiped the dead man's face with a handful of snow.

Seemingly unfazed by the grisly state of the corpse, Parsons bent over and peered at the face of the dead man, which was just about visible now that Hayden had wiped away some of the filth coating it.

'Well, I be blowed,' he exclaimed, straightening up and staring at them. 'It be Harold Hapgood, hotel manager. How'd he end up in slurry pit?'

'More importantly,' Kate said grimly, 'who the hell put him there, and why?'

* * *

Parsons hurried back to the house and returned with a large bed sheet, which Kate and Hayden used as a shroud in which to wrap the body. Then insisting that Parsons returned to the hotel, they carried the dead man round to the outhouse at the front as quickly as they could to avoid attracting the attention of any of the other guests. Kate was reminded of many of the hospital mortuaries she had attended over her career in the force as she unlocked the door and they carried the dead man inside to join the corpse of Jimmy Caulfield on the concrete floor. She mused that the outhouse was fast becoming a mortuary itself and if things continued like this, the place would soon become jam-packed with corpses. She just hoped that neither she nor Hayden became one of them in the future, recalling that with the incident in the barn a short time before, she herself very nearly had.

That chilling thought coupled with the bitter cold of the outhouse sent a sudden involuntary tremor through her and she swayed for a moment as she straightened up.

'You okay?' Hayden asked, giving her a hard stare.

She nodded. 'Let's just get this over,' she said and, switching on the outhouse light, got down on her knees to carry out a cursory examination of the new victim. At first she couldn't see any wounds or other signs of injury. But then she turned the body over on to its side and the likely cause of death became immediately apparent despite the filth covering it. It wasn't due to drowning or asphyxiation in the slurry pit either.

'Seems our killer deviated from his or her usual MO this time,' she said, pointing.

Hayden bent down to take a look and grimaced. What looked like a length of thin metal was projecting from the back of the victim's neck. 'Looks like some sort of long metal skewer,' he suggested.

'Maybe from Daphne Parsons' kitchen,' Kate agreed, allowing the body to fall back again. 'Probably the last time it was used was for roasting a beef or turkey joint. But it must have been driven in with considerable force.'

'I will never eat a roast joint again,' he retorted drily.

* * *

It was completely dark by the time Kate and Hayden returned to the hotel via the back door. They found Tom Parsons sitting in his usual chair in the kitchen, the stem of his smoking pipe gripped fiercely between his teeth and another mug of what looked like tea on the chair arm beside him. Daphne Parsons was nowhere to be seen, but a pile of peeled vegetables and a roasting tin containing what seemed to be chops of some sort stood on the draining board. Kate couldn't help wondering if the skewer embedded in Hapgood's neck had previously protruded from a joint of beef roasted in that very tin . . .

'Dinner be a bit late tonight, I fancy,' Parsons said soberly after removing the pipe from his mouth. 'Daphne took real bad by news 'bout Mr Hapgood.'

'Where is she now?' Kate asked.

Parsons jerked the stem of his pipe in the direction of the hall door. 'Lyin' down in her room,' he said. 'Pretty shook up, she be.'

Kate nodded. 'Just as well she's there for now. My colleague and I would like to have a quiet chat with you.'

'Thought p'raps you might.'

Kate leaned back against the sink while Hayden found a three-legged stool in a corner and dropped on to it.

'Why do you say that?' she went on.

Parsons shrugged. 'I ain't daft, Sergeant,' he said. 'I knows you thinks I might be your murderer.'

Kate didn't confirm or deny his assertion. 'So what were you doing out there just now,' she said. 'Getting a bit dark for ground maintenance, wasn't it?'

'I weren't out there for no maintenance', he replied. 'Missus were puttin' stuff in waste bin and sees you coming out of barn. Said I should take a look at what were goin' on.'

'Did you go into the barn then?' Hayden asked.

Parsons took a sip of his tea and shook his head. 'Time I got me clobber on you was both at slurry pit.'

Kate forced a smile and nodded towards the mug of tea he'd replaced on the chair arm. 'I must admit, you've certainly taken the death of your former boss with commendable fortitude. In your situation I would probably have hit the brandy or whisky bottle over the shock.'

He met her gaze without flinching. Kate got the impression, rightly or wrongly, that he saw through her ostensibly "innocent" compliment and the trap she had set for him.

'Not fer me, Sergeant,' he said. 'Me and Daphne don't touch stuff on account of us bein' strict Baptists, see.'

For a second Kate felt rattled. She hadn't expected her hidden invitation to him to comment on his own drinking habits to be so easily kicked to touch. There was more than a little ire in her tone when she continued. 'Yet you provide alcohol for your guests at the hotel. There's even an honesty box in the bar and your wife complained that drinks were not being paid for. So how does that fit in with your beliefs?'

He raised one hand in a deprecating gesture. 'Ain't fer us to tell 'em as be outside our faith what be right and wrong. 'Sides, we has to do what them as pays our wages tells us to do.'

There could be no answer to that and she quickly changed the subject.

'When did you last see Mr Hapgood?'

He scratched the stubble on his chin with the stem of his pipe, a thoughtful frown on his face. 'Must ha' been 'bout two to three weeks past. In the hall it were when rest of staff was all dismissed. Give us a nice bundle to stay on till last guests that was expected had left. Said we'd get other half after like.'

Kate emitted a short, humourless laugh. 'Doesn't look like you'll be getting that now, does it?' she said.

He shook his head mournfully. 'Didn't 'spect this carry on neither. You done now, Sergeant? I got to see to Daphne.'

He didn't wait for an answer but climbed to his feet and knocked his pipe out into his nearly empty mug before leaving the room.

'You didn't mention the hideaway in the barn?' Hayden pointed out as they both left the kitchen.

'No point,' she said. 'He'd only deny knowing anything about it and we're not in a position to prove he's lying.'

'Except by asking Daphne.'

'I plan to do that at the next opportunity, but he's probably already priming her now.'

He followed her up the stairs. 'So, do you still think he's our man then?'

She paused on the landing and turned to face him. 'I don't know what the hell to think, Hayd,' she said. 'The more I delve into this business the more confused I get.'

'There's one thing we do know, though,' he replied gloomily as he followed her along the corridor to their room.

'What's that?'

'If Daphne doesn't get her skates on pretty soon, we may not get dinner at all.'

* * *

In fact, dinner was eventually served on the stroke of eight amid profuse apologies by Mrs Parsons, and it turned out to be beautifully cooked lamb chops with the usual trimmings, followed by a tasty trifle. Mrs Parsons certainly took her duties very seriously indeed, despite the shock she had endured earlier, and it put an appreciative smile back on Hayden's face. Especially when he managed to get a second helping of the sweet this time.

All the remaining guests were there at their long table, but they were a sullen, uncommunicative bunch and there was little conversation to compete with the scrape of cutlery during the course of the meal. The two bottles of wine that had been placed on their table were hardly touched and everyone left as soon as the meal was over with scarcely a glance in Kate and Hayden's direction on the way.

'Cheerful bunch,' Hayden commented, gulping some more of his wine and belching behind a big, white handkerchief.

'Can you blame them?' Kate said. 'They must be wondering who's next for the chop.'

'Well, I've just eaten my chop,' he replied. 'Very nice too, it was.'

She ignored the recourse to his familiar flippancy. 'What I can't understand is why Hapgood was murdered in the first place,' she went on in a low voice. 'He doesn't appear to have been connected to this uni crowd. The fact that he must have been stiffed prior to their arrival here suggests he was either part of the murder conspiracy or he found out about it and had to be silenced. I can't think of any other explanation, can you? Maybe this business has nothing to do with the drowning of Francis Templeton at all in spite of what we've been told so far?'

He slurped his last drop of wine with a genial look that suggested he wasn't in the mood to consider the issue either way.

'Do we have to think about that right this minute?' he asked. 'It's after nine and I think it's time to turn in. My mind will be clearer after a good night's sleep.'

'What about speaking to Mrs Parsons about this Baptist thing?'

'What, now? I reckon she'll be in bed, or at least heading for it and we should do the same.' He climbed a little unsteadily to his feet. 'It will keep now till the morning.'

She stared critically at him and then at the empty wine bottle, acutely aware of the fact that she had had only one glass.

'You go ahead,' she said. 'I'll be up in a minute. I'll just scout round to see if she is still about.'

She watched him leave the room and head unsteadily for the stairs, then made her way to the kitchen. She heard the metallic clang of something even before she reached it and found Mrs Parsons putting a roasting dish away in a lower cupboard.

The other turned and straightened as she entered the room. Her face was strained and pale and her eyes looked haunted.

'Thought I'd come to see how you were, Mrs Parsons,' she said. 'Your husband told me you were suffering badly from shock after what happened to Mr Hapgood.'

The woman threw her a narrowed glance and busied herself putting other cooking utensils away. 'Did he now? Well, it were an awful thing right enough. But I be fine, thank you, Sergeant. I had me a little lie down. Sorry 'bout late dinner.'

Kate shrugged off the apology. 'No idea as to who could have murdered him, have you?'

Parsons shook her head. 'Such a nice gentleman too, he were. Not an enemy in world, far as I knows.'

Kate grimaced, thinking how many times before she had heard that said about victims of violent crime.

'Do you think he may have upset one of the staff by dismissing them and they came back and dumped him in the slurry pit as a form of revenge?'

She snorted. 'Revenge, poppycock. There were only Ginny, hotel receptionist, and Mavis an' Jill what done rooms, then "waited on" at dinner in evening. All come from village like Tom an' me. Ginny were 'bout sixty an' walked with a stick, an' Mavis an' Jill was only kids really. No more'n twenty, I'd say. Nice girls I know'd since they was born.' She gave Kate a hard look. 'None of 'em would've hurt a fly, so 'tain't right to go 'ccusing folk'.

'I'm not accusing anyone, Mrs Parsons,' Kate replied. 'I'm just trying to work out why anyone would want to kill Mr Hapgood. Er, did the staff actually stay here?'

Parsons shook her head. 'None of us done that. No need. We all come up each day from village. Me and Tom only stayin' here now temporary like till last guests go, on account of place bein' empty. Tom be in room Mr Hapgood 'ad 'afore he went.'

'And you didn't see him again after the day he paid you both to stay on?'

'Never saw him again. 'Spected him back today to close place up an' pay us rest of our money. Thought 'afore you found him that snow had stopped him gettin' through.'

Kate took the plunge. 'As the weather will have stopped you getting to church yesterday too, I suppose.'

Parsons frowned. 'Church? Don't go to no church. Don't have no truck with that stuff no more.'

'Oh? But Tom told me you were both strict Baptists.'

To Kate's astonishment she let out a loud guffaw. 'Strict Baptists? Old bugger 'avin' you on, girl. We *was* Baptists, true. But not these ten years past. Got throwed out, see, on account o' Tom's drinkin' . . .'

'His drinking? But he said he was teetotal.'

Another loud laugh. 'Teetotal? Tom? Oh, he is now, but only 'cause I told him I'd leave him if he didn't give it up, and he knows I catch him at it anymore we be finished.'

Parsons frowned again. 'But dunno why he'd say we was Baptists.'

Kate could feel her heart thudding away with excitement and she made a strong effort to conceal her sudden breathlessness from the curious stare of this perceptive country woman. It was plain that her husband had said nothing to his wife about the barn. No doubt hoping he had put the two detectives off the scent. Kate reasoned it was better to let him think that he had got away with it until she had the chance of confronting him again. So she made no mention of it now in reply to Daphne Parson's query.

'Oh, I was just talking to him about how much drink your guests seemed to get through, and he said, as Baptists, you didn't drink at all.'

Parsons relaxed. 'Did he now, ol' bugger? But he be right 'bout them folk we got stayin' here. Criminal waste, all that liquor is. Still, Mr Hapgood tell us to let 'em have much as they wanted. No limit, he said. Make sure they's comfortable.'

Kate smiled. 'Well, if that's what he said, why worry about it? Now I must be off to bed. It's getting late. Sorry about Mr Hapgood, *and* the other dreadful traumas you have been subjected to over the weekend. Let's hope we are able to get to the bottom of it all and we can get some help in here once the thaw arrives.'

Parsons shook her head again. 'I'm awful feared none of us will be livin' an' spared be then, Sergeant,' she said. 'Somethin' evil be loose in Warneford Hall, you mark me words, an' ain't nothin' goin' to stop it till it's done.'

On that note, Kate left the troubled woman to finish her chores and headed upstairs. There was a triumphant gleam in her eyes when she went to join Hayden in the bedroom, eager to say a big "I told you so" to her cynical other half. But disappointment awaited her. The snores issuing from the swollen lump in the double bed told her that Hayden was in no fit state to listen to anyone. He was out for the count.

She made no effort to try and awaken him; there was no point. After all, delaying her revelations a few more hours wouldn't change anything. The die was already cast and one thing was abundantly clear: good old Tom Parsons would have some very serious questions to answer when she confronted him in the morning.

Undressing and climbing into bed beside her husband, she was only vaguely aware of the wind rattling the window panes before she drifted off into a deep, troubled sleep, populated by nightmare hooded figures and rows of grinning corpses with skewers protruding from their heads. But unbeknown to her, another real drama was shortly to unfold in the snowbound wilderness beyond the hotel that would ultimately throw all her plans into further turmoil . . .

CHAPTER 13

Lenny Welch was up in the early hours of the morning, shivering in the cold room as he pulled on several layers of warm clothes, including a thick pair of corduroy trousers and a woollen hat with a flashlight attached to it by means of an elastic strap. The shin-high boots he had brought with him on the off chance of fitting in some serious walking over the weekend were already on the floor beside his bed, a thick woollen sock in each, and he quickly forced his feet into them and tied up the laces. Okay, so the gear wasn't ideal for a six- to seven-mile trek through thick snow to the village the Parsonses had spoken about, but it was all he had, so it would have to do, and with his current level of fitness, he felt confident that he could manage it. He had no idea what the village offered in terms of shelter and communication with the outside world, but anything was better than staying at Warneford Hall waiting to be attacked by some homicidal psychopath. He felt no guilt about running out on his former housemates. After all, it wasn't clear whether the killer of Abbey and Jimmy might not be one of them anyway and as far as he was concerned, with Abbey gone, it was everyone for themselves. He was sorry to leave his nice new Mercedes convertible behind, but consoled himself with the thought that he could easily arrange for a garage to collect it in the next few days once the snow had thawed sufficiently.

Making some coffee, he filled a flask and slipped it into his rucksack with some sausage rolls, pork pies and apples he had helped himself to from the kitchen earlier. Then he left the room with the rucksack strapped to his back over a fleece-lined khaki coat. Prepared as much as he could be for the challenging hike ahead of him.

The corridor outside his room was still in darkness, but his flashlight enabled him to see his way clearly as he quietly headed for the stairs and descended to the hall. It was deserted. The front door was unlocked and opened easily, admitting a blast of cold air and what felt like some fine rain. Exactly what was needed to help disperse the snow. Maybe the much awaited thaw was on the way, he thought. But if it was, he had no intention of waiting for it.

Outside, the scene had a magical quality in the light of a misty moon. It resembled a clip from a Walt Disney fairy-tale production. But he was not interested in the aesthetics of the situation, only in the depth of the snow, which rose halfway up his calves when his booted feet sank into it. Hugging into his coat, he crunched his way across the forecourt on to the tree-lined driveway leading towards the main entrance, forced to lift his feet in an exaggerated stride at virtually every step to make any real headway.

After just a few yards he began to feel quite pessimistic. If this was what lay before him for the next six miles, even someone with his level of fitness faced a daunting challenge. He just hoped he didn't end up too exhausted to complete it. Stuck out here in the cold with no proper shelter and the possibility of snow beginning to fall again, there was a real risk he had bitten off more than he could chew.

A fox burst from the hedgerow just after he had passed through the entrance gateway, making him start back with a gasp of alarm, and he cursed himself for his cowardly reaction. Anyone would think a horde of demons had suddenly jumped out on him. So much for the big, tough guy he claimed to be. Scared of nothing and willing to take on all-comers. If only . . .

He reached the shaky wooden bridge he had driven over on his way to the hotel three days before, though it was so thickly covered with snow that he only knew it was there by the wooden posts supporting the safety rails on each side. He stopped halfway across and, leaning on one of the rails to peer over the edge, he picked out the glint of water. It appeared that although much of the river had iced over sufficiently to support deposits of snow, there were patches of clear water where the ice had collapsed, creating a few small pools which eerily reflected the light of the moon.

It was a rather beautiful sight, but not one he felt like admiring for long in the present circumstances and he made to turn away from the rail to continue his trek towards the top lane, when he heard the distinctive crunching sound of other footsteps in the snow behind him. Alarmed at the sound, he swung right round and found himself confronted by a tall, hooded figure holding something out towards him in one hand. His last clear recollection was of the hood slipping back slightly off the head of the apparition, a hideous ruined face glaring at him in the moonlight. Then he was enveloped in some sort of numbing, sweet-smelling spray before pitching backwards against the disintegrating wooden rail and smashing through the ice into the river's paralysing grip.

* * *

Kate only slept until around two in the morning, waking with a muffled cry as her nightmares reached a grisly climax that faded into the depths of her subconscious within seconds of opening her eyes. She found herself lying on her back in a heavy blackness bathed in perspiration. Beside her, Hayden muttered and snorted in the midst of his own colourful dreams, but otherwise the night was very still. She couldn't sleep at all after that. Her mind was too active. Instead, she lay there for at least another hour, turning things over in her mind without coming to any real conclusions about anything, apart from the conviction that Tom Parsons was not a very good liar and although he didn't yet know it, he had unwittingly been shot down in flames by his own wife.

Finally, round about three o'clock, she gave up trying to sleep and, rolling off the bed and stripping off her nightdress, she headed to the ensuite for a shower. She heard the sound of a door closing, followed by soft footfalls in the corridor, at just after three while she was drying herself in the bedroom. But by the time she got to the door with a towel wrapped around her and had managed to unlock it to peer out, whoever had been there was on the way down the staircase and she saw nothing but the glow of a torch gradually draining away into the main hallway.

Quickly pulling on some clothes and her walking shoes, minus her socks, she left the bedroom to investigate, masking her torch in one hand to reduce the spread of the beam. She got to the landing at the top of the stairs and stopped to listen. Nothing moved, but moonlight seeped into the hallway below through the windows and the large roof skylight. At first the hall appeared to be deserted, but then quite suddenly she stiffened. A tall figure had emerged from the shadows to the left of the staircase and was crossing the tiled floor in the direction of the front door. A figure clad in a long dark coat with a hood. For a few seconds she could do nothing but stare at the sinister manifestation, transfixed by the bone-chilling sight. But then as she snapped out of her temporary paralysis, the apparition was through the front door, closing it very carefully behind them, and had struck out through the snow across the moonlit forecourt. Finally galvanising herself into action, she took the stairs two at a time, skidding on the tiled floor at the bottom in her reckless haste to get to the front door. But a bank of cloud was already moving across the face of the moon. By the time she reached the door the cloud had blotted out the pale yellow disk completely, returning the forecourt to darkness. When the moon reappeared perhaps a couple of minutes later, the figure had completely vanished.

Where the nocturnal marauder had been going was a total mystery, but that they had been up to no good seemed very likely after all that had been happening in the last few days. Cursing herself for her momentary hesitation, Kate was left with no option but to admit failure and make her way back to her room. Once there, she sat in the chair at the dressing table for at least another hour, bemoaning her lot and trying to come to terms with the fact that she had let a possible killer simply walk away from her at the very moment that she could have nailed them.

Yet, as it transpired minutes later, the shenanigans of the night were still not over and she was about to climb back into bed when she heard another series of soft footfalls in the corridor outside. Lurching from her chair, she raced to the door and threw it open, just as another door creaked shut further along the corridor. The corridor was deserted, but she was just in time to catch a glimpse of a bar of light showing below the door of one of the rooms, before it was abruptly extinguished and silence reigned once more.

Kate's heart was racing again with the excitement of the moment. So her efforts that night had not been completely wasted. Although she could not be absolutely certain, she felt fairly confident that she knew from which room that brief flash of light had emanated. It was the room occupied by Jeffrey Cartwright.

* * *

'Seems we've got two main suspects to choose from now then?' Hayden said later that morning.

He had been surprisingly non-committal about the night's events. She had expected him to fly off the handle as soon as she told him about her risky exploits. But he had just scowled his disapproval and left it at that. Maybe he had finally given up trying to reform the unreformable? She really hoped so. They had had more rows over the years about her reputation as "go it alone Kate" than anything else.

'I'm still keeping an open mind,' she replied, 'but I must admit, they've got pride of place in my thinking at the moment. Parsons plainly lied about the stuff left in the barn and he's certainly strong enough to have been responsible for pushing that generator off the loft. As for Cartwright, I've never trusted that little worm from the start and he is, after all, one of the ex-uni crowd, so he has the right connections and could have the motive we're looking for . . .'

'Which would be what?'

'No idea, but maybe something to do with Francis Templeton's death, or some grudge he is nursing about the others.'

'Bit pie in the sky.'

'Maybe, but where had he been during the night to return to his room in the early hours of the morning? I couldn't tell whether the figure in the hooded coat was male or female, as I said during my earlier encounter with it, but Cartwright looks about the same build and he always seems to pop up in the most unexpected places. Like when he took the mick about us checking the hotel loft that time.'

'Hardly evidential.'

'No, but it's a start. We shall just have to keep an eye on him, that's all. But first, we need to have words in Tom Parsons' shell-like. Preferably away from his old lady. That way he might be more prepared to open up a bit more to us. Especially if we suggest the alternative would be passing the info we have about his liquor and porno mags in the barn on to her.'

'If they *were* his?'

'Who else could they belong to?'

'As we said before, maybe one of the staff the hotel let go. Perhaps Mr Hapgood himself.'

She nodded. 'Also possible, I agree, but it's Parsons' lies that suggest otherwise. Why come out with the claim that he was a strict Baptist and a teetotaller, when it was completely untrue? Why not just say, "I don't like whisky"? There was no need for him to go into all that twaddle. It was almost as if he sussed what we were looking into and was trying to pre-empt any questions being asked about it.'

Hayden considered that and shrugged, again apparently in agreement.

'See your point. So when do we interview him? After breakfast, I hope. I'm starving.'

Kate sighed. 'Tell me something new,' she said.

* * *

There were only four others in the dining room when Kate and Hayden went downstairs after Kate had finally told him what Daphne Parsons had said to her — Ronnie Brewer, Victoria Adams, Jeffrey Cartwright and Tammy Morrison. Of Lenny Welch there was no sign.

'Lenny's gone,' Cartwright announced in a loud voice, which ended in a fit of coughing and sniffing.

'How do you know?' Kate asked sharply, experiencing a sinking feeling in the pit of her stomach.

Cartwright wiped his nose on the back of his hand and flashed one of his sneering grins at her. 'Saw him, didn't I?' he replied. 'Heading off along the corridor to the stairs. Well togged up he was too, with a rucksack on his back.'

Kate's eyes narrowed. So that *was* Cartwright she had heard closing his door and briefly turning his bedroom light on and off.

'What time was that?' she asked.

He looked suddenly uneasy. Perhaps realising that blurting out the news just to impress everyone with his first-hand knowledge on everything that was going on might on this occasion have been a bad idea.

'Haven't a clue,' he replied quickly. 'Late at night, though.'

'So, how come you happened to see him go at that hour then? Out for a walk in the snow, were you?'

He shook his head and smiled self-consciously. 'No, no, no. Just couldn't sleep and heard a noise outside my room again. Saw him when I went to check on it.'

'You didn't speak to him then?'

'None of my business what he was doing.'

'Good riddance,' Brewer interrupted in a growl. 'He always was an arsehole and now he's proved it by running out on the rest of us.'

'Maybe we should be relieved he's gone,' Cartwright went on more enthusiastically. 'Could be he was the one who did for Jimmy and Abbey.'

'You don't really believe that, do you?' Morrison said sharply. 'Lenny was a bit of a hard nut, but he wouldn't have murdered anyone. What possible reason would he have had for killing Abbey or Jimmy?'

Cartwright lit a cigarette and sniffed again from behind the smoke. 'Nutters don't need a reason,' he said. 'They just get off on it.'

'And you'd know all about that, would you, Jeff?' Adams said meaningfully.

Cartwright's eyes narrowed and he threw a quick, embarrassed glance at Kate as the full implication of Adams' words struck home. 'Stands to reason,' he mumbled in a more mollified tone. 'Why else would they do it?'

Morrison unwittingly let him off the hook. 'I've told you all who's behind this,' she put in, her voice trembling now.

Brewer erupted immediately, cutting her off. 'Not that bollocks about Francis again?' he snarled. 'Just shut up about the little shit, will you, Tam? He ended up as fish food and that's that. The only way he'd ever come back is in a tin! Even then he would probably be well after his "best before date".'

Then, as the sick humour of his spontaneous remark suddenly occurred to him, he dissolved into a fit of laughter, with Cartwright willingly joining in.

Morrison jumped to her feet. 'I hope you still think this is funny when you end up the same way, Ronnie Brewer,' she shouted angrily. Throwing her linen napkin at him she stalked from the room.

'You pig!' Adams snapped at Brewer. 'See what you've done now?'

Climbing to her feet she went after the young woman, her face set in a tight mask. After a few minutes Brewer and Cartwright left also. Cartwright sniffing as usual, a cigarette in his mouth trailing smoke behind him and Brewer scowling at Kate and Hayden as he passed their table.

'Like one happy little family,' Hayden commented after the door had closed behind them. 'This weekend has certainly turned out to be a memorable reunion for them.'

Kate emitted a short laugh. 'Just goes to show how quickly friends can fall apart when under pressure,' she said. 'And Brewer continues to show his true colours.'

'Interesting what Morrison shouted at him about ending up the same way as Templeton, though, wasn't it?' Hayden added. 'Sounded a bit like a threat.'

'That's what I thought. Perhaps our nice, sensitive Tammy isn't all she purports to be. I did say at the start that I suspected there was a lot more going on in her head than we appreciated. Let's just hope it's not thoughts of murder.'

Hayden pushed his plate away and finished his coffee. 'I thought you had already decided on your two main suspects?' he said. 'Welch and Parsons off the list now, are they?'

'Not at all,' she replied. 'But it seems Welch is away on his toes, so the only way we'll know he wasn't our man is if the killings continue, heaven forbid. As for Parsons, the jury is out on him at least until we have had our little chat with the man.'

She gave him a little smile, then added, 'But to plagiarise George Orwell's *Animal Farm*, Hayd, "All the people are suspects, but some are more suspect than others".'

He smirked at the witticism. 'Then our next move is to root out Parsons, eh?' he said.

She shook her head. 'No, after what Cartwright said just now, I've thought of something else we should do first, so a slight change of plan.'

'And that is?'

'Depends on what I find.'

Mystified, he followed her out into the hallway. Opening the front door, she stared out across the forecourt. 'Look at that,' she breathed.

145

Hayden followed the direction of her gaze. He could see nothing but footprints in the snow.

'Footprints?' he commented, slightly puzzled.

'Exactly. Heading towards the entrance gates, by the look of it. Assuming Cartwright was telling the truth and he did see Welch leave, I guessed they would be there, since we don't seem to have had any further heavy snowfalls during the night.'

'Okay, but so what? To start with, they could have been made by anyone, maybe even Tom Parsons doing his maintenance work. On the other hand, if they *were* made by Welch, it merely supports Cartwright's claim. It doesn't exactly get us anywhere.'

'I disagree. If you look again, you will see that there are in fact two sets, merging together in places, which indicates that two people followed the same route.' She threw Hayden a hard, sideways glance. 'One set of tracks was made by Welch, I am certain of it, but who was responsible for the other set and why were they heading in exactly the same direction? There can only be one explanation. Welch was being followed. I have a bad feeling about this, Hayd, and I think we need to check things out.'

'What? You mean follow them on foot?'

She made a wry grimace. 'Unless you have a spare four by four handy?'

Twenty minutes later, dressed in their anoraks and still damp walking shoes, the two detectives left the hotel to trudge through the snow towards the main entrance, Kate leading the way and Hayden, ashen-faced and muttering his disapproval, stumbling along three paces behind her.

They reached the practically buried bridge over the river a few yards after the main entrance and noticed straight away that the footprints in the snow ended halfway across it. Beyond, the track continued its twisty way up to the distant top lane, unblemished by disfiguring feet.

They noticed something else too. A section of the safety rail was broken in half on one side, the splintered ends left

146

hanging down limply from the posts, as if as the result of some sort of collision. At first they thought the damage might have been caused by one of the small sheep-herding tractors often to be seen racing about the fields, which a local farmer had unwisely used to try to get through the snow. But peering over the edge of the bridge looking for the smashed remains of the steel carcass in the river below, they saw something else instead. It looked like a bundle of old clothes three-quarters submerged in the water and jammed against one of the bridge supports. But with a joint feeling of dread, they realised it was nothing of the sort. Very carefully edging their way down the bank below the bridge they knelt down side by side and succeeded in getting a grip on a thick waterproof coat. Then using every ounce of strength they possessed, they slowly set about hauling what was obviously a body up out of the water. Twice they nearly pitched headfirst into the river, but then, with Kate clinging with one arm to the branch of a convenient willow tree for support close to the water's edge, the two of them finally managed it, pulling the body out and falling back in the snow completely exhausted with the effort.

It was a few minutes before they recovered sufficiently to be able to turn the body over, but they were sure of its identity even before they did so and they were not mistaken.

'Victim number four,' Hayden said soberly as they stared down at the contorted face and staring eyes of Lenny Welch.

CHAPTER 14

The main CID office at Highbridge police station was virtually deserted and Acting Detective Inspector Charlie Woo was on the warpath. It was gone ten in the morning, yet the department's only detective sergeant had not yet put in an appearance.

'Have you seen or heard from Kate Lewis today?' he snapped at the dapper, tousle-headed detective constable sitting at his desk in the general office.

Jamie Foster shook his head.

'What about Hayden? The pair of them usually come in together.'

Another shake of the head.

'But they both finished their leave yesterday. They should have been back on duty from eight this morning.'

'Sorry, guv,' Foster replied. 'Can't help you.'

'So, with Fred Alloway sick again and Indrani Purewall and Ben Holloway on leave this week I've got just two DCs, you and Danny Ferris, to manage with.'

Foster grimaced. 'Not Danny, guv,' he corrected. 'He's giving evidence in a crown court case for at least a couple of days.'

Woo raised his eyes to the ceiling in a gesture of despair. 'Ye gods, I'd forgotten all about that,' he acknowledged. 'So where the hell *is* Kate? This is not like her. I've rung her mobile and her home number repeatedly, but I've got nowhere.'

Foster nodded. 'Maybe she got stranded at the hotel she and Hayden were going to for their break?' he suggested. 'You know how bad the weather's been in the Southwest for the past few days due to this freak storm, and it's moving rapidly up from Cornwall. I gather they were going to some place near Chard and that part of the county has already been hit pretty bad, apparently.'

Woo waved a hand dismissively. 'Yes, yes, I'm fully aware of all that. But then why hasn't she or Hayden called in?'

'Maybe the phones are down where they are, or there's no mobile signal?'

Woo snorted. 'Yeah, and maybe they've both been kidnapped by the bloody *hinky-punks*,' he retorted sarcastically.

Foster smirked briefly but said nothing. It was inadvisable in the circumstances.

Woo dropped a piece of paper on his desk. 'Kate's annual leave form,' he said. 'At least she filled that in properly before she went, so we know where the pair of them were staying. I've been ringing the hotel half the morning, but they're not answering. Keep trying for me will you and let me know if you get any result. I'd better pay a visit to Kate and Hayden's cottage in Burtle village while you're doing that, just to make sure everything's okay there.'

Foster glanced ruefully at the mountain of paperwork in his tray and pushed the report he had been checking to one side with a resigned sigh. 'On it right away, guv,' he said.

Heading for the double doors of the office, Woo snapped his fingers and half-turned. 'Oh yes, if no joy there, you might check around to see if we've reports of any accidents between here and where they were staying.'

'Anything else you want me to do, guv?' Foster asked with a slight edge to his tone.

Woo grinned. 'Not at the moment, Jamie. But that should stop you being bored for the rest of the morning, shouldn't it?'

* * *

The body of the hapless Lenny Welch was heavy. But Kate and Hayden had no choice but to carry him back between them to the hotel. In normal circumstances, as with the other deaths that had occurred, they would have left his corpse in situ to await the arrival of the police surgeon or pathologist and scenes of crime team and would also have cordoned off the scene. These were not normal circumstances, however, and he could hardly have been left lying there on the bank. Welch was a big lad, though, and would have been hard enough to carry even in favourable weather conditions. With the deep snow, the task was made doubly difficult and they were forced to complete it in stages. When they finally reached the outhouse beside the hotel, which to all intents and purposes was fast becoming an unofficial mortuary, they were almost beaten. To make matters worse, their return had not gone unnoticed. Jeffrey Cartwright chose that moment to poke his head outside the door of the hotel, a cigarette clamped firmly in his crooked mouth.

'Shit, is that poor old Lenny?' he exclaimed, sidling over as the detectives laid the corpse on the ground while Kate hunted for the outhouse key in her pocket.

'Sadly, yes,' she said. 'It seems he failed to make it.'

Unlocking the door, she helped Hayden carry the body into the outhouse and deposit it in the last vacant space alongside the other two.

'So that makes it three of us already?' Cartwright called out through the open door. Then he broke off and stared. 'But who's that other stiff?'

Kate glanced quickly at Hapgood's corpse and inwardly cursed her negligence in leaving the door open. The sheet they had used to carry him from the slurry pit had fallen open and much of his body was now clearly visible, including part of a gold watch chain dangling from his waistcoat, which gleamed through the filth still coating much of his body as if in defiance of any attempt to conceal it.

'Nothing to do with the present situation,' she replied quickly and closed the door on him.

'That's torn it,' Hayden murmured, peering through the window at Cartwright hovering outside. 'Of all people to clock us. He's bound to blab about all this to the others. So what now?'

'We lock up, we go back to the house and we avoid answering questions from anybody,' she replied, 'aside from confirming that Lenny Welch was found dead. Then if anyone says anything that betrays the fact that they know where we found him, it would indicate they could be the perp we're looking for.'

He nodded. 'Fair point, I suppose, though unless they're totally stupid, I would think any of them could make a reasonable guess as to where he was found, knowing he was on his way out of here and that all the deaths so far, except that of Hapgood, have been from drowning.'

'Well, it's all we've got and that would at least give us an "in" for a proper interview. Talking of which, I think it's time we had our little chat with Tom Parsons.'

'If we can find him, of course,' Hayden replied. He waved an arm at the corpses laid out behind them. 'But we need to get a result of some sort pdq. Couple of these bodies are already showing significant signs of deterioration and the last thing we need is for them to turn ripe before they can be subjected to a proper forensic examination.'

She sighed heavily. 'Don't you think I know that. Hence my earlier thought about one of us following Welch's lead by trying to get to the village.'

His gaze hardened. 'You know my views on that, and after the level of difficulty we experienced getting just the short distance from the hotel to the bridge — even before we had to carry Welch's body back here — I am convinced more than ever that neither you nor I would be able to cover the six miles necessary in such conditions without coming a cropper.' He hesitated. 'That's, of course, if our mystery assassin actually allowed us to get any further than Welch did in the first place.'

* * *

151

The thatched cottage in the small village of Burtle may have had a picture postcard appearance in the snow, but it looked completely dead to the world. After knocking repeatedly on the front door, Charlie Woo made a point of completing a circuit of the whole property, peering through side windows and the securely locked patio doors on the way. It didn't look as if anyone had been there for some time and although Hayden's distinctive Mk II Jaguar was parked in the run-in down the side of the place, Kate's MX 5 was nowhere to be seen. Obviously the pair had not been back to the cottage since going on their break to Chard.

Calling Jamie Foster on his mobile, Woo said, 'No sign of life here. Did you manage to get hold of the hotel they were staying at?'

'Affirmative, guv,' Foster replied, and he sounded worried now. 'They said their telephone line had been down, but it was now back up. They confirmed Kate and Hayden were staying there . . .'

'Were?'

'Yeah. They cut short their break and checked out on Friday to try and beat the bad weather.'

'Anything else?'

'Well, I've been in touch with our HQ control room and though there's been loads of accidents, none so far involving serious injury or anything else and no casualties involving anyone with the name Lewis.'

'Shit!' said Woo, slowly and distinctly. 'Then it looks like we've got two missing police officers!'

* * *

Kate and Hayden spent a while longer in the outhouse, carrying out a cursory examination of Welch's body, but they found no evidence of any obvious external injuries and it seemed certain from the condition of his corpse that drowning had in fact been the sole cause of his death. They then carried out a thorough search of both Welch and Hapgood's clothing, with Hayden checking on Welch and Kate concentrating on Hapgood. Hayden drew a blank with Welch, finding only a wallet, some loose change, car keys and other personal effects. Kate fared no better with Hapgood at first, turning up the same sort of irrelevant items. But then as she pulled back his jacket, which was stuck to his other clothing by congealing slime, something made a clinking sound and, feeling round his waist, she found a bunch of keys on a keyring attached to his belt by a hook. With a sharp exclamation, which quickly drew Hayden's attention, she detached the keyring and examined the keys carefully while he peered over her shoulder. They were largely made up of Chubb or Yale keys, but there was one old-fashioned looking cast iron key in the bunch that stood out.

Kate held it up on the ring in front of her husband. 'What do you think?' she said, her excitement palpable. 'The clocktower lock? I saw when I was up there that the door seemed to have an old-fashioned lock that this key could fit.'

Hayden bent closer to study it. 'Well, it certainly looks vintage. Maybe it's an original from when the place was first built. All the other locks in the hotel appear to be of the modern Yale or Chubb type. They were no doubt installed when the new owner bought the hotel. For some reason whatever this fits was not changed.'

'And as the manager, Hapgood would obviously have had keys to every room, so he might also have had the key to the clocktower.'

Hayden grunted. 'True. There's an even chance that, from what you've said, this could fit the clocktower lock and that the killer forgot about Hapgood's keys when he was dumped in the slurry pit. There's only one way to find out.'

Kate nodded. 'Tonight would be good, when everyone else should be in bed.'

'Everyone except the killer, you mean. If this *is* a "hider in the house" job, we could walk slap-bang into the nasty beggar.'

'That would be an ideal time to introduce ourselves then, wouldn't it?'

By the time they finally left the outhouse and locked up, Cartwright had gone and as Hayden had said, he was no doubt already blabbing the news of Welch's death to the others. What was more worrying was the fact that he was probably also telling them about Hapgood's corpse, which was almost certain to produce the awkward questions they both feared. All it needed was for Tom or Daphne Parsons to tactlessly come out with something about Hapgood's demise on top of it all and the febrility of the atmosphere in the hotel would only intensify. But there was nothing they could do about it now. The cat was well and truly out of the bag and all they could do was, as Kate had already suggested, stay tight-lipped about it and give nothing away.

As it turned out, however, they were able to avoid any immediate confrontation with anyone. The hotel seemed to be dead and they guessed that the other guests had gone back to their rooms. Maybe Cartwright hadn't yet managed to spread his dramatic news? That at least gave them a head start on their proposed interview of Tom Parsons and the chance to quiz him before anyone else.

They found him back in the kitchen. Seated in the same chair as before, with another half-full mug of what looked like tea on the arm, but there was no sign of his wife. His pipe was gripped tightly between his teeth and he was staring into space at something only he could see. His face was unnaturally pale and there were dark patches under his eyes, suggesting he hadn't slept at all the previous night. Here was a very worried man, Kate deduced. So much the better for them.

He snapped out of his dream-like state when they walked into the room and focused his gaze warily on Kate as she dropped into the chair facing him from the other side of the Aga cooker.

'Thought we'd have another chat with you, Mr Parsons,' she said quietly.

He withdrew the pipe from his mouth and dumped it in a tin lid beside his mug. It wasn't producing any smoke at all and she guessed it had expired a while before, which suggested he had been sitting on his own in the kitchen for some time.

'Did you now?' he replied and his voice was strained and husky.

'You happy for us to do it here?' she went on as Hayden found his three-legged stool again and sat down awkwardly beside her.

'Do what you want. Daphne done the buffet and havin' another lie down. Won't be back fer hour or so.'

'You know why we've come to see you again, don't you?'

He nodded. 'Done a stupid thing. Told you a lie 'bout bein' a Baptist. Just panicked.'

'The lie was about a lot more than being a Baptist. It was also about your alcoholism. Your wife told us what happened with the church.'

'Aye, had a right go at me after, too. Wanted to know why we was talkin' 'bout it at all.'

'Did you tell her the truth?'

'What, 'bout the booze in the barn?' He shook his head. 'Think I'm cracked? She be gone if I done that. Just told her we was talkin' 'bout how much them others was drinkin'.'

'So you admit the bottles of whisky in the barn are yours?'

He nodded. 'I goes there for a smoke and a top up when I gets the need. Can't help meself, see. But Daphne wouldn't understand.'

'Why not just help yourself from the bar? No one would know.'

'She'd know. Eyes like hawk she has. Safer in barn where no folk can see.'

'What about the porno mags. They yours too?'

He stiffened, his eyes widening. It was plain he hadn't realised they'd been discovered as well. Then he shook his head vehemently.

'As God be my witness, they got nothin' to do with me. They was in that drawer already. Must've been left by feller workin' farm 'afore we come here. I ain't no pervert . . .'

155

Kate waved her hand to cut him off. 'To be frank, Mr Parsons, I'm not really interested in the magazines or your stash of booze,' she said. 'But answer me this. Why did you try to kill me?'

The manner in which Kate suddenly dropped the question into the conversation was a deliberate tactical move. An intention to shock and throw him off-kilter in the middle of more low-key issues while he was already on the defensive. For a second he just gaped at her. 'K-kill you, Sergeant?' he stammered once he could get the words out. 'What you talkin' 'bout?'

'You know exactly what I'm talking about. The generator you pushed off the barn loft when I was standing underneath it yesterday afternoon. Getting too close to the truth, was I? Is that why it was necessary to murder me like you did all the others?'

'Murder you?' Parsons lurched to his feet, fists clenched by his sides and eyes blazing. 'That's a damned lie. I never done that to you, nor them other folk. Never would. What you tryin' to do to me? Fit me up like they does on telly?'

Hayden tensed, but Kate didn't flinch and she stared Parsons out. 'Sit down, Mr Parsons,' she said sharply. 'I haven't finished yet.'

For a moment it was touch and go as to whether he would comply in his overwrought state, or whether he would lose it altogether and storm out of the room. But the next instant his body seemed to sag as if all the energy had gone out of it and he simply dropped back into his chair with his head in his hands.

'I done nothin' to no one,' he muttered half to himself. ''Tain't right bein' 'ccused of somethin' like that.'

Kate frowned. She placed great store by her intuition and the gut feelings that had developed in her years dealing with manipulative criminals. His response, coupled with the body language that had accompanied it, had not seemed like that contrived by a guilty man who had anticipated the question and was seeking to brazen things out. In fact, his whole demeanour had been entirely believable and convincing. Doubts about his culpability for the attempt on her life had now begun to creep into her mind, but she wasn't about to let up on him just yet in case she was wrong.

'So, how come you were over to the slurry pit so soon after we got there?' she continued. 'How could you have known we were in the compound unless you were already close by? Like in the barn next door, for instance?'

He raised his head and met her stare with a sort of weary resignation. 'As I tell you when we last spoke,' he said, 'missus and me was in kitchen when she sees you come out of barn an' she says I were to go and see what were goin' on . . .' He paused for a second as if in the middle of saying something else and his gaze suddenly sharpened. 'But that be it, don't it? If I were in kitchen with missus when you come out, it couldn't ha' been me in barn, could it?'

Kate's mouth tightened. She now remembered him telling her that before, just as he claimed, which meant he was right. He had the perfect alibi. Unless . . .

'How long had you been in the kitchen with your wife?' she persisted.

He hesitated, his new confidence draining from his expression. 'Er, dunno rightly. Was there for me tea.'

'We can always ask your wife if you can't remember?'

She saw his Adam's apple jerk in his throat as he swallowed quickly. She smiled. That nervous reaction was always a dead giveaway. She had learned that long ago. Now her own confidence increased.

'Well?' she prompted. 'If you have a bad memory, I'm sure Mrs Parsons would be able to tell us.'

''Bout ten minutes,' he blurted. 'Been clearin' snow out front. But I never went into that barn then an' I done nothin' to you neither.'

She decided to end things there. It was obvious that he wasn't going to admit to anything, despite the fact that he had been shaken by her questions. Furthermore, they had no way of proving anything against him. Better to leave it there and let him stew for a while. If he was guilty that was when he was likely to make a mistake, though deep down she had to admit to herself that he was no longer a front-runner in her mental list of suspects.

'Thank you, Mr Parsons. We'll bear that in mind,' she said abruptly and stood up. 'Drink your tea before it gets cold.'

'He's not our man, is he?' Hayden commented after following her out into the hallway.

She clicked her teeth. 'Looks doubtful, but on the other hand he could easily have followed us into the barn, done the deed and got to the kitchen in time for Daphne to see us leave.'

'Seems to me we're fast running out of potential suspects now Welch is dead.'

'Not quite. Don't forget, we've still got the clocktower and Cartwright's "hider in the house" to check out tonight. We could get lucky.'

'And we could end up looking stupid.'

'What have we got to lose? If the key fits and we find nothing of interest there, who's to know we were ever in the clocktower? So cheer up, and let's take a break and have some lunch.'

He grunted. 'I thought you'd never mention it.'

* * *

The remaining guests were already in the dining room. Brewer, Adams, Cartwright and Morrison. All helping themselves from the lunch buffet table, although Kate gained the impression from the way they looked up, with only lightly filled plates, as soon as she appeared, that in reality they had been waiting for them.

'So Welch didn't make it?' Brewer called out, his face set into a cold, hard slab.

Kate joined them at the buffet table and began helping herself without looking at him. 'Unfortunately not.'

'What happened to the poor bastard then?' Cartwright said, allowing his plate to dip and losing a roll in the process, which bounced away from him across the floor.

'He died,' Hayden replied drily.

'What of?'

'Shortage of breath.'

'Another drowning, was it?' Adams asked quietly.

Kate nodded. 'Looks like it.'

'Where?'

'Sorry, but I'm not prepared to say at the moment.'

'Must have been in the river near the main entrance,' Cartwright continued.

Kate's gaze fastened on him. 'Why do you say that?'

He hesitated. 'Well, it's obvious, isn't it?'

'Why there more than anywhere else? The lake for instance?'

He looked uncomfortable, but before he could think of an answer, Brewer was off again. 'But Jeff tells us there's another corpse in the outhouse. Who is he and where did you dig him up?'

Kate sighed and stared at him levelly. We didn't "dig" anyone up, Mr Brewer.'

'So who is he then?'

'Again, no comment, I'm afraid.'

Brewer's face contorted into an ugly scowl. 'We have a right to know.'

'You have no right to anything,' Hayden said, stepping forward to stand beside Kate. 'This is a police investigation.'

Morrison put in for the first time, showing no interest in the mystery corpse. 'That means there are just three of the original housemates left,' she said. 'Francis will come for another of us next.'

Her voice was no longer verging on hysteria, but strangely flat and matter of fact, with a dullness in her eyes that suggested she had lapsed into some form of worrying dissociative condition. Kate had seen this before in trauma victims and she knew it could sometimes result in a complete mental breakdown.

But with characteristic insensitivity, Brewer proved himself to be totally oblivious to her deteriorating condition and wheeled on her angrily. 'Shut your mouth about Francis, you silly cow,' he snarled. 'No one wants to hear that psycho claptrap from you anymore.'

'Nice one, Ronnie,' Adams snapped, once again jumping to Morrison's defence. 'You really are a pathetic arsehole, just as Kate said before. Can't you see the girl is traumatised?'

Brewer was clearly taken aback by a repeat of the venom in the tone of his own girlfriend, following on as it did from her earlier referral to him as a pig, but he wasn't about to apologise. 'We're all bloody traumatised,' he growled and, dumping his untouched plate of food back on the table, he turned on his heel and walked out.

An uncomfortable silence reigned after that, with no further questions being directed towards Kate or Hayden as they ate their meal quietly at their table by the door. There was little conversation between Cartwright and Adams seated at the long table by the window either, while Morrison spent the whole of her meal well apart from them, eating slowly and almost mechanically as she stared down at her plate in an apparent dream-like state.

Cartwright finally got up and left the room after hastily gulping down his food between revoltingly loud fits of sniffing. No doubt, Kate thought with a wry smile, on his way to the bar to commiserate with Brewer. As for the remaining two women, Adams and Morrison also left perhaps fifteen minutes after Cartwright, and Kate was struck by the way Morrison held on to Adams' arm as they crossed the room to the door. Morrison looked like someone in a trance and Adams was clearly concerned about her mental stability. It was a touching gesture and seemed to indicate a deep-felt sympathy for the young woman, which was illuminating to say the least.

'I wouldn't like to be in Adams' shoes when she meets up with Brewer again,' Hayden commented as they also got up to leave. 'He seems to be a pretty violent-tempered individual and he won't forgive her for making him look a fool in front of everyone yet again.'

Kate pursed her lips reflectively. 'Oh, I think Victoria Adams is a match for our Ronnie,' she said. 'He is the sort of man who is all bluster and he'll probably just lapse into childish sulks for a while.'

'Not a potential killer then?'

She made a face. 'At the moment I can't see who could be a potential killer out of those we are left with,' she said. 'Whoever committed these murders did so coldly and clinically, following a lot of planning, and while they couldn't have foreseen the snow imprisoning their intended victims here, everything else was, in my view, carefully thought out days, maybe even weeks, before.'

'And Hapgood? What about him? Was his murder also planned?'

'I believe so. I think he may have been party to the plot or at least used by the killer to — unwittingly or otherwise — set things up. You know, get rid of the staff, apart from the Parsonses who were duped into staying on for the express purpose of looking after those due for the chop. Then, when he was no longer needed, he was simply stiffed to keep him quiet.'

Hayden nodded slowly. 'All very plausible, but what about the owner or owners of the hotel? How would they fit into all this? Was the sale of the place just a blind so they had a safe venue for multiple murder, or were they duped as well?'

Kate shrugged. 'No idea, any more than I can fathom what this Francis Templeton has to do with this business, if anything.'

'Revenge by someone for his death?'

'Who? And why go to such lengths?'

'Maybe you're right and we will find the answer to it all in the clocktower room tonight. But the Parsonses won't be too pleased about us poking our noses in there.'

'I don't intend telling them, do you?'

CHAPTER 15

Superintendent George Rutherford, or "Birdie" as he was nicknamed by those working under him because of his joint passions for birdwatching and golf, had had many unusual issues to deal with in his long career in the police service, but this time he was faced with something totally unique.

Rotund and balding with a neat military moustache and a permanent puckered frown, he was a former army major, with thirty-five years' service in the force, and was very much a member of the old school of policing. Straight-laced with no time for the current trend towards political correctness, he was a traditional copper's copper, who did things by the book and he was well respected by the rank and file for his fair, no-nonsense approach to everything. But he was acutely aware of the fact that the top hierarchy saw him as past his sell-by date and were anxious to squeeze him out at the first opportunity and replace him with a younger, more dynamic version. In his rank, he had the option of staying on until he was sixty, but he knew full well that the knives were out for him and one wrong move would be enough to finish him. The problem Acting Detective Inspector Charlie Woo had brought to him had the potential for doing just that and he knew he had to tread very carefully indeed.

'Disappeared?' he echoed and stared at Charlie Woo in astonishment from under tufted brows. 'Both of them?'

Woo made a grimace and nodded. 'Seems like it, sir,' he said. 'Should have been back on duty at eight this morning and they never appeared. The hotel where they were staying near Chard says they checked out on Friday, but they've not called in and there's no answer from either of their mobiles. I've also been to their home in Burtle, but there's no sign of them, or DS Lewis' Mazda sports car.'

Rutherford looked at his watch. 'H'm, well it's now after five, so I can understand your concern, but perhaps they made a mistake and thought they were due back tomorrow.'

'I can't see that, sir. Both are experienced officers and the dates of their leave are clearly stated on their annual leave forms.'

Rutherford cleared his throat and sat back in his swivel chair with his elbows resting on the arms of the chair and his fingertips together in a steepled gesture.

'It seems a very strange business,' he said, to all intents and purposes giving the issue careful thought.

Deep down, however, his thoughts were in turmoil. Do nothing, and face a nightmare of recriminations if the two officers turned out to be seriously hurt. Send the balloon up with a major, force-wide search, and be made a laughing stock if they reappeared safe and well, having cocked up on their leave dates.

'Have you spoken to the DCI?' he asked.

Woo shook his head. 'No, sir. He's also on leave at present.'

Rutherford blew his nose on a big white handkerchief. Procrastination had never been one of his weaknesses, yet he sensed that his DI was beginning to think that that was exactly what he was doing. Damn it! Maybe he *was* getting too old for this job as some others thought.

'I don't think this matter warrants a full-scale search at this stage,' he said, adopting a middle course. 'It is possible in this foul weather that the officers could have got stranded in the snow somewhere and have no mobile contact. I gather that heavy rain and a thaw is expected tonight and it's certainly a lot milder, so we can anticipate the major roads being freed up later tomorrow. In the meantime, I suggest you get the registration number of their car circulated on a low-key basis to all patrols between here and their hotel, and if they haven't turned up by tomorrow morning, let me know, and, er, we'll consider further action.'

'What about informing the chopper, sir? I know it's been up on road surveillance because of the weather. Maybe this matter could be passed to the crew so that they can carry out a sweep? You know, eyes in the sky and all that.'

Rutherford shook his head quickly. 'Be dark shortly, Inspector,' he said. 'They'll be returning to base and . . . I . . . um . . . want to avoid this being seen as a major incident. If the press get hold of it — you know, missing police officers and all that — heaven knows where it will lead. Just circulate DS Lewis' car registration to all mobiles as a vehicle of general interest and have any sightings reported to Control for your information. Nothing more than that. By all means have Air Support also advised when they resume road surveillance in the morning if nothing transpires, but keep it all low-key for the time being. I'm sure that's for the best . . .'

Woo was plainly not happy, but he nodded and rose from his chair. 'Understood, sir,' he said. 'I'll keep you informed of any developments.'

But as he walked back to his office, he was a very worried man.

* * *

Cartwright and Brewer were the only two sitting at the long table when Kate and Hayden walked into the dining room in the evening and apart from being treated to a hostile glance by Brewer, the detectives were completely ignored. Instead, the pair of ex-grads engaged in another of their secret conversations like two schoolchildren involved in playground conspiracies. The meal itself was late again, and the sausage casserole had not been cooked properly and was nearly cold. As for Daphne Parsons herself, she was in a dark, non-communicative mood, which suggested she and her husband might not be on speaking terms. Everything was crumbling, Kate decided, and it wouldn't be long before relationships at Warneford Hall became so toxic that they provoked a reaction as serious as anything that had happened so far.

Cartwright and Brewer left before Daphne Parsons returned with the sponge and custard sweets and she delivered them with the aplomb of a waitress at a seedy backstreet café, spilling some of the custard in front of Hayden when she virtually slammed the plates down on the table and drawing a sharp rebuke from him as it splashed on to his shirt.

'Something must have upset the lovely Daphne,' he murmured, wiping his shirt with his napkin. 'Could it be something to do with what husband Tom's been up to, I wonder?'

'Maybe she found the porno magazines,' Kate replied, 'and she's suddenly realised what she's been missing all these years.'

He grunted and to her surprise he pushed his untouched sweet away from him to join his abandoned main course. It was the first time she had ever known him refuse food.

'Not eating then?' she asked, following his example.

'Probably full of rat poison,' he commented sourly. 'We're obviously not flavour of the month as far as she's concerned.'

She stood up. 'We are likely to be even less so when she finds out we've screwed the clocktower room,' she said, turning for the door. 'Especially if we turn up something we're not supposed to find.'

The hotel seemed dead to the world when they finally left their room later that night. Nothing moved. No rafters cracked, no windows rattled. There were no snores behind the closed bedroom doors. It was as if everyone had gone and they were the only ones left in Warneford Hall. They and the ghost of Mawgana Keegan.

The corridor was in darkness again. No one had bothered to turn on the wall lights. Kate masked the torch in her hand as they crept towards the alcove and the stairs up to the clocktower. Twice the floorboards cracked under their weight and each time they paused, listening. But no one responded to the sounds and they moved on.

They made the clocktower landing without incident and Kate remembered with a shudder the last time she had been there and the hooded apparition she had encountered, as the torch swept around the walls and then focused on the old wooden door.

Hayden withdrew the bunch of keys he had washed in the bathroom basin earlier and selected the cast iron key. Taking a deep breath, he inserted it in the lock in the beam of Kate's torch and turned it to the left. Nothing happened and it seemed to meet an obstruction. He turned it back the other way and again it seemed to jam. Throwing Kate a quick glance he tried it the other way again. Still no joy. He straightened slightly, flicked it backwards and forwards in the lock, then eased it out a fraction and turned to the left again. He felt movement, heard a click and the key turned fully in that direction. Trying the handle, he felt the door give and the next moment it opened on what appeared to be well-oiled hinges.

'They ought to have oiled the lock as well,' he commented. Removing the key as a precaution, he stepped into the room ahead of Kate as she closed the door behind them.

Her torch picked out a dark carpet spread across the wooden floor, but its beam then became superfluous with the blaze of a more powerful light as Hayden reached to one side of the door and snapped on a wall switch. Now the whole room was brightly lit, its contents fully exposed, together with some surprises.

It was only about eight feet square and they could see dominating the left-hand side of the wall the reverse of the big, mechanical tower clock facing the front of the hotel, which had had its back plate removed exposing its rusted mechanism. A small window with a roller blind pulled down over it graced the wall opposite the clock and a thick, blue carpet covered the floor. In the far right-hand corner a wooden ladder was visible rising to a trapdoor in the ceiling, which was shut: possibly installed to enable maintenance to be carried out to the crenelated roof.

Of greater interest was a cork board displaying several photographs and printed documents, which was screwed to the wall to the right of the clock and directly opposite the door. Beneath it there was a small table carrying a single portrait photograph of a smiling, dark-haired young man, set in an expensive looking gilt frame. This had been placed on top of a portable, marble urn vault encircled at the bottom by a wreath of what were plainly artificial silk flowers. An unlit candle in a brass holder stood on either side of the vault and an ashtray of spent matches stood next to one of them.

'Gordon Bennett!' Hayden exclaimed. 'It's a shrine of some sort.'

Kate made no reply, but moving closer to the table, she peered at a brass plate attached to the front of the urn vault. It read simply: *RIP FRANCIS.*

'Francis Templeton,' she breathed, swinging round to stare at Hayden. 'This must contain the ashes of the lad who was drowned!'

But Hayden had pushed past her and was studying the material on the cork board.

'It's all here,' he breathed. 'The motive for it all.'

She stared past him at the board. There were exactly six colour photographs presented in a neat line-up, and all were easily recognisable as the ex-uni crowd who had attended the party weekend at Warneford Hall. Under each photograph was a narrow printed note, bearing the full name of the person, giving their home, work and email address, their private mobile and landline number and the make, model and registration number of their car, plus details of their associates and regular habits.

'Bloody hell, this shows real planning,' Kate breathed.

Hayden released his breath in a rush. 'You can say that again,' he agreed, 'and precise targeting.'

He tapped each photograph in turn with his forefinger, drawing attention to the red crosses that disfigured the portraits of Jimmy Caulfield, Abbey Granger and Lenny Welch.

Kate's mouth tightened. 'So just the people involved in the fatal spiking of Templeton's drink,' she summarised, 'and only three now without crosses. Brewer, Cartwright and Morrison. Which means one of them has to be next and though we now have the motive for these murders, we still don't have the ID of the killer.'

'Maybe not, but it can't be one of them, can it? After all, there's no one missing from the photographs. So unless the killer intends committing suicide after knocking the other two off, like in that Agatha Christie novel, *And Then There Were None,* it's got to be someone else.'

'The "hider in the house",' Kate said.

He shrugged. 'Who else? But if that's the case, they're not using this place as a doss. There's no bed or any other signs of occupation. Just that?'

He pointed to a coat hook sticking out of the wall in the corner by the door. 'For hanging up the hooded coat perhaps?'

She stiffened. 'But if it was . . .'

'Exactly. The coat's not there now, so our killer could already be out there on the prowl.'

Even as he said that, the door burst open and Tammy Morrison stood there staring at them.

* * *

Instead of a nightdress or pyjamas, the young woman was fully dressed, in tight grey trousers, a blue, woollen sweater and a pair of stout, black shoes, as if she had been out somewhere. Her eyes were no longer dull and vacant, as they had been the last time they had seen her. They were staring past Kate and Hayden, rigidly fixed on the photograph displayed on the urn vault. Then as Kate stepped forward, she pushed past her and made to reach out towards the picture frame. Hayden grabbed her in time and bodily hauled her back, trapping her in his arms as she emitted a choking cry: 'It's Francis!' After which she collapsed in a dead faint.

Morrison was only just stirring again as Hayden carried her back to her room and laid her carefully on her bed, propped up against her pillows. Kate followed soon afterwards after switching off the light in the clocktower room and locking the door behind her.

Then slipping off the young woman's shoes, Kate fetched a glass of water from the ensuite bathroom and held it to her lips as she opened her eyes and stared at her blankly.

'You fainted, Tammy,' Kate said gently. 'Drink it slowly.'

Coughing at first and then taking several swallows from the glass Morrison nodded, then pushed the glass away.

'It was Francis,' she said slowly and distinctly. 'He's here.'

'It was a photograph,' Kate replied. 'Just a photograph.'

Morrison closed her eyes tightly for a few seconds, then shook her head quickly as if to clear away something she didn't want to see. 'He's come back. He's here, hiding . . .'

Kate threw Hayden a thoughtful glance. 'Why were you up there on the clocktower landing, Tammy?' she asked.

Morrison's pale face contorted into a heavy frown. 'I think I went for a walk,' she replied.

'You *think* you went for a walk?' Hayden echoed. 'Don't you know? Anyway why would you go for a walk in the middle of the night?'

'Don't know,' Morrison replied in a low monotone as if she were trying to put the pieces of her memory together. 'But I saw you with a torch . . .' She frowned. 'Yes, that's right, I saw the torch and followed you to see where you were going.'

'When you went for your walk, weren't you frightened that you could run into Mawgana?' Kate put in, recalling how the young woman had previously voiced fears about the alleged ghost.

Morrison shot up on the bed, making Kate jump. 'There isn't any Mawgana,' she said excitedly. 'Don't you understand? It's him. It's all down to Francis.'

Kate studied her face intently. Her eyes had in an instant become unnaturally bright, as if a light had suddenly been turned on inside her head. Yet they didn't appear to be focused on either her or Hayden but seemed to be staring at something over Kate's shoulder. Kate felt her skin crawl and quickly glanced behind her, but there was no one there. She shivered and turned back again. Morrison was either still traumatised or she was a very good actress. The question was which?

'Did you put the photograph and the other things up there?' Kate went on. 'Did you do it in memory of Francis? A sort of shrine to him?'

The light in Morrison's eyes had faded and she was looking straight at her now. 'Don't be silly. Only Francis would have done that.'

Kate sighed. Whether Morrison was truly mentally ill or not, it was plain to see that they would get nothing more out of her that night. It would have to wait until later the following day.

'You must stay in your room now,' Kate said, playing her game — if that was what it was — and talking to her as if to a small child. 'You mustn't go out there again. Do you understand?'

Morrison nodded and sank back on to her pillows. 'I'm tired,' she said, and promptly closed her eyes. The next moment she was asleep.

Hayden had crossed to the bedside table on the far side of the bed and he now signalled to Kate to come over to him. As she approached, he held up a small box with an official looking label attached to it before carefully lifting the flap to show her a single foil strip inside holding a number of tablets.

'Some local chemist by the look of it,' he said close to her ear, putting the tablets back. 'Something called diazepam. Isn't that Valium? You were on it at one time, weren't you?'

Kate started, her mind flashing back to the near nervous breakdown she had suffered and the pharmacological treatment she had undergone at a special clinic. Morrison was plainly asleep and snoring softly, but she played it safe.

'Not here,' she said and waved him towards the door.

Closing it quietly on the sleeping woman, they both returned to their own room and Kate swung on Hayden immediately.

'Diazepam is a benzodiazepine,' she said. 'One of the psychoactive tranquillizers used to treat anxiety. It can cause drowsiness, disorientation, confusion and hallucinations. Believe me, I know from personal experience. Also, in extreme cases it can actually become addictive. If she's taken diazepam and has been drinking alcohol as well it could explain her present mental condition.'

Hayden's expression was grim. 'But it wouldn't explain why the name I saw on the box was that of Miss Abbey Granger,' he said.

'Granger? You sure?'

'Positive, and the question is, did Granger give Morrison the tablets to help her with her nerves over Templeton, or did she simply help herself?'

Kate's gaze locked on to his. 'And if she helped herself, what the hell was she doing in Granger's room in the first place and when was she there? Before or on the very night Granger was drowned in the bath!'

He nodded. 'Which on top of the way she just happened to materialise in the clocktower room just now, rather suggests Miss Tammy Morrison has quite a bit of explaining to do.'

CHAPTER 16

Jeffrey Cartwright was a watcher. He had been a watcher ever since he was old enough to appreciate the power of knowing what was going on around him. Particularly with things that others wanted to keep to themselves. That was how he had got on in life. He had watched what people were up to and used that information to his own advantage. Often to the detriment of those he had been watching. Quietly passing on what he had learned to other interested parties where it suited him or agreeing to withhold that information in exchange for financial gain, or as a means of bettering his own personal position. He had snooped and eavesdropped on the pupils at his school, carried on the "tradition" with his fellow students at university, then taken it with him into the world of work. It had earned him a nice living and ultimately a succession of promotions in his current career working for a big accountancy firm.

He felt no guilt about his disreputable behaviour. To him it was just business. A way of improving his lot and making a success of his life. Even if that meant ruining others or bleeding them dry in the process.

Unsurprisingly, since the death of Jimmy Caulfield he had felt no guilt about keeping a wary eye on everyone at

Warneford Hall either, although this time it had been for a very different reason. One of self-preservation. Despite the brash, derisive comments he had come out with in the company of the others, deep down he had been as one with Kate Lewis all the way. He had never believed the drowning of Jimmy Caulfield and then Abbey Granger to have been accidents, and he had been proven right. Furthermore, he was not surprised that Lenny Welch had ended up as the third victim after seeing him leave his room early that morning. Lenny had been asking for trouble trying to "quit the sinking ship" like that. The phantom killer was bound to have been aware of his intentions after he had made them so public and had obviously targeted him as a result. Cartwright knew, despite being denied any form of confirmation from the two detectives at the outhouse, that Welch had been drowned like the other two, this time in the river just beyond the hotel. He had seen them carrying the cadaver back from the main gate and they could only have come from the river bridge. He wasn't a watcher for nothing. But he took no comfort from the fact that someone seemed determined to wipe them all out, since that almost certainly included him as well.

Not that he was that optimistic about his life expectancy anyway. Addiction to both alcohol and cocaine had seen to that. Brought up in a cosseted, well-to-do environment as a child, he had wanted for nothing and the only stress he had had to cope with was boredom. Like many dissolute rich kids, it was perhaps inevitable, that he would one day turn to first alcohol and then illegal, so-called recreational drugs as a form of escape from his drab, privileged world. Initially, he had experimented with soft drugs like cannabis and amphetamines. But before long this had led to his transition to what he saw as a more satisfying alternative known by the street name "C" or coke, short for cocaine.

Rather than halting his one-way ticket to self-destruction, university had stimulated his abuse. Once on campus it hadn't taken him long to discover that a whole variety of recreational drugs were freely available to those who had the necessary cash and the right contacts. Introduced to some like-minded abusers through his early association with Ronnie Brewer, he had cemented a place among their tight-knit group with a few freebie handouts of coke and rounds of drinks at the local pub, which had earned him, if not respect, then the necessary brownie points to gain acceptance. But the downside to it all was that his level of alcohol addiction and dependency on cocaine had increased and with it his craving for more and more of the drug when the euphoric "highs" he had previously experienced produced less of a stimulative impact. By the time he graduated, cocaine had gained almost total control over him.

The tragedy was that it was at this point that he had been given a lifeline. Following university, he'd met a decent young girl whom he'd fallen for in a big way. Through her influence and support he had actually managed to reduce and then halt both his alcoholism and drug addiction altogether after many months of gruelling treatment in a specialist rehab unit and had been clean for almost three years. But then, with the shock of Rosemary's sudden, unexpected death in a head-on car crash, he had lapsed, falling back into his bad old ways and once again becoming a slave to the crystalline white powder.

Snorting the stuff over the years had not only caused substantial damage to his internal organs, but also to the internal structure of his nose and sinuses and, according to his doctor, his septum had developed a perforation that would only get bigger over time and could lead to the total collapse of the nasal valve. He was always sniffing and constantly experienced a runny nose as well as heavy nose bleeds. His appetite had zeroed, with insomnia reducing his sleep patterns to little more than catnapping. In short, he had become a wreck and his alcoholism had only made things worse by adding to the damage caused to his liver and kidneys. He knew his organs would soon start failing and that death was the inevitable consequence. But his joint addictions had gone too far for him to try and quit now. Yet in a strange way life was still worth clinging on to for as long as possible and there was one thing he was very sure about: there was no way he was going to end up as another drowning victim like the others if he could prevent it.

For that reason, despite the tightening grip cocaine had on him, he remained as vigilant as possible. Especially at night. In fact, somewhat perversely, he was actually grateful to the magical white powder for the way the snorted lines seemed to produce a greater alertness in him and a hypersensitivity to sight, sound and touch for a brief period, even if it did mean the sacrifice of a normal sleep pattern. At least with his heightened senses he could feel confident that whoever the phantom killer was, they would find it very difficult to sneak up on him. But at the same time the drug had another effect on him that he failed to appreciate in his semi surreal state. By creating a false reality, it imbued him with a reckless disregard of risk, emboldening him to the extent that he felt almost invincible.

It was in this surreal state of mind after another fix that he quietly left his room armed with a torch shortly before Kate and Hayden headed for the clocktower. He'd discovered to his chagrin that the bottle of vodka he'd stolen from the bar the day before was now completely empty and the need to satisfy his other craving for alcohol by locating a replacement bottle drew him downstairs to the bar as if from the pull of a giant magnet.

It had started to rain as he left his room and within seconds it was lashing against the windows, driven by the force of a maniacal wind, which drowned any sound of his departure. That suited him to a T and he smirked at the thought that at least that interfering woman detective wouldn't hear him making his way along the corridor.

He reached the head of the stairs and paused for a moment to peer down into the hallway. It was pitch black. He switched on his torch and directed the beam into the shadows, swinging it slowly round to cover every corner. He could see no one. He felt disappointed. He wanted to share his new sense of wellbeing with someone. Even to shout it out loud. It was the same heady exhilaration that always gripped him after snorting a line of cocaine, but this time it was even more pronounced. Maybe because he had increased the dose to guarantee him a better high. In any event, the tactic had worked. His euphoria was mounting by the second. Man, it was unreal . . .

He stumbled down the stairs and stood in the middle of the hall giggling inanely for a few seconds. Then wiping his dripping nose, he headed unsteadily to the bar. His torch picked out the rows of bottles on the shelf and he shook his head several times to improve his focus. Several malt whiskies, gin, brandy, a couple of bottles of something else he couldn't quite make out, but no vodka. He felt cheated. Surely there had to be at least one bottle of vodka left? He checked under the counter and in the cupboard behind it. Nothing but wine.

Swaying even more unsteadily after bending down to peer into the cupboard, he straightened up, then headed back out into the hallway. Maybe the replacement liquor was stored in a cupboard or a rack in the kitchen. It was worth checking anyway. Otherwise he would have to put up with malt whisky.

The kitchen smelled of damp and stale cooking, but there was no sign of a bottle rack. Just two large chest freezers and a tall refrigerator against one wall. He found lots of drawers and cupboards, but they contained nothing but cutlery and crockery. Brilliant! Some hotel, this. No wonder they were closing down.

It was then that he saw the small wooden door and went across to it. It was unlocked. The beam of his torch revealed a flight of narrow wooden steps plunging away from him into darkness. Of course! The cellar. That's where replacement liquor was likely to be stored, well out of sight. He pushed the door right back and ducked his head through the opening, steadying himself with one hand against the wall as he felt his way down the steps.

His torch picked out the gleam of water just in time and he stopped dead, almost pitching forward at the same moment. No vodka here, he thought. The bloody place was flooded. Whisky then. It had to be the whisky he'd seen in the bar. That would have to do.

He was in the process of turning round, awkwardly clutching at the wall with his free hand for balance, when he heard the measured footsteps coming down the steps towards him from the kitchen. Shining his torch up towards the open door, he glimpsed a dark, hooded figure making its way purposefully towards him. Even in the fading stages of his temporary drug-induced euphoria, the horrible truth suddenly hit him. Despite his long held conviction, neither cocaine nor alcohol were going to be the cause of him shuffling off his mortal coil, but something else entirely . . .

* * *

Kate once again found it impossible to get to sleep after the night's events and she lay there listening enviously to Hayden's snores for a long time as she turned things over and over in her mind. Had they at last unmasked the killer? Was it likely that the outwardly gentle, sensitive young woman who had expressed her feelings of guilt over Francis Templeton's death so convincingly and had exhibited such terror over her apparent belief in his return from the dead, was in reality a ruthless, cold-blooded murderer? Had she and she alone been responsible for luring her former university housemates to Warneford Hall for the express purpose of killing them one by one? Solely in an attempt to gain some kind of atonement for her involvement in spiking Templeton's drink all those years ago? The very thought seemed absurd. It seemed equally absurd that a slip of a girl like her could have had the strength to overpower and drown fit young men like Lenny Welch so easily, even with the aid of some powerful knockout spray.

Yet at the same time her claim that she had just happened to spot Kate's torch in the gloom of the corridor, had followed it out of curiosity, then accidentally walked in on the search of the clocktower just didn't hold water. Furthermore, for someone allegedly frightened of every shadow and nursing a paranoid fear that the hotel was haunted by a vengeful ghost to have even contemplated venturing out of her room on her own in the middle of the night simply to go for a walk, was well beyond the bounds of credibility.

Whatever the truth was, it was clear that an in-depth examination of the entire episode was needed before any conclusions could be drawn from what had taken place. Something that could only be achieved through further intense interrogation. Which was not going to happen lying there wrestling with the problem in the dark but would have to wait until after breakfast at the earliest. With that thought in her mind, Kate closed her eyes and went straight off to sleep.

The sound of sharp tapping awakened her to two important facts. One, that someone was knocking on the bedroom door and two, that both she and Hayden had slept through breakfast.

Throwing off the bedclothes as Hayden stirred beside her, she pulled on her dressing gown and went to the door. A fully dressed Victoria Adams stood outside in the corridor, her face once more pale and grim.

'I thought you ought to be told as soon as possible,' she said. 'Tammy seems to have gone.'

Kate ran a hand through her long, auburn hair and tried to focus on what she had just been told. 'Gone?' she echoed. 'What do you mean, gone?'

'Left the hotel type "gone",' Adams replied tightly. 'She didn't come down for breakfast and I was worried about her after the state she was in yesterday, so I took her up a cuppa.' She shrugged. 'I knocked and got no reply, so I took a peek into her room. It was empty.'

'So how do you know she's left the hotel?'

'I checked the room and all her belongings have gone as well.'

'But where the hell could she have gone? It's thick snow outside.'

'Not any more, it isn't. It's more like an extension of the lake. It poured all night and there's been a heavy thaw.'

Kate took a deep breath. 'Th-thanks for telling me. I'll be out shortly.'

Adams treated her to a twisted smile. 'Heavy night, was it?'

Kate glanced over her shoulder at the large pyjama-clad mound rising up in the bed and nodded ruefully. 'You could say that,' she said, closing the door, 'but not the way you're thinking — unfortunately.'

Hayden was not in the happiest of moods. The news that they had slept in and missed breakfast came as a nasty shock to him and he put the blame squarely on Kate's shoulders.

'You should have wakened me,' he protested. 'You know how deeply I sleep.'

But Kate was not interested in his chagrin. She was already pulling on her clothes and she didn't even bother to argue the point. 'Get dressed,' she snapped. 'That was Victoria Adams. She says it looks like Tammy Morrison has done a bunk.'

He made a disgruntled face. 'She could have told us that earlier. Then we would at least have been in time for breakfast.'

She left him still muttering to himself as he got dressed and went straight to Morrison's room. The door was ajar, but she didn't bother to knock. She found Adams back inside going through a chest of drawers. The curtains across the single window had not been pulled back and the bedroom light was on.

'Just thought I'd double check,' Adams said and she raised both hands in a *fait accompli* gesture. 'But the place has been cleared out completely.'

Kate stared carefully around the room, as she had been taught to do at every potential crime scene. First impressions were usually the most important part of any investigation. The bed had not been made but looked as though Morrison had simply thrown the bedclothes back and left them in an untidy bundle hanging over one side, touching the floor. There was a half-full glass of water on the bedside cabinet and a used coffee cup standing on the dressing table beside the coffee percolator, but otherwise, apart from the unmade bed, there was no sign of any previous occupation.

'Must have been gone a while,' Adams commented, seeing Kate cross the room to place one hand against the coffee percolator. 'Maybe everything got too much for her and she just panicked into running off somewhere.'

Kate went to the window and peered out. It was still raining and what she could see of the hotel grounds was no longer carpeted in white, but disfigured by large patches of brownish slush floating on several inches of sluggishly moving water.

'I don't see how she could have got far in that,' Kate commented, turning to face Adams as a still scowling Hayden chose to join them. 'It looks like the grounds of the hotel are flooded. Therefore the track up to the lane will be in an even worse state, and she couldn't have tried to drive out after all the car tyres were slashed.'

Adams shook her head. 'She didn't have a car here anyway,' she replied. 'Ronnie told me she travelled down to Somerset by train and Abbey Granger picked her up from Taunton railway station. He laughed about it and said that although she had come all this way to "party", she arrived looking more like an Eskimo, in knee-length winter boots and a hooded anorak, but with just a holdall for the whole weekend, which wouldn't have held a lot of fancy party clothes.'

She shrugged. 'Perhaps as she was dressed for the weather and wasn't burdened with heavy luggage, she decided that she could risk chancing her arm and leaving on foot.'

Kate crossed to the wardrobe standing against the far wall and found it was as Adams had said. It was completely empty. It was the same with the chest of drawers Adams had been going through when Kate had walked into the room, and the bathroom told an identical story. There were no personal toiletries on the tiled shelf inside and the towels had been left in a heap in one corner. Clearly, the room had been vacated.

'Strange that she should suddenly choose to leave last night,' Kate said coming out of the bathroom.

'She seemed very upset after Ronnie had a go at her again at lunch yesterday,' Adams replied. 'On the face of it, not far off losing her mind completely. To be honest, I think she has a deep-seated paranoia about the death of this chap, Francis Templeton, and is suffering from some sort of guilt complex. Ronnie told me what happened to Templeton and from the way she's been behaving over the last few days, it seems like she has taken it all on her own shoulders — even though the rest of the group, including Ronnie, were obviously just as complicit in the unfortunate prank as she was.'

She hesitated. 'The thing is I feel very sorry for the girl, really I do, but there's something about her that bothers me. It's as if there are two people inside her, the gentle, caring young woman and . . . well, another different kind of person altogether.'

Both Kate and Hayden were studying her fixedly now.

'You mean like Jekyll and Hyde?' Hayden said.

Adams looked embarrassed and gave a little self-conscious laugh. 'Look, I'm probably being stupid. Forget I said anything.'

'Not at all,' Kate replied. 'You seem to have formed a close bond with Tammy Morrison over the last few days, and therefore you could be in a much better position to form an opinion of her than anyone else. Did she ever suggest to you that her former housemates deserved to be punished for what they did?'

Adams appeared to be inwardly squirming. 'Not exactly, no. Please, I shouldn't have said anything. I'm probably imagining things. It's just that, well, you know, her running off like this . . .'

Kate pressed her point home. 'You use the phrase "not exactly". Are you saying she *did* say something?'

Adams gave a heavy, resigned sigh. 'Just that they needed to feel what it must have been like to drown the way Francis did.'

Kate stiffened. 'A strange thing for her to come out with, I would suggest?'

Adams was quick to try and explain the comment away. 'Oh, I don't think she meant that literally.' She gave a shaky laugh. 'I can't see Tammy being the type of person who would resort to drowning someone in their bath or skewering them and dumping their body in a slurry pit, even if she was suffering from some sort of mental aberration. Furthermore, I don't think she would have had the physical strength to do it. She didn't strike me as a muscular sort of person.'

Kate pursed her lips reflectively. 'Looks can be deceptive, though, can't they?' she said. 'So did she say anything about running away?'

Adams seemed to be edging towards the door, as if she were reluctant to become involved any further. 'Er, not to me, and the last time I saw her was at lunch yesterday. Now I should be getting back to Ronnie. I promised to meet him in the lounge after breakfast.'

Kate smiled. 'Thanks, Miss Adams. You've been most helpful.'

'So, what do you think?' Kate said to Hayden after Adams had left.

He didn't answer, and she was surprised to see that his scowl after missing breakfast had gone and there was now a curious gleam in his eyes.

'Check the bed,' he said abruptly.

She stared at him, uncomprehending. 'Check what?' she exclaimed.

For reply, he stepped forward and got down on his hands and knees beside it. She glimpsed some sort of black material sticking out from between the mattress and the frame. As she watched, he lifted the mattress up slightly with one hand and rummaged beneath it with the other, pulling whatever it was further into view. Then releasing the mattress he used both hands to tug it completely free. Climbing back on his feet he shook out what appeared to be some sort of black, full-length hooded coat.

'Well, I'll be damned,' Kate breathed. 'It looks like the coat my assailant was wearing on the clocktower landing.'

'Probably because it is,' he replied, handing it to her. 'Otherwise, it would seem to be a most peculiar place to keep a coat. Let's see if there's anything else.'

Pulling the pillows off the bed, he hauled the undersheet right back and made an exclamation. Then turning slowly he held up a ragged looking facial mask made out of some sort of greyish cloth and inserted two fingers grotesquely through the eye holes.

'Tammy Morrison's complete Mawgana outfit by the look of it,' he said. 'I wonder if this was the last thing the victims saw before their heads were forced under the water?'

Kate looked puzzled. 'But-but why on earth would she do a runner and leave incriminating evidence like this behind? She must have known it would be found.'

He shrugged. 'Maybe she felt she didn't have a choice. She knew the game was up after she'd blundered into the clocktower room but didn't want to risk being caught with the coat and mask in her possession. Also in relation to the coat itself, don't forget Adams said she arrived here wearing an anorak and carrying just a holdall, so she probably couldn't have managed a bulky garment like this as well. She was just desperate to get away from here as quickly as possible.'

Kate frowned. 'But if she didn't have the coat with her when she arrived, then that suggests it must already have been here. Coupled with what we found in the clocktower room, this means she must have been to Warneford Hall beforehand to set everything up. These murders were obviously not spontaneous acts at all, but were carefully planned. Hence those bogus invitations that were sent out in the first place to entice everyone here.'

Hayden nodded slowly in agreement. 'If that's the case it also means Morrison must have had very personal connections to Warneford Hall. You couldn't just arrive at a hotel like this out of the blue and set up a shrine in the clocktower room without someone's help or connivance.'

'Harold Hapgood,' Kate breathed, her eyes shining. 'Of course, it's as I said before, he was in on it! As the hotel manager, he must have been. Then when he ceased to be of any use to the killer he was wasted.'

'It certainly makes sense. Maybe the jigsaw pieces are starting to come together at last. It's just a pity we can't do anything with them until we can get some contact with the outside world . . .'

But Kate was no longer paying any attention. She had suddenly stiffened, raising one hand to cut him off. 'Listen!' she snapped.

But he had heard it as well. The unmistakable rapid thudding of an approaching rotary engine.

'A chopper!' she exclaimed, lurching for the door. 'Quick, outside!'

As they both raced for the stairs they couldn't help but be heartened by a new sense of optimism, for it sounded very much like the outside world was at last coming to them.

CHAPTER 17

The powerful police EC135 Eurocopter swooped low over the M5 motorway, just south of Taunton like some monstrous, flying bug. It left behind a stream of backlogged traffic struggling through a part snow, part slush landscape in driving rain, and headed back across country towards Glastonbury. Up since dawn on the third day of their surveillance of what up until the day before had been a snowbound whiteout of the Southwest, pilot Dick Riccard and his youthful police observer, Sergeant Janine Cope, felt the helicopter jolt periodically in the turbulence created by an uncomfortable bout of windshear.

Riccard, an RAF veteran of the Afghan conflict in Helmand Province, threw a glance at his companion and noted her white face with a grin.

'Feeling sick?' he asked. 'Don't be shy. You know where the sick bags are. Just not on the floor, please.'

She made a face at him. 'You just keep us in the air, Dick,' she said, 'I'll look after my stomach.'

He chuckled as the machine dipped briefly when the strong headwind suddenly reduced and the helicopter was sucked downwards with the descending column of air before righting itself and making a slow climb.

'Whoops!' he said, adding, 'time to be heading back to base anyway. It's getting a bit naughty out here at the moment and an over-late breakfast calls, me thinks.'

They passed over the A358, also choked with slow-moving traffic, and glimpsed ahead the hilltop tower of Burrow Mump, rising above the vast sheet of flood water created by the dissolving islands of grey-white slush like a sinister finger pointing at the sky.

'Bit of a desolate area this. Even without the melting snow,' Riccard commented. 'Give me civilization any day.'

But Cope cut him off before he could say anymore. 'Hold it, Dick. What's that there in the lane close to that big house? See it?'

Riccard followed the direction of her gaze. They were crossing a curious pattern of half-buried hedgerows and willow trees and at first he couldn't see what she had spotted. Then the next instant he clocked the car and slowly reduced height in a carefully controlled hover mode a few yards behind the vehicle. It looked like some kind of sports car — he wasn't good on car recognition — and it was parked close to a hedge.

'So it's a car,' he said. 'I expect there are loads of them abandoned all over the Levels after the weather we've just had.'

She shook her head impatiently. 'You're missing the point. It's a Mazda MX5 and if you remember, a Mazda MX5 was circulated by Control this morning for general observation. It may be the one they're interested in.'

'Roger to that, I suppose,' he said, now recalling the last-minute circulation they had received when they were taking off. 'And there was me thinking we were supposed to be up here monitoring traffic flows. So who does this car belong to then? Someone important or just another local thug?'

'No idea,' she replied. 'Ours is not to reason why and all that. Just to report the precise location so a road mobile can be sent to check it out.'

'Just like the bloody mushroom treatment we got in the military,' he complained, thinking of his previous service. 'You know, kept in the dark and fed on bullshit.'

She grinned, but didn't respond to the comment, having heard it all before from her cynical partner. 'Can you go any lower?' she asked instead.

He shrugged. 'Land on the roof if you like,' he said sarcastically.

She made a wry grimace. 'A dekko at the registration plate would be good enough, thanks,' she retorted.

Seconds later she groaned. 'Looks like it could be the car,' she said, 'but I can only see a part number. Three digits. Rear plate's still caked in snow and the front plate is almost buried in the bank. I'd better let Control know so they can get a mobile out to do the business.'

Riccard looked to be gloating as he took the helicopter up again, still maintaining hover mode. 'How disappointing for you, Sergeant,' he said. 'Maybe we can now pop back for some breakfast then?'

Her grin returned. 'Excellent idea,' she laughed. 'Then I can treat you to a double shot of bromide to go with those special bullshit mushrooms you're so keen on.'

* * *

Kate was as usual way ahead of Hayden as she ran down the stairs and she saw the helicopter hovering low over the fields the moment she burst through the front door of the hotel.

'It's the police chopper, Hayd,' she shouted excitedly back to him as she sloshed her way across the flooded forecourt towards the hotel's main entrance. Trying to run one second, kicking up mini water spouts in the process, and the next stopping briefly to wave her arms at the helicopter in a desperate attempt to attract attention. 'It looks like they've spotted our car.'

Hayden was too far behind her to hear exactly what she said, but he got the general gist of it and lumbered after her.

Almost tripping over in the ice-cold water as he tried to catch her up while simultaneously focusing his gaze on the most wonderful sight he had seen in days.

But it was all in vain. Even as Kate got to the open gates and the track leading up to the top lane, the helicopter's engine note increased in pitch and the machine started to lift out of hover mode. Within seconds it had become a fast reducing dot, heading north-east.

'What rotten luck,' Hayden understated breathlessly, finally catching up with her a few yards along the track beyond the hotel entrance. 'So near and yet so far.'

She half-turned towards him, her expression bitter. 'It's a lot worse than that,' she replied and pointed.

Staring past her, he suddenly saw what she meant. Where the rickety wooden bridge spanning the river had once been, just a couple of lopsided wooden posts marking the edge of a gaping hole remained. The bridge itself had completely disappeared and from where he stood he could see splintered pieces of timber floating in the swollen river beneath, which had burst its banks and now extended out across the marshy fields on both sides for several feet.

'Gordon Bennett!' he exclaimed. 'This is a bit of a pickle and no mistake.'

She sighed heavily. 'No, Hayd,' she corrected. 'It's not a bit of a pickle, it's actually pretty deep shit! Even when the flooding finally subsides, we'll still be stuck here like inmates in a bloody prison.'

He shrugged. 'Well, look on the bright side, old girl. The chopper seems to have spotted our car, otherwise why would it have been hovering over the spot like that? It's very likely they'll do a vehicle check, then send someone out to look for us.'

'I won't be holding my breath for that,' she retorted as they sloshed their way back to the hotel. 'They were proba-bly just doing a bit of road monitoring. There are probably dozens of abandoned cars around after the blizzard hit and were they to send someone out here to physically check our motor, with the bridge down they'd not be able to get to us now anyway.'

He hissed his disapproval. 'Don't you ever call me a pessimist again! At least now that the snow has virtually gone and Tammy Morrison with it, the threat of more killings has been removed. As soon as the flood water also goes down we'll be able to concentrate on finding ways of getting out of this hole rather than worrying about who's likely to be next on the hit list. Things are beginning to look up, old girl.'

But he was wrong about that. Just a few yards from the front door of the hotel they were met by a series of hysterical, blood-curdling screams, which cut through the air like the slice of a butcher's knife.

* * *

They almost collided with Ronnie Brewer and Victoria Adams emerging from the bar as they blundered into the hallway.

'The kitchen,' Adams shouted over her shoulder as the couple ran down the passageway ahead of them. 'The screams came from there.'

They found Daphne Parsons partially collapsed in one of the chairs by the Aga with her husband bending over her, looking pale and lost. She was hyperventilating between long, gasping sobs and it was plain that he hadn't the faintest idea what to do.

'What is it?' Kate said more harshly than she had intended. 'What the hell is all this about?'

Daphne was caught up in a shaking fit, but she glared almost insanely at Kate, her eyes bulging from their sockets as she raised one hand and pointed across the kitchen. 'There,' she choked. 'In there.'

Brewer and Adams stood there gaping as Kate swung round to stare across the room. The first thing she noticed was that the door to the cellar was wide open and the light was on inside. Before she could investigate further, Hayden had beaten her to it, stopping at the head of the wooden steps to stare down into the poorly lit gloom. Kate peered past his bulk and saw that the cellar was flooded to an even greater extent than on her previous visit and the water now covered the lower steps. She could also see that something bulky was floating there up against the steps, and she didn't need to be any closer to it to be able to determine that it was a body.

Nudging Hayden to begin the descent, she followed him down the steps as far as they could go until water was once more over their shoes.

'It's Jeffrey Cartwright,' Hayden said, bending down to peer more closely at the corpse, although Kate had already guessed that from the sight of the long, black hair floating on the surface like a halo around the corpse's head. 'Victim number five. Morrison must have done the business either earlier in the night or just before she fled.'

'But what could Cartwright have been doing down here in the first place?'

'He was an alkie as well as a junkie, wasn't he? Probably thought it was the wine cellar and that there was liquor down here.'

'Why bother with the cellar? There's a bar full of the stuff just down the hall.'

'Maybe not his usual poison, though?'

Kate grunted. 'I didn't think alcoholics were that particular, and we'll probably never know now anyway. Let's get him up top.'

Conveniently, the corpse had jammed itself in the narrow space between the walls on either side. But there was insufficient room for Hayden and herself to crouch down alongside each other to try and haul it up on to the steps above the water line as they had done when retrieving Welch's body from the river. In the end, Hayden had to be left to do the job on his own while Kate crouched behind him and held on to his waist as tightly as she could to prevent him from pitching over.

It took their combined efforts ten to fifteen minutes to do what was necessary and at one stage there was near disaster when Kate nearly let go of her husband with a sharp cry of loathing as a big black spider sprang from the corpse and raced up Hayden's arm and across the back of her hand, resurrecting her long-held fear of the creepy-crawlies. At the same time back up in the kitchen Daphne Parsons' hysterical sobbing went on and on without pause. Something they could have well done without. But the hapless woman's distress was understandable under the circumstances. They simply had to grit their teeth and try to shut out the nerve-grating sounds altogether as they struggled with their grim task.

Once the cadaver had been hauled up on to the steps, they were able, with some degree of effort, to carry it up to the kitchen between them. But they had the good sense to leave it just inside the doorway and to close the door afterwards to prevent further distress being caused to Daphne Parsons and to avoid satisfying the morbid curiosity of Brewer and Adams. By now the shocked woman had recovered sufficiently to be able to speak more coherently between gulps of the very large brandy Tom Parsons had brought to her from the bar.

'You found him, Mrs Parsons?' Kate asked gently.

'Found who?' Brewer called out from a few feet away, but Kate ignored him.

Parsons shuddered. 'Only went down into cellar 'cause I see door part open an' light on,' she said. 'He-he were just floatin' there. 'Orrid, it were.'

Kate nodded. 'Did you see anyone else come out of the kitchen as you went in there this morning?'

The woman shook her head. 'Not a soul.' She stared up at Kate. 'What were he doin' down there anyways, that's what I want to know? No business bein' in cellar. Nothin' there but floodin'.'

'Maybe he thought that was where you kept your drink?' Kate suggested. 'We know he was an alcoholic, so it seems likely he was looking for some liquor that wasn't in the bar.'

'Good grief, it's Cartwright, isn't it?' Adams exclaimed.

Kate threw her a sideways glance but said nothing in reply.

'So who done him?' Tom Parsons growled beside her.

'How do you know anyone did?' Kate replied. 'Maybe he just slipped and fell in the water. Then he couldn't get out again.'

The other snorted. 'Bit of a coincidence though, ain't it?' he said. 'Seein' as how all them others was said to have been murdered.'

'We know who the culprit is anyway,' Brewer snarled. 'That psycho bitch, Tammy Morrison.'

'You don't know that for sure, Ronnie,' Adams interjected.

'Don't I?' Brewer retorted. 'Then why has she bolted? It's as plain as the nose on your face. She always was a nutty cow. Keeping on about Francis Templeton all the bloody time. Probably had something going with him at uni, and when he croaked she set this whole weekend up to take her revenge.' He gave a short, derisory laugh. 'Well, she's shit out now, hasn't she? *I'm* still alive and kicking, so she didn't get all of us before she scarpered.'

Kate studied his flushed, contorted face and compressed her lips into a thin, hard line. 'You know what they say, Mr Brewer,' she said. 'It isn't over till the fat lady sings, and you'd be wise to remember that.'

The sneer froze on Brewer's face and there was a flicker of something in his eyes. 'You saying Morrison's still hiding around here somewhere?'

'I'm saying nothing of the sort. We have no idea where she is. But we cannot be certain that she *was* our killer anyway. It could be anyone — you, for instance.'

'Me?' Brewer gave a guffaw. 'Don't be bloody stupid. Why would I want to murder all my old housemates? Anyway you forget I have an alibi for every murder that's occurred so far: Victoria. They all seem to have been committed at night and as Vic and me sleep in the same bed, it would be impossible for me to leave the room without her knowing about it. And who's to say it wasn't one or both of those two.' He waved an arm in the direction of Daphne and Tom Parsons who had been listening to the altercation and were staring at them all with a mixture of trepidation and astonishment.

Tom Parsons' reaction was predictable. 'You hush your mouth,' he said and lurched towards the other man. Hayden quickly stepped in his way.

'Enough!' Kate shouted. 'This is getting us nowhere. Just go with Miss Adams back to your room or to the bar, Mr Brewer, and I mean right now!'

Victoria Adams nodded quickly and took hold of her boyfriend's arm, firmly turning him towards the door. 'The sergeant is right, Ronnie,' she said. 'Cool down and let's go and have a drink.'

After they had left, Kate fixed Tom Parsons with a hard, uncompromising stare. 'I suggest you control your temper, Mr Parsons,' she said. 'It will only get you into even more trouble than you are in already. Don't forget, until we get to the bottom of this business, no one is above suspicion and that certainly includes you.'

Parsons scowled, then relaxed and nodded. 'Sorry, Sergeant,' he said. 'But that there feller gets me goat, he do.'

Then, bending over his wife, he helped her to get up from her chair and led her, still sobbing, out of the kitchen.

Kate followed their departure with her brows furrowed in thought and Hayden expertly read what was behind her expression.

'Genuine shock, do you think?' he asked. 'Or just another example of good acting?'

She grimaced. 'You could well say that about any of them. There seems to be more deceit here than I've ever encountered on an investigation before.'

'You're certainly right there, and with this latest killing, I must admit, I'm beginning to have some new doubts about things.'

'Go on?'

He shrugged. 'Well, if we are to believe Tammy Morrison *is* our killer, and *prima facie* the evidence does point that way so far, why on earth would she have decided to pay that visit to the clocktower after only just stiffing Cartwright? It wasn't as though she was intending to return the coat and mask to her hideaway, as we found those hidden in her bedroom. If she is our killer I can see why she would have regarded flight as her only alternative once she had dropped herself in it by walking in on us during our search. But why risk going to the clocktower at all? It doesn't make any sense to me.'

'Perhaps she went there to commune with Francis Templeton at his shrine and to tell his ghost about her latest hit. She's got to be crackers after all, so that would be feasible.'

'Do you really believe that?'

She affected a humourless smile. 'No, I don't. In fact, I must also admit it's one of the things that has been bothering me about this whole scenario.'

'So like me, you believe she could have been telling the truth in the first place. You know, about following us to the clocktower out of curiosity, however weak that might have sounded at the time? That maybe she fled the hotel solely out of fear for her life?'

'It's certainly plausible when you think about it. But on top of all that, I don't feel we should get hung up on the hooded coat and mask. As far as I know, the one person who has actually seen the suspect killer in their fancy dress getup is yours truly during that confrontation on the clocktower landing, and I reckon it's fair to assume that any others who might have seen the same apparition are now all dead . . .'

'So the clothing itself is irrelevant?'

'Not irrelevant, no. Obviously, if it was being worn by the killer when committing the murders, it could ultimately provide vital DNA evidence under forensic examination. But its value to us at this moment in time might be more about something else entirely.'

She paused for a second, then studied him fixedly. 'Doesn't it strike you as odd that someone who had so meticulously planned this weekend of murder, and showed themselves to have the agility of mind to be able to adapt to all situational changes as they occurred, would make the clumsy mistake of keeping potentially incriminating evidence in their bedroom rather than up in the clocktower where it couldn't be directly connected to them?'

'You're saying it was planted by someone else?'

'I'm saying it's a possibility. I mean, as it stands everything seems a bit too convenient, doesn't it? Virtually handed to us on a plate at exactly the right moment.'

'The purpose being to convince us of Morrison's guilt and thereby shut down the investigation?'

'Exactly and if the clothing was planted by someone else it could only have been to influence my thinking, and mine alone, as no one else knew about it but the killer and myself.'

'So who are we looking at?'

'It can only be one of our four remaining survivors — or maybe all four acting together.'

'Not to mention the ghost of Francis Templeton,' he said drily.

She grimaced again. 'With this inquiry I'm beginning to think that even that is possible,' she acknowledged, 'and there's something else too.'

'Which is what?'

She shook her head. 'That's the trouble. I can't put my finger on it, but something has been nagging at me ever since we found Jeffrey Cartwright's body. Something significant I either saw, was said to me, or I just picked up in conversation . . . I just can't nail it down, although I sense it's important.' She tapped her head. 'It's buried somewhere deep inside my head. Stuck there like . . . like some momentous fart you can't release.'

Hayden winced. 'Eloquently put, as always, Kate,' he replied sarcastically. 'You do have a way with words, don't you?'

'I might have an even better appreciation of them if I knew what the hell they were trying to tell me,' she retorted.

* * *

The liveried police SUV with its blue-and-yellow painted "cushions" and distinctive roof strobe churned through the flood water which ran down the country lane like a river and pulled in behind the Mazda MX5 abandoned by Kate and Hayden.

'Bit wet out there,' Police Constable George Hooper commented, peering out the side window of the BMW's front passenger seat.

'Bit of water won't spoil those nice shiny shoes of yours,' Sergeant Griff Davies said in the rich lilt of the Welsh Valleys from behind the wheel. 'Control said we were to check it out.'

'What for?'

'Haven't the foggiest, bach. CID job apparently.'

'Bloody secret squirrels. Why didn't they drive down here to check it out themselves?'

'Ours is not to reason why,' Davies said, unknowingly repeating what the helicopter observer had said. 'So you'd better give it the once-over while I check the RO on the system.'

'*I'd* better check it out? Why can't you? After all, you've more experience than me.'

Davies was not the most energetic of skippers and he was conveniently near the end of his thirty-year service. Unsurprisingly therefore, he was in no rush to prove himself and simply grinned, tapping the chevrons on the arm of his tunic. 'RHP, bach,' he retorted. 'Rank Has Privileges.'

Hooper snorted his contempt and opened the door to climb out into the rain, stepping gingerly into the stream running past the car. He didn't see the hole in the road and one shoe was filled with cold water in a second. Cursing, he checked the car's boot, but it was locked. Both the driver and passenger doors turned out to be the same. It was plain that there was no one in the car, but the bonnet was not closed properly, suggesting the vehicle had broken down. He didn't examine it. After all what would that tell him? Instead, he sloshed back to the police car, scowling at his colleague who was bent over the steering wheel in hysterics. Emptying the water out of his shoe he slumped back in his seat.

'Locked,' he said unnecessarily.

Davies nodded. 'Guessed it would be,' he replied, still chuckling.

Hooper fixed him with a critical stare. 'So who's the RO? You said you were going to check.'

Davies consulted his open pocketbook. 'Some bird. Katherine Lewis. Lives in a village near Highbridge apparently. Wonder what she was doing out here in the wilds and where she went when the car broke down?'

Hooper sniffed. 'And why CID are so interested in her. Hey, maybe she's a serial killer or a terrorist?'

'Yeah, and maybe she reversed into the chief constable's car in the supermarket.'

Hooper grinned now. 'Hanging offence, that. Now, I know this neck of the woods pretty well. Used to live not far from here when I was a woodentop. There's nothing for around six or seven miles until you get to the village. Just a couple of farms — oh yes, and an old hotel down a track.' He pointed. 'Right where that finger post is. Warneford Hall. Up for sale, I hear.'

Davies started the engine. 'Seems a good enough place to start then,' he said. 'Might even get a nice hot cup of coffee while we're at it, eh?'

* * *

It would have been easier and more appropriate for Kate and Hayden to have deposited Cartwright's body with the other three corpses in the outhouse where, like them, the cold temperature would have assisted in delaying natural decomposition. But the place was already overfull with logs and equipment and it had never been built to serve as a mortuary or charnel house. As a result there was insufficient room. They were therefore forced to take the body up to his room where they placed him in the empty bath in the same way as they had Abbey Granger.

It was there that they were able to carry out a cursory examination and they found the injury to his head immediately. The wound was to his right temple and at an angle which suggested he had been struck with some heavy blunt instrument. The wound was much deeper than that sustained by Jimmy Caulfield and it seemed almost as if it had been inflicted with either particular savagery or as a result of the assailant losing their balance at the crucial moment and resorting to much more force than they had originally intended.

'Whatever he was hit with,' Hayden commented, 'I wouldn't be surprised if he sustained a fractured skull.'

'Which means he would have been in no state to try and save himself from drowning,' Kate added. 'Maybe the killer didn't use the knock-out spray this time or it didn't work because Cartwright sussed them at the critical moment and tried to defend himself.'

Hayden nodded in agreement. 'The narrow steps leading down into the cellar would not have been the ideal place to try and overpower someone. Especially if the target spotted the assailant behind them. But as the killer would have been at a higher elevation, in the end they would have had the advantage.' He raised his hand and brought his balled fist down in a hammer-like motion to illustrate his point. 'Hence the injury Cartwright sustained to that side of his head.'

Going through the dead man's sodden clothing they found two small plastic packets in one of his pockets containing some sort of white powder and several empty packets, together with two empty bottles of vodka, in the room's wastepaper bin.

'Looks like cocaine,' Kate commented, peering at one of the packets. But she refrained from resorting to the nonsensical act so often depicted in fictional TV dramas of dipping a wet finger into the powder to sample it. That would have told her nothing and risked her own health by her ingesting the drug itself.

'Looks very much like it,' Hayden agreed, strolling across the room to take a look inside the wardrobe. 'But the way he seems to have simply dumped those empty ones in the bin suggests he wasn't too bothered about anyone sussing what he was up to anyway.'

Kate returned the packets to the dead man's pocket and turned her attention to the chest of drawers. 'I don't suppose he anticipated anyone would be in his room to see until after he had left the hotel at the end of his stay,' she replied.

'Or,' Hayden added grimly, 'that he would be dead before anyone did!'

A few minutes later, after checking out the dressing table and bedside cabinets and finding nothing else of interest, they both stood for a moment in the middle of the room, staring around them as if they half-expected the walls to provide them with some information.

'So, five stiffs and a suspect who may be away on her toes, or be someone hiding in plain sight,' Kate summarised. 'Not exactly the most glorious investigative result in our careers, is it? We could end up being laughed off the department after this.'

'We could always try sheep farming in New Zealand,' he quipped.

'Not funny, Hayd,' she admonished. 'I'm convinced there's more to this business than meets the eye.'

'Such as?'

'You tell me. But for a start, I think we need to check out that clocktower room again.'

'Looking for what?'

'Inspiration perhaps.'

CHAPTER 18

The police SUV, which had been sloshing through the five to six inches of snowmelt gurgling down the sharp incline of the track leading to the hotel from the upper lane, came to an abrupt halt just before the wooden bridge over the river. Or at least, it came to a halt before what remained of it, and the police officers inside sat for several minutes staring at the gaping hole, which was practically all that had been left behind after the bridge had collapsed into the swollen, bubbling race of discoloured water.

'Well, that's it then, isn't it?' Sergeant Griff Davies growled. 'No way through here anymore and it's goodbye to that nice hot cup of coffee by the look of it.'

For a moment George Hooper quietly studied the floodwater emerging from under the front wheels of the car on its way down from the upper lane and watched it tumbling over the edge of the track where the bridge had once been.

'So what about the car up top?' he asked. 'Are we just going to leave it at that?'

Davies shrugged. 'What else can we do? Looks like the bridge may have been weakened by the weight of all the snow over the past few days, or had rusted bolts which snapped, and was then completely finished off by the flood when the thaw set in. If we can't get through, it's doubtful whether the driver of the Mazda managed it either. So I suggest we start checking out other properties in the vicinity. You said there were a few outlying farms. At least we can then say we've done our bit and can head back to base for a shot of caffeine.'

Hooper shook his head doubtfully. 'We don't know when the bridge caved, do we? The car looked as though it had been left there a while, so the driver could have made it to the hotel before the thing collapsed, which means they might have been marooned there ever since.'

'So why didn't they call for a breakdown or ring the police control room on their mobile phone?'

'Provided they had a mobile phone. Not every person carries one, you know, and anyway, this area is known for its poor cell reception.'

'If it's a hotel, there's bound to be a landline.'

'True enough. So let's get Control to get hold of their number and ring them. That way, we may be able to find out straight away if this Katherine Lewis is there or not?'

Davies shrugged. 'I suppose it's worth a try.'

The control room took only ten minutes to respond, following Hooper's situation report and request for them to make the phone call, but it was a waste of time. 'No reply,' the operator came back to them. 'Line may have come down in the storm. Please attempt direct contact.'

Davies released his breath in an exasperated hiss as the control room cut off. 'So what the hell do they expect us to do, George?' he said sarcastically. 'Strip down to our Y-fronts and swim across the river, or maybe try to jump the gap in the Beamer like they do in all the best cop chase films? I wouldn't give much for our chances if we did.'

Hooper gave a sheepish grin. 'It just seems to me that the hotel would be the most likely place the driver would have made for if they'd broken down in the lane. After all, it would have been right there for them. Couldn't we call up the chopper to do a recce for us?'

Davies held on to his sarcasm. 'The point being what? I expect any SOS message that was carved out in the snow would have been washed away by now!'

Hooper's face reddened. 'I was just trying to think of a solution to the problem,' he snapped.

'That's your trouble, "Mastermind". You spend too much time thinking. It can give you a sore head. Me? I just let problems take care of themselves.'

'But seeing as the RO is a woman, she could have been on her own, which means we should make every effort to find her.'

'We *are* making every effort. Did you see a body lying by the side of the track as we drove down here? No. Did you see one floating in the river? Again, no. Is it feasible for us to get across the river or to the hotel or to carry out a search of the flooded fields. Absolutely not.'

Davies started the engine and with his eyes on his rear-view mirror began to reverse towards a passing place he had spotted a few yards back. 'So, let's go through the motions by checking a couple of those farms you said were along the lane. That should be enough to satisfy the powers that be that we've done all we could. Then we can get back to base for that coffee and maybe a currant bun, eh?'

* * *

The clocktower door opened a lot more easily this time. Kate didn't wait for Hayden to enter the room but pushed past him. Everything appeared to be exactly as they had last seen it. The marble vault, the portrait and the candles forming the shrine, and the photographs and printed information pinned to the cork board on the wall behind it. Nothing seemed to have changed.

'Doesn't look like anyone's been in here since we locked up last night,' Hayden said. 'I would have been surprised if anyone had, to be honest. So I don't know what you expect to find.'

Kate began chewing her lip and wandered over to the shrine, bending down to peer at it more closely.

Hayden made an impatient tutting sound. 'Look, we're wasting our time up here. If Morrison *is* our killer then our bird has well and truly flown, and there's nothing more we can do about it until the flooding has gone down and we can get in contact with the police control room.'

But Kate didn't respond. She had suddenly reached forward and seemed to be prising something away from the stalk of one of the candlesticks where the wax had solidified in the small brass cup. 'Look at this,' she breathed and turned to hold it up in the light streaming through one of the clock-tower windows.

Curious, Hayden walked over to her and screwed up his eyes to examine what she was holding between a finger and thumb. It was a strand of dark hair.

'Now what the hell is this doing here?' she exclaimed.

He shrugged. 'So it's a hair. What about it?'

'Well, obviously it was inadvertently shed by whoever was handling the things on the table at the time, maybe even setting the shrine up. We all shed minute strands of our hair when we are moving around. It's a perfectly natural process, particularly with people who have long hair. Mine often attaches itself to furniture and pillows. You are always complaining to me about it.'

'Dead right too. Sticks to everything . . .'

'And in this case, you have to admit, its presence here is pretty significant.'

'In what way?'

She shook her head irritably, guessing he was being deliberately obtuse. 'Cut it out, Hayd. Just look at the colour.'

He sighed. 'Okay, it's dark and Morrison's hair is ginger. I do see what you're getting at.'

'That's a relief anyway.'

She turned back to the table, reached down and produced a further strand of dark hair, this time from the corner of the photograph frame.

'And look, here's another one, the same colour. Yet not a trace of a single ginger hair as far as I can see.'

He grunted. 'So someone other than Morrison was in here doing the business.'

'Not just *someone*, Hayd, but the person who set up this shrine in the first place. And on the basis of what I've just found, it looks as though that person could not have been Tammy Morrison.'

'Well, I agree, it certainly supports the doubts we aired earlier about her culpability for the murders. But on its own it is hardly conclusive evidence and until we are actually able to get the hair samples to the lab . . .'

The loud crack as he stepped back cut off the rest of what he was about to say and he froze as if he had stepped on the pressure plate of a landmine, staring down to see what he had crushed under his size nines. It turned out to be a pair of spectacles and he moved his foot to one side and bent down to pick them up before moving more into the light.

It became immediately apparent that the spectacles had been completely smashed. His weight had snapped the blue plastic frame where it fitted over the bridge of the nose and completely destroyed one of the lenses. But the other lens, although badly scratched, was whole enough for him to see that it appeared to be lightly tinted with a particularly strong magnification.

Kate quickly joined him and taking the spectacles from him studied them for a couple of seconds. 'Tammy Morrison,' she exclaimed. 'I'd know these anywhere.'

'Then how did they get here?'

'More to the point, how did we miss them when we came in?'

Hayden glanced around him, then nodded towards the adjacent wall and the point where he had trod on them. 'Must have been right by that wall and as they are of a similar colour blue to the carpet they were easy to miss. Also, if you look there, you can see a slight bulge in the pile. No doubt it hid them from our view and to be perfectly honest, we weren't really looking at the floor anyway. But the fact that they are here does rather suggest Morrison must have come back again before she did her runner.'

'Or more likely, that they fell off last night when she walked in on us and we just didn't notice them when we picked her up and took her back to her room. Either way it could be a critical piece of evidence.'

'How so?'

'Do you remember right at the beginning of things, the night Jimmy Caulfield was killed, I came across her struggling to shut the front door, which we initially thought to have blown open? Well, she wasn't wearing her glasses then and in conversation she told me that she couldn't see far without them, as she was very short-sighted. Strange then that she should suddenly decide to pack her bag and take off in the middle of the night without them, don't you think?'

'Perhaps she had a spare pair.'

'Perhaps she did. But together with the strands of black hair I've just found, it would suggest to me that, despite what someone has tried to trick us into believing, she never left Warneford Hall at all, but is still here, no doubt lying stiff and cold in some secret place where the real killer finally dumped her after silencing her for good.'

'Which would mean our real murderer is still resident at Warneford Hall.'

For some reason as he was talking, she moved away from him, then raised a cautionary finger to her lips to point at the half-closed door. He cottoned on straight away and carried on talking as she tip-toed the remaining few feet to the door.

'Well, seeing as Brewer appears to be the last of the gang left,' he said in a slightly louder voice, 'if he is not the killer himself, he is likely to be the next one on the killer's list, so we need to keep an eye on him . . .'

Kate reached the door, flung it wide and leaped out across the landing. Hayden lumbered after her and caught a glimpse of her disappearing down the stairs. But even as he started down the stairs himself, she reappeared coming back up, panting heavily.

'They've gone,' she said irritably.

'Gone? Who's gone?'

'Someone was out there listening to our conversation,' she said. 'I heard the crack of the floorboards as they moved. But I wasn't quick enough. They must have sensed that I had heard them and they bolted.'

He stared around him, dubiously. 'Bolted must be an understatement for them to have vanished as quickly as that.'

She nodded. 'They had probably heard enough and were already making tracks when I heard that floorboard crack.' Then seeing the doubt in his expression, she released her breath in a familiar exasperated hiss. 'There *was* someone out there, Hayd,' she insisted. 'I'd swear to it — on your life.'

'Hey, steady on,' he exclaimed. 'No need to go that far. I believe you.'

Back in their room after Kate had locked the clock-tower door and pocketed the key, she lowered her voice conspiratorially.

'Whoever our eavesdropper was, Hayd, it had to be someone able to move freely around the hotel without attracting any attention, so it couldn't have been Morrison returning to finish the job. But one thing is very clear. If it *was* our killer they will now be aware from our conversation that their attempt to set Morrison up as the murderer to stall the investigation has failed, which will put them even more on their guard from now on.'

'So what do we do?'

She gave a tight smile. 'We rattle their cage to flush them out. We embark on an intensive search of the hotel, including all bedrooms. The pretext being that we are look-ing for specific undisclosed material to support new evidence we have obtained, which could lead to the identification of the murderer.'

Hayden looked far from happy about that. 'You mean to wind them up?'

'Exactly. It is in moments of panic that dangerous criminals like this are prone to making mistakes.'

'Yeah,' he said gloomily, 'and it's in moments of panic that they are also prone to rubbing out those who cause them to panic in the first place.'

She smiled. 'Then we shall have to keep our eyes open, won't we? Better bring a torch for all the nooks and crannies, just in case . . .'

* * *

Sergeant Griff Davies was not a happy member of the Traffic Department — or Roads Policing Unit, as it had been renamed by some bright spark in cloud cuckoo land — and it sounded like the cup of coffee he had been looking forward to was not going to happen any time soon. George Hooper's call to the control room reporting on the result of the check on the abandoned MX5 car had gone down like a lead balloon. Just ten minutes after they had left the scene and were just a few miles down the road the metallic voice was back on air, querying why they had not persisted with their check on the Warneford Hall Hotel and telling them to return to the same location to await further instructions. Now stopped just behind the sports car with the engine cut, Davies showed his frustration by slamming the palms of both hands several times against the steering wheel.

'What further instructions?' he snarled. 'Are they deaf as well as stupid? Don't they know what the term "road impassable" means?'

Hooper, well used to his colleague's hot-headed temperament, grinned and thrust a Mars bar under his nose from the lunchbox now resting in his own lap. 'Have a nibble of that, sarge,' he said. 'It'll help to stabilise your blood sugar.'

Davies glared at him, but he still took the Mars bar and tore the wrapper off with his teeth as if he were pulling the pin of a grenade.

'Bloody civvies,' he continued, stuffing his mouth. 'Sitting there in their nice, warm, air-conditioned control room. Need a rocket up their arses, that's what they need.'

'Seems like there must be something special about this car, though, sarge,' Hooper cautioned. 'As you heard, some DI is hopping up and down over it.'

Before Davies could answer, the radio activated again with their call sign, and the metallic voice was back. 'Detective Inspector Woo, Highbridge CID, will liaise with you at location,' it said. 'ETA approximately twenty minutes.'

'DI Woo?' Davies muttered under his breath. 'What kind of a sodding name is that? It's like something from a comic strip.'

'I don't know,' Hooper replied with a grin, 'but if he's one of the graduate entry boys, maybe he can actually walk on water for us!'

CHAPTER 19

'Search our room? You've got a bleeding nerve.'

Ronnie Brewer stood squarely in the doorway of the bedroom, hands on hips and head thrust forward in a mood of pure aggression.

After a quick bite of the cold lunch, which Daphne Parsons had somehow managed to put out in the dining room for her remaining guests despite her shock over her discovery of Cartwright's body, Kate had pressured Hayden into beginning their search of the hotel, and the sour-faced investment banker had been the first on her list.

Kate stood her ground with the big man. 'So, what have you got to hide, Mr Brewer?' she said. 'Something you don't want the police to see?'

Spittle formed on Brewer's lower lip and his body tensed. 'Don't you come that with me, you arrogant little cow,' he snarled. 'I don't have to explain myself to you. You're not even on duty.'

'What is it, Ronnie?' another familiar voice called from inside the room and the next moment Victoria Adams pushed in beside him.

'Can I help you, Kate?' she asked with a smile.

'The bitch wants to search our room,' Brewer almost spat before Kate could say anything. 'Like hell she will!'

Adams made a face and sighed. 'If she wants to do a search, Ronnie, I'm sure it's a necessary part of her investigation,' she said. 'You haven't found Tammy yet, Kate, I suppose?'

Kate shook her head. 'But we've uncovered new material that indicates she cannot be the person responsible for the deaths at the hotel,' she explained, 'and we have reason to believe she may have come to harm.'

Adams went pale and raised a hand to her mouth. 'You mean she could be another victim and the killer is still here with us in this hotel?'

Kate nodded. 'And we are now looking for specific additional evidence that we believe could finally establish who the real killer is.'

'What sort of evidence?'

'I'm sorry, I can't tell you that.'

Brewer raised one large, clenched fist. 'Well, whoever this arsehole is, they won't get past me,' he said.

Kate stared at him for a moment. On the face of it Brewer was nothing more than an overweight, loud-mouthed braggart, and it seemed totally inconceivable that he could have planned and carried out the series of ruthless murders that they were investigating. But on the other hand, his boorish behaviour could be nothing more than a carefully constructed front. He was an intelligent, well-educated man who had the sort of callous, unfeeling nature and very powerful build that would lend itself to the task of cruelly overpowering someone and holding them under water to drown, if it was to his advantage to do so. The only problem was what advantage? What possible motive could he have had? Except, as she had already recognised, the intent to ensure that the circumstances surrounding the death of Francis Templeton never reached the public domain to destroy his reputation and his position in society. After all, others had killed for a lot less. She was tempted to quiz him a little to see if she could shake something loose, but in the end resisted the temptation and ignored him instead.

At which point Adams put in again with a slightly strained laugh. 'Well, I can assure you we haven't got a body hidden under our bed,' she said, 'and we haven't hit anyone over the head with any blunt instruments lately either.'

Kate smiled. 'I'm sure you haven't. But you will understand that we need to carry out searches of every room for elimination purposes anyway.'

Adams stepped back and beckoned Kate and Hayden inside, forcing Brewer to move out the way muttering angrily to himself. Then she swept an arm around the room. 'Please help yourselves. We've nothing to hide.'

The room was identical in layout and size to Kate and Hayden's, with similar old-style furniture and fittings. Splitting up, as if in accordance with some sort of telepathic agreement, the detectives wandered around the room, casually opening drawers, checking inside the wardrobe and glancing at items on the bedside cabinets. It wasn't the kind of rigorous professional search they usually carried out in the course of official criminal investigations, but that wasn't the intention this time. They were there primarily to make a statement and Kate was sure that what they were doing would soon get to the ears of the killer, whoever that might be and wherever they might be hiding. Whether in plain sight or in some bolthole known only to themselves. As it was, they turned up nothing of glaring interest and after Kate had finally poked her head inside the ensuite bathroom to check out the bottles and cartons on the glass shelf above the basin, they quickly left, thanking the couple — tongue in cheek in relation to Brewer — for their 'cooperation'. But Brewer couldn't resist one last snipe.

'Off the suspect list now then, are we, occifer?' he commented with a sneer.

Kate stared at him contemptuously for a couple of seconds, a thin, humourless smile hovering over her lips. 'That will depend on what you have done, Mr Brewer,' she said, 'and whether in a few hours' time you end up being arrested for multiple murders, or are found in a bath or a lake with your lungs full of water like the other victims.'

Then she left him glowering after her as she followed Hayden back to their room.

'Well, that was a waste of time,' Hayden commented as they walked in.

'Not entirely,' she murmured.

'Oh? What did you find then?'

'On the face of it something quite innocuous,' she said, 'but which could put a whole different complexion on everything.'

'Like what?'

'Like the small box of tablets contained in foil wrappers I came across on the bathroom shelf. I recognised them from the weeks I spent at the clinic undergoing pharmacological treatment for my breakdown. They were benzodiazepines, sleeping tablets, and they had been prescribed to one Victoria Adams.'

He looked underwhelmed. 'So, she has trouble sleeping. What of it?'

'Well, think about it. All along, Brewer's get-out as a possible murder suspect has been the fact that he sleeps with Adams at night and she would know if he left the room after they'd turned in. But what he didn't tell us was that she takes sleeping tablets. That means she would have been completely sparko once they were in bed, allowing him to go anywhere he wanted without her having the slightest inkling of the fact.'

He pulled a face. 'Certainly worth bearing in mind, old girl. But it doesn't really get us much further, does it?'

'It's a start at least and maybe we'll stumble on something else that connects the dots somehow before we've finished what we have to do.'

Fortunately, the other bedrooms along the corridor proved to be a lot easier to access than Brewer's. Essentially this was because they were either empty with unlocked doors or as in the case of Abbey Granger and Jeffrey Cartwright, were occupied solely by corpses who could no longer protest about anything. But the search results in every room were just as negative. Except in the case of Abbey Granger, where the sweet, nauseating smell of death, which greeted them the moment they stepped over the threshold, served as a grim reminder of just how long the young woman's corpse had been lying in the bath since her demise. A quick visual check revealed the tell-tale blueish tinge to her fingers, toes and lips, which indicated that degeneration had already begun to set in. Both left the room grim-faced and tight-lipped, wondering by just how much the corpses in the outhouse might also have since deteriorated since they last checked, particularly that of Harold Hapgood who must have been dead for considerably longer than any of the others.

'If we don't get hold of a police investigative team soon,' Hayden commented, 'there will be nothing of any real value left for forensics to find.'

Kate nodded. 'So, let's get this business over with as quickly as we can,' she said. 'Then if nothing results from the chopper's sighting of our car before dark, one of us is going to have to somehow try to get across that river and go for help.'

'That's uncommonly decent of you to volunteer to do that,' he said sarcastically. 'I just hope your doggy paddle is up to it when the time comes!'

* * *

Charlie Woo stood beside Jamie Foster and stared grimly at the river swirling below the track. They had met up with the two Traffic officers by the broken-down Mazda in the top lane and after giving the sports car the once-over Woo had left his car parked behind it and got Davies to take them all down the track in the big four by four so he could see for himself where the bridge had collapsed.

'That's the hotel entrance just around that bend, you say?' Woo snapped over his shoulder to George Hooper who was standing behind them.

'Sir,' Hooper confirmed. 'We're quite close, yet not close enough unfortunately.'

'And there's no other way across the river?'

'Not unless you swim across,' Griff Davies put in, privately enjoying the DI's obvious frustration and unwisely releasing a chuckle.

'Think this is funny, do you, Sergeant?' Woo said icily, turning to face him.

Davies' grin vanished. 'Not at all, sir.'

'Good, because missing police officers are not a subject for mirth!'

Davies gaped. 'Missing police . . . ?' he blurted. 'You're saying those who were in the Mazda are "job"?'

Woo nodded. 'DS Kate Lewis and her partner, Hayden, from Highbridge CID.'

'But then why weren't we told?'

'Because we didn't want the information getting out to the press and stirring up a hornets' nest for nothing. The fewer people who knew about it the less likely that would happen.'

Hooper made a face as he thought about Davies' earlier comments about mushrooms, but he said nothing and as usual, Davies said it for him.

'But I mean, we just thought . . .'

Woos eyes glinted. 'Thought what? That if it was just some lone woman on her own, that that didn't matter?'

'No, sir, not at all. But there's nothing else we could have done. We can't get across the river and there's nothing to say your DS and her oppo are actually in the hotel anyway.'

'Broken down on a lonely road in thick snow with a hotel just down here in the dip? I reckon there's every chance they'd have gone for it, don't you?'

'There's a couple of farms further along the lane,' Hooper said. 'We were on our way to check them out when we were told to rendezvous here. Maybe they know of another way across the river?'

Woo nodded quickly. 'Then what are we waiting for? You can take us there in your Beamer. My motor only just managed to get us here in all this floodwater.'

Walking ahead of the two detectives to the patrol car parked a few yards away in the same passing place Davies had earlier used as a turn-around, Hooper threw him a quick smirk. 'Pity about that nice hot cup of coffee you were after, sarge,' he mocked. 'Still, they do say too much caffeine is bad for you.'

Davies glared at him with undisguised venom. 'Shut your face, Hooper!' he said.

* * *

Kate and Hayden found Tom Parsons closeted in his room and, unsurprisingly, he was just as unhappy about their intrusion as Ronnie Brewer had been. 'This be private. You got no right to force your way in here,' he protested angrily.

The Parsonses occupied two separate, adjoining bedrooms along the passageway, to the right of the hotel staircase. He answered the door in his sock soles, dressed in army combat style khaki trousers and an aertex vest, which exposed a distinctive tattoo on his bicep of a winged dagger with a banner underneath carrying the words "Who Dares Wins". His hair was in disarray and he looked half asleep — or maybe hungover, Kate thought, going by his previous history.

'Sorry, Mr Parsons,' she explained, 'but we need to check every room in the hotel in connection with the disappearance of your missing guest, Miss Tammy Morrison.'

'We was told wench were murderer and she done a runner,' he retorted.

'That was just Mr Brewer speaking out of turn. After uncovering new evidence, we don't believe she killed anyone but may actually have come to harm herself, and we are now close to identifying the real murderer.'

He hesitated, then seemed to relax and moved to one side. 'In that case, do what you have to do, girl,' he growled. He gave a crooked grin. 'Wanna strip search me too?'

'That definitely won't be necessary,' she said with a wry grimace.

The bedroom was very small and contained just a single bed, a wardrobe and a chest of drawers. There was an even smaller ensuite bathroom opening off on the left and when Kate poked her head inside she saw that it was well-equipped with a basin, WC and a bath with a shower visible through a plastic curtain. There was nowhere anyone could be hidden, but she checked the wardrobe just to make sure.

'Satisfied now?' Parsons asked. 'Be you thinking I might ha' done her in and stuck her in bath?'

'It would certainly fit the pattern,' she replied candidly, then changed the subject. 'But where's your wife now?'

'Far as I knows she be back in kitchen,' he said. 'Got dinner to do, ain't she? Tell her there be another one less now, will I?'

'You might as well. But first we need to check her room too.'

'She won't like that. But help yourself anyways. 'T'aint locked.'

As it transpired, Daphne Parsons' bedroom, which in layout was identical to her husband's, produced nothing more of interest than his own and Kate glimpsed a mocking glint in his eyes as he watched them go through the motions.

'Nice tattoo, Mr Parsons,' she said as they were finally leaving the room. 'Special Air Service, isn't it?'

He merely nodded and straightened his stance, either out of a sense of pride or as a mark of respect towards his old regiment or possibly both.

'You served then?'

'Wouldn't be wearin' tattoo if I hadn't, would I?'

'You never mentioned being in the armed services before?'

'Why should I? Tain't nothin' to do with anythin'. You done here now?'

She didn't bother to reply and as he returned to his room and closed the door behind him, she and Hayden made their way slowly back along the passageway to a deserted hallway now lit solely by a single wall lamp. There they paused for a moment to take stock as the shadows lengthened outside with the approach of dusk and the gurgling of the floodwater in the gutters and drains created the only sound to intrude upon the uneasy, sepulchral stillness which had fallen upon the hotel.

'Well now, Parsons certainly kept quiet about his service in the SAS, didn't he?' Kate observed as she stared out of one of the hall windows at the white twists of mist that had now begun to drift past it in the flickering glow of an external security light. 'Hidden depths with him, I would say.'

Hayden nodded. 'And with you too, it seems — to recognise that tattoo.'

She raised her eyebrows. 'Even though I'm a mere woman, you mean? Well, you learn something about people every day, don't you? It may interest you to hear that I also know the original insignia of the regiment was designed as the flaming sword of Damocles. Another little snippet for your edification.'

He winced but thought better of responding to the censure. 'Anyway,' he said quickly, anxious to move on, 'Parsons must be a bit of a tough nut underneath that country yokel persona if he served in that particular regiment. Has probably already killed a few people in his time.'

Kate smiled at his obvious discomfiture but didn't pursue her advantage. 'You're thinking he may have practiced his old skills here?'

'It's possible, you must admit.'

She gave a long sigh, her frustration abruptly resurfacing. 'We seem to be doing nothing else but going from one suspect to another,' she said. 'One minute the killer is Parsons, the next it's Morrison. Now we're back to Parsons again. We keep changing our minds.'

He shrugged. 'With crime investigations that's always the nature of the beast, isn't it? You have to alter your thinking as new facts emerge, and we've had plenty of new facts to chew over in the past twenty-four hours.'

'You can say that again. There's been more twists and turns to this multiple homicide than I've ever encountered on an inquiry before.'

'No idea yet about the thing you said had been troubling you since Cartwright's death?'

She pulled a face. 'I wish there were.' She tapped her forehead as she had done when first mentioning it to him. 'It's trapped in here somewhere as tight as a duck's arse. It might turn out to be of little importance in the end, but if so why has it continued to nag at me ever since?'

'It probably needs some sort of trigger to release it from your subconscious. It will come when it's ready.'

'Yeah, and so will bloody Christmas!'

'And in the meantime, we do what, now that we seem to have searched all the rooms in the hotel?'

She stiffened, her gaze suddenly focusing on something she had spotted through the window behind him, and she snatched at his arm. 'We find out why a light has just flashed on and off in the outhouse!' she breathed.

CHAPTER 20

Theodore Farm was around two miles away. It was approached along a concrete driveway peppered with potholes beneath the two to three inches of melted snow which had flooded off the adjoining fields on to it. Potholes seemingly designed specifically to cripple the most sturdy of off-road vehicles. In the rapidly gathering dusk it provided Griff Davies with every opportunity to justify his Class 1 advanced driving ticket, which all Traffic officers were required to hold.

The farmhouse itself was situated on the far side of a tarmacked spur off the main drag, which ended just beyond it in an untidy yard crammed with patched-up barns, outhouses and milking sheds. A Massey Ferguson tractor stood idle in the middle of the yard with chickens and geese flapping around it and an elderly man in dungarees stared at the liveried police car with undisguised amazement from halfway up a ladder propped against the wall of the house.

He left what he was doing to scramble down the ladder and limp towards them as they pulled up beside an old Land Rover.

Charlie Woo and Jamie Foster lost no time in climbing out of the police car to meet him. Woo quickly introduced himself, receiving a non-committal 'Oh, ah,' in return, and told him about the collapsed bridge to the hotel.

'Down at last, is it?' the farmer replied. 'Surprised it stayed up so long.'

'The point is,' Woo explained, 'we have to get to the hotel — police business — and so I need another place for crossing the river. It is quite urgent.'

'Hotel be closed now,' the old man replied. 'What you be wantin' to go there fer?'

'I'm sorry, I can't tell you that, but do you know of another way to get across the river?'

The old man thought about that and said, 'Only place I knows be old stone bridge down track, back o' my barns.' He shook his head. 'But 't'aint somethin' I would try in that nice, shiny motor o' yourn, 'specially now with fields all flooded like. Ghost Marsh be a bad place fer them what don't know her and she can swaller a full growd beast whole if she's a mind to. There be only one safe way to cross that place.'

'And you know it?'

'Aye, I knows it.'

'Then will you show us?'

The other sniffed at the air. 'Dark soon and mist be comin' down. Hens need to be put away too on 'cause o' them foxes.'

Woo took a deep breath. 'Will you show us the way or not?'

The farmer sighed. 'Aye, I'll show you, but you'd best take care. It will take more'n my tractor to pull you out if them *hinky-punks* takes to doin' their mischief.'

'The what?' Woo commented as the farmer turned away from them towards the Land Rover.

'Marsh spirits, guv,' Foster murmured close to his ear. 'Local superstition. Will-o'-the wisps and all that.'

The DI closed his eyes for a second in resignation. 'Of course, the marsh spirits,' he repeated wearily. 'That's all I need right now. Remind me to hang on to my crucifix, will you?'

* * *

The mist was starting to drift in, adding to the gloom of the night, as Kate and Hayden quickly slipped out the front door. But creeping towards the outhouse, despite the reduced visibility, they could see that the door was standing ajar. Pausing by the bottle-laden skip they listened carefully, but there was not a sound The night was perfectly still. Either the intruder had gone or they were hiding somewhere inside the building.

Kate produced the torch they had brought with them at the start of the search and masked it in her hand. Then directing the narrow beam briefly at the middle of the door, she tapped Hayden on the arm and pointed. A key was clearly visible in the lock. So someone else had had a duplicate all the time. But the point was where were they now?

Deciding on a bold approach, she pulled the door open and reached inside to switch on the light, recoiling slightly from the stench of putrefaction which immediately assailed her nostrils. But the move met with no physical response, suggesting the intruder had already fled. In fact at first sight, apart from the presence of the key in the open door, there was nothing to indicate that anyone had been there at all. Everything looked the same as it had on their last visit. The three bodies lay exactly where they had previously been deposited seemingly untouched. The only noticeable change related to the corpse of Harold Hapgood, which was now clearly in a state of advanced degeneration, and Kate did her best to avoid looking as she stepped over it gingerly to check the remainder of the building where the light from the single overhead bulb failed to reach.

She got to the far end and probed the two corners, but the only movement the beam picked out came from the spiders retreating away from the light back into their cobweb lairs.

With a shiver, she turned and played the beam along the pile of logs, which did not appear to be as neatly stacked as before.

Meanwhile, true to form and regardless of the reason they were in the outhouse, Hayden was giving the mini tractor the once over.

'Boys' flaming toys,' she breathed in exasperation, then snapped, 'We're not here to look at bloody tractors, Hayden.'

'Just curious,' he replied. 'It's a particularly powerful little beast and whoever's been using it isn't very security minded. The key's been left in the ignition.'

'Who cares?' she retorted. 'We're not thinking of going for a joyride, are we? I'm more interested in what someone was up to in here.'

'Whoever it was,' he replied, joining her, 'they must have split in such a hurry on our approach that they didn't even have time to lock up afterwards.'

'They were certainly in a panic,' Kate replied thoughtfully. 'Which suggests they were up to no good. Maybe our searches spooked our killer into taking some sort of spontaneous action over something. But what?'

She ran the torch over the logs again. The spiders fled before the beam as before, like a rippling black sea. She sighed and started to turn to check the other side of the building, then stopped short, the hairs rising on the back of her neck.

'Hayden,' she said very quietly. 'Would you come here a moment.'

Overcoming his distaste of the corpses, he joined her. 'What is it?' he asked, his curiosity aroused by the tone of her voice and the fact that the torch was trembling in her hand.

'Look you there,' she said.

He peered more closely at the logs, but at first he couldn't see a thing. Then suddenly he saw what she had glimpsed.

'Gordon Bennett!' he breathed.

The eye was staring straight at him from the midst of the log pile, and wisps of red hair were now plainly visible curled around one of the logs like fine thread.

'I think we've found Tammy Morrison,' Kate said.

* * *

The track led out from behind a large barn between wire fencing for about a mile and a half until it reached an arched stone bridge over the river. The ground was a fair bit higher here than the area around the Warneford Hall Hotel. But nevertheless, the fields beyond were plainly saturated and Woo and Foster gave them a dubious once-over from the top of the bridge.

The old farmer had stopped his Land Rover just in front of the police car and he ambled over to them with a broad grin on his wrinkled face.

'Looks bad out there,' he said, 'but you'll be all right long as you follers the reflectors on the line of posts you can see and keeps river side of marsh. Track crossing the fields been built up with load of hardcore, which should be solid enough.'

'You're not leading the way then?' Jamie Foster asked.

The old man shook his head. 'No need to,' he said and pointed into the gathering dusk. 'You can see clocktower on roof of hotel there. Just foller the river t'wards it.'

He raised a warning finger. 'But don't fall for the tricks o' them hinky-punks with their lanterns. They'll try to lead you off into the marsh in the mist.'

'Mist?' Woo echoed. 'What mist?'

'It be comin', the other said. 'I smells it. Now I got to get back to put them chickens away.'

Then he climbed up into his Land Rover, swung away from them in a half circle and moments later was on his way back to his beloved chickens.

'Do you think we should chance this, guv?' Foster said to Woo. 'Looks a bit risky to me.'

Woo nodded. 'I realise that,' he replied, 'but we've got two missing police officers and I am convinced they would have found some way to call in by now if they had been able to. The fact that their car was seemingly abandoned in blizzard conditions and the nearest habitation to it is the hotel suggests to me that this Warneford Hall is where they would most likely have sought shelter, so we have to check it out.' He forced a smile, jokingly adding, 'After all, what could possibly go wrong?'

They found the start of the track as soon as they drove down the slope on to the marsh. The first white-painted post with its attached red reflector marking the edge of the marsh was clearly visible and the steering shook in Davies' hands as the wheels detected the rough, bumpy hardcore strip beneath the vehicle, its solid presence imbuing the four policemen on board with some measure of confidence despite the uncomfortable ride they were having to endure.

For a change, Davies said very little, apart from an occasional muttered expletive as they negotiated a particularly bad patch. Crouched over the steering wheel, peering into the rapidly fading light, he was too busy concentrating on the task in hand to start a conversation. Within minutes of setting off he had even more to think about too as darkness finally swept in across the waterlogged fields, blotting out everything. The mist crept in shortly afterwards. Smoky wisps at first, which floated spookily in front of the headlights. Then it thickened appreciably, developing an almost luminescent quality. Inevitably this reflected the twin beams back on to the windscreen, making it even more difficult to see ahead despite dipping the headlights and using the powerful fog lights. The posts with their red reflectors were soon gone altogether, swallowed up in the shifting nothingness, and in the absence of any reference points, Davies had no choice but to come to a stop.

'It's no good, sir,' he said to Woo sitting in the front seat beside him. 'It would be madness to carry on in this.'

Woo nodded and, climbing out of the car, walked a short distance in front of the vehicle, peering into the gloom on both sides. The next instant he raised a shadowy arm, waving agitatedly. In response, Davies eased the car forward and found him standing beside one of the posts with its reflector glowing redly in the headlight's beam. The only problem was the post was on the wrong side of the car.

'You're on the marsh,' Woo shouted. 'I was trying to tell you to pull over to your left.'

At which point, the car suddenly heeled over slightly and first the front and then the back wheel settled at an obtuse angle into a patch of soft sticky earth with a sucking, gurgling sound.

'Well, we can't blame those so-called hinky-punks for this,' Foster commented drily.

But Charlie Woo simply stared at the hapless Davies in a cold fury.

* * *

It didn't take Kate and Hayden long to clear the logs away, but they felt no sense of satisfaction at having their suspicions confirmed. The body *was* that of Tammy Morrison and her holdall was dumped beside her. She was dressed in the same clothing she had been wearing when they had last returned her to her room from the clocktower in a dead faint, so it was almost certain that she had been murdered that same night. The cause of death was not difficult to establish. The killer had not bothered to remove the plastic bag which had been pulled over her head and it was still fastened tightly with a drawstring around her neck.

'The bastard suffocated her,' Kate said, staring bleakly at the dead woman, 'and my guess is that she was stuck in here under the logs as the least likely place we would think of looking for her. But then they came back to satisfy themselves that the corpse was hidden well enough. Hence the mess they made of the log pile.'

Hayden nodded. 'They needed to ensure she couldn't be found in order to perpetuate the myth that she was the killer and had fled the hotel to escape justice.'

'Looks like my idea to rattle their cage and flush them out with those searches had the desired effect,' she said. 'It forced them to stick their head above the parapet.'

He frowned. 'What bothers me is what, in their desperation, they might do now that we've found Morrison.'

He got his answer a lot quicker than he'd expected. Suddenly the outhouse door slammed shut with a resounding bang and they heard the key turn in the lock with a sharp, metallic crack.

* * *

Hayden shook the handle of the outhouse door a couple of times to confirm it was indeed locked and sighed heavily. 'Should have taken the key out before coming in here,' he commented, significantly leaving out the royal "we", which by implication served to exonerate him from the lapse.

'*We* didn't think of the swine having the nerve to double back, did *we*?' she replied tartly, correcting his blatant cop-out. 'At least I've still got the key I took from Tom Parsons.'

She bent down beside the lock, thrust her key in and tried to turn it, but it wouldn't budge. Just like the clocktower room door. She tried the other way and the same thing happened. She straightened up and stared at him, her eyes widening.

'It won't turn,' she said. 'The arsehole must have left their own key in the other side or jammed something in the lock.'

He tried her key himself, with a similar result. Stepping back slightly with a concerned frown, he threw his not inconsiderable weight against the door. It quivered, but that was all. Muttering under his breath, he tried twice again, but then had to admit defeat and turned away, rubbing his shoulder.

'Well, that's not going to work,' he said. 'Looks like we're stuck in here until someone lets us out.'

'And who's going to do that?' Kate retorted. 'It'll be completely dark outside now and no one is likely to be going for a stroll in the mist, are they? Also, there are only two guests left in the hotel, plus the Parsonses, and one of those four is likely to be the killer.'

'True,' Hayden agreed. 'Unless there *is* some other maniac hiding away somewhere, like Cartwright suggested, which I'm again beginning to think is still a possibility. But whoever all this is down to, with us shut up in here, the field is clear for them to do whatever they want to do.'

'All the more reason for us to get out pdq.'

He stared around him. 'Easier said than done,' he said. 'The windows are too small to climb through and there are no other exits.'

She nodded towards the back of the outhouse. 'What about all the tools that are lying around? There must be something we can force the door open with or use to cut out the lock?'

He treated her to a tolerant smile. 'In a James Bond film perhaps, but I don't think we're in that league.'

Her eyes narrowed. 'Don't you patronise me, Hayden,' she snapped. 'Just take a look, will you.'

He shrugged and wandered away, only to return within minutes. 'There's a busted chainsaw and some loppers,' he said, 'but not much else of any use . . .'

'Ssh!' she cut in, holding up one hand, to silence him. 'Someone's out there.'

Almost immediately there was the distinctive clink of bottles.

'They're going through the stuff in the skip we saw there,' he said in a low voice.

'The skip?' she echoed. 'Whatever for?'

'Perhaps it's Tom or Daphne Parsons dropping off more empties from the bar.'

Kate reacted instantly, making for the door and hammering on it for all she was worth.

'We're in here,' she shouted. 'Can you unlock the door?'

There was no reply, but the clinking abruptly stopped.

She shouted again, hammering on the door even more heavily and kicking against it. There was still no response.

'Maybe it was a squirrel or a cat then,' Hayden said, changing his mind. 'You know, foraging for stuff.'

'Whoever or whatever it was,' Kate replied, 'either they didn't hear me, or they didn't give a shit anyway.'

He ran a hand through his mop of untidy blond hair. 'Then we'd better prepare for a long, cold night in here,' he said with a shiver. 'Because there's nothing else we can do.'

But unbeknown to either of them at that moment, cold was about to become the least of their worries. After wasting another half hour trying to clear the blockage from the lock with a broken screwdriver Hayden had found on the floor, they were startled by a sudden splintering crash as one of the windows shattered. Moments later a bottle trailing flames from the neck flew through it and landed among the logs in the wood pile. Exploding on impact, it ignited one of several bundles of old newspapers dumped there and sent a stream of burning accelerant racing across the concrete floor.

'Bloody hell!' Kate screamed. 'It's a petrol bomb . . .'

Even as she sprang across the floor to try and stamp it out two more petrol bombs were lobbed through the window in quick succession, one exploding among the stored equipment, propelling flaming accelerant everywhere. The box of newspapers and some of the seasoned logs in the pile were already alight, filling the outhouse with choking smoke. Just as Hayden stumbled towards the second burning missile, which had landed close to the mini tractor, Kate spotted to her horror the flames from the third device licking round the base of a steel cradle in the far corner which held a large orange coloured propane gas cylinder.

Her skin crawled. They were trapped and she didn't need a science degree to know that with the outhouse alight and several propane gas cylinders for company, they had just seconds to say their goodbyes . . .

* * *

The BMW seemed well and truly stuck. All efforts to free her by easing the heavy vehicle slowly backwards and forwards, using the manual box in a higher gear instead of relying on automatic transmission, only seemed to make things worse. Even four-wheel drive didn't help and while Woo fumed in frustration, the mist seemed to close more tightly around them all like a wet, clammy shroud.

Woo was on the point of delegating someone to walk back to the farm for help when headlights emerged in the murk behind them. Moments later the big red tractor drew up behind them, but further over, sticking to the hardcore track.

The farmer was grinning like a Cheshire cat when he jumped down from his cab. 'Know'd you'd get stuck,' he said, 'so after I puts chickens away I says, "Hiram, you'd best take a look".'

'I'm glad you did,' Woo replied. 'But can you pull us out?'

'I can try, but you be in pretty deep,' the old man said with a chuckle. 'I'll hitch up me chain anyways. But it might take a bit of time.'

'We haven't *got* time,' Foster shouted abruptly. 'Look at that!'

Woo spun round and saw that what looked like a bright red flower had suddenly sprung up in the depths of the mist way ahead of the stranded Traffic car. Seconds later it began to expand and as it did so, it increased in intensity until it had blossomed into an angry devouring blaze. At which point, there was a violent explosion, which rolled right across the marsh, and a ball of fire seemed to blast through the mist itself, sending out blazing embers wreathed in coils of black smoke, writhing like serpents in their dying agonies.

'Bless us all,' the old man exclaimed as he stood there gaping. 'That got to be Warneford Hall.'

'Then God help them!' Woo breathed, raising a hand to his forehead in despair. 'For one thing's for sure, we aren't able to.'

CHAPTER 21

The black and white feral cat was by nature an opportun-
ist and his nocturnal wanderings usually took him to the
back of the Warneford Hall Hotel, where there was always a
chance of picking up some kitchen scraps from the dustbins
to feed his ever hungry belly. He had already half completed
his rounds this particular night, putting up with the couple
of inches remaining of the recent flooding, and had just made
his way to the front of the hotel, intending to see if there was
anything there to scavenge, when he smelled the smoke and
heard the shouting coming from inside the outhouse next to
the hotel. Most animals have an inherent fear of fire and he
was no exception, but he was also curious and had obviously
never heard the phrase about curiosity killing the cat. So he
approached the skip full of empty wine and spirit bottles
close to the outhouse and crouched down beside it, sniffing
the air and trying to peer round it and under the door. The
next instant he felt his hackles rise as a river of fire raced up
one side of the building, then burst through the roof like
a multitude of licking serpentine tongues with a crackling
roar. Fleeing across the forecourt into the sanctuary of a small
shrubbery on the corner of the garden, he crouched down

under the low-level branches, watching with terrified fascination as the whole building was wreathed in flames.

He heard the roar of an engine, but he had no idea what it was. Seconds later what looked to him like a monstrous abomination burst through the front of the outhouse in the midst of a massive apocalyptic blast that blew the walls of the building apart from the inside and hurled sections of the burning roof and other debris in all directions. The terrified moggie didn't wait to see any more but was off well before the mini tractor careered diagonally across the forecourt into the hotel garden, churning through the standing water and creating a miniature bow wave. The next instant the two figures clinging to the machine parted company with it just before it plunged into the lake and came to an abrupt stop in the shallows with a last choking hiss.

For a few moments there was silence, broken only by the roaring of the flames that continued to devour the rest of the dismembered building. But then, as it dawned on Kate and Hayden that they had got clear of the inferno intact, their shocked reaction to the nightmare episode was entirely predictable. Suddenly convulsed with a bout of unnatural laughter that was a mixture of hysteria and relief at their miraculous escape they struggled unsteadily to their feet and hugged each other more tightly than they had ever done in their lives before.

'Worst bloody driver I've ever known,' Kate said, still wheezing in the midst of her laughter, and shivering with the cold as she patted Hayden affectionally on the back. 'Just haven't got a clue, have you, Fangio?'

'Haven't got a licence for a tractor either,' he retorted with a choking hiccup.

Then his gaze focused on the flames still burning in the gutted outhouse over her shoulder and he gently prised himself free, no longer laughing. 'Gordon Bennett,' he said humbly, 'that really was a close one. We weren't expected to survive that.'

Kate's unnatural humour also died and she turned to stare in the same direction. 'Holy shit!' she exclaimed. Then she said, 'But where is everybody?'

Hayden ran his hands down his trousers, futilely trying to rub the wet patches dry. 'What do you mean?'

'Well, an outbuilding next to your hotel suddenly catches fire and blows up and no one comes out to investigate? Bit strange, wouldn't you say? Unless they're all deaf or . . .' She broke off. 'Quick, we need to check things inside pdq.'

Scrambling to their feet, their sodden clothing pressing coldly against their bodies, they headed across the still partially flooded forecourt to the main door of the hotel.

All the lights were on, but there was no sign of anyone in the hallway and not a single sound to break the heavy silence that reigned. They checked the bar first and then both the lounge and the dining room. All were deserted and the tables weren't set in the dining room even though dinner was practically due. No smell of cooking emanated from the deserted kitchen. A worktop boasted four plates loaded with green salad and an extra-large grill pan containing what looked like uncooked steak kebabs on long wooden skewers. But there was nothing on the Aga.

Acutely conscious of the fact that they hadn't had any dinner, Kate was unsurprised by Hayden's reaction to the sight of the food. Bending over to sniff at it he turned towards her with a grimace. 'That's all I need,' he complained. 'My stomach already feels as if my throat's been cut. I could eat that as it is.'

She managed a brief, sympathetic smile. 'Maybe later, Hayd,' she patronised. 'If you're a really good boy, that is.'

He cast her a scathing glance. 'I can do without the facetiae, thank you,' he said, pompously drawing on his public school Latin. Then he peered more closely at the meat dish. 'Bamboo sticks by the look of it. I wonder if our Daphne also uses metal skewers like the one that killed Hapgood. After all who would know if one had gone missing?'

He rummaged through the drawer under the work top and there was the clink of cutlery. '*Exactment*,' he said triumphantly, and held up a long sliver of metal. 'Looks just like the one that was embedded in Hapgood's neck.'

But Kate was now staring at him fixedly, a new light dawning in her eyes. 'But of course!' she breathed. 'The skewer, and there was that remark about the blunt instrument too, wasn't there? You're a genius, Hayd.'

He threw her an indulgent smirk. 'Well, I don't know about that, but people have often told me . . .' He broke off as her words suddenly struck home. 'What are you on about? You're talking in riddles.'

'No time now,' she snapped. 'Tell you later. We need to check on Tom and Daphne Parsons first. I have a bad feeling about this.'

'What do you mean?'

But she was already heading for the hallway, leaving him no option but to follow at a shambling run.

The door to Tom Parsons' room was locked. Kate knocked and called out several times, but no one responded. She tried Daphne's room, but it was exactly the same.

'Break it down,' she snapped.

Hayden frowned. 'What? We can't do that. We've got no right . . .'

Kate stepped back and put her shoulder to it. It flew open with hardly any resistance.

Daphne was lying on her back in the middle of her bed, fully clothed. She didn't stir at the sound of the door bursting open.

'Strewth, is she dead?' Hayden exclaimed.

Kate tapped her on the arm twice, but there was no response. She checked the pulse in her neck, then bent over her and put her ear close to her mouth.

'Deep sleep,' she said. 'My guess is she's taken something.'

'What, just before dinner? That doesn't make sense. Her husband said she was already preparing dinner when we searched these two rooms earlier.'

Kate shrugged. 'Well, she seems to have prepared it, but never got round to putting it on the cooker. Just as well, really, as she's well out of it now. Let's check next door.'

Tom Parsons' door offered no more resistance than his wife's. He was asleep on his bed too and in a similar comatose condition to Daphne.

'Drugged,' Kate surmised grimly. 'It's the only explanation.'

'But by whom? And why?'

She tossed her head in exasperation. 'Come on, Hayden, keep up. You're usually ahead of the game. Who do you think? The same person who tried to cremate us in the outhouse. As to why, that's now obvious. They want to complete any remaining unfinished business in their vendetta to avenge the death of Francis Templeton, and they don't want any witnesses around.'

'But under the circumstances that unfinished business could only be Ronnie Brewer, which means he can't be the killer after all.'

'And he's not.' Kate's eyes were shining again. 'He's the final target on the agenda.'

'Then Victoria Adams must also be in great danger too.'

'What, the lovely Victoria?' she said with a sneer. 'Don't you believe it. Adams is completely safe, I would stake my own life on it.' She put a hand on his arm. 'Hayden, there is no outside killer, no psycho sleeping rough. There's not even a "hider in the house". There's just Victoria bloody Adams. *She* is our serial killer and I should have seen it sooner.'

He started to say something, but she waved him irritably to silence. 'Listen to me. Remember what you said a while ago about my needing a trigger to let what has recently been bothering me out of my subconscious? Well, you activated that trigger in the kitchen when you said about the metal skewer. It was like a door suddenly being blasted open and it's all clear to me now.'

Seeing his dubious expression, she took a deep breath. 'When Morrison disappeared, Adams said to us that she didn't see her as the sort of person who would "drown some-one in their bath or skewer them and dump their body in a slurry pit". How could she have known how Hapgood died or where we found him unless she committed the murder herself? We released that information to no one.'

'Tom Parsons knew he was dumped in the slurry pit.'

'True, but I doubt whether he would have discussed it with Adams — why would he? And anyway, he didn't know about the cause of Hapgood's death. We only discovered that when we examined the corpse in the outhouse. Then there was the flippant comment Adams made when we were searching her room to the effect that they hadn't "hit anyone over the head with any blunt instrument lately". Again, no one but you and me knew that any of the victims had been hit over the head and the use of the term "blunt instrument" was a real giveaway. The only way she could have known what sort of weapon was used was if she had been the one using it?'

He still seemed reluctant to accept what she was saying. 'But how could she have committed the murders when she's been sharing a bed with Brewer? She would have disturbed him had she got up in the middle of the night to leave the room. Remember we've always discounted him for the same reason and it works both ways. Also, don't forget she was on sleeping tablets — you found them yourself in the ensuite — so she would have been out of it when the murders were committed anyway.'

Kate shook her head. 'It was just her name on that box, that's all. I don't believe for one moment she was taking sleeping tablets. It was just a blind. Remember how Brewer was a heavy drinker and always seemed aggressive and hungover in the mornings when we saw him? I am willing to bet it was because she slipped a couple of those tablets into his bedtime booze each night, knocking him out completely. Probably did the same to the Parsonses just now with her chloroform spray, then some kind of similar sedative.'

Hayden shook his head unhappily.

'It seems unbelievable that an attractive, sophisticated, young woman like her could be responsible for all this mayhem. Or that she could have been posing as Brewer's girlfriend all this time and actually sleeping with the fellow when she planned to kill him in the end. It beggars belief. I mean, she came across to me as a genuine peacemaker. She even tried to help and then defend Tammy Morrison when Morrison came under suspicion.'

'It was all part of the image she wanted to create, Hayd. To present herself as this nice, inoffensive, caring person while all the time she nursed hatred and murder in her heart and was prepared to ruthlessly take out anyone who got in her way. Hapgood and us, for instance.'

She waited a second for her words to sink in, then went on, 'And don't forget, she was the one who came to tell us that Morrison had done a runner. On the face of it appearing to reject the possibility of the woman's guilt while at the same time cleverly stoking up our suspicions with a few seemingly innocent but incriminating disclosures about her and leaving the hooded coat and mask in her bedroom where she knew we would find it. We are dealing with a cunning, very dangerous psycho, Hayd, and we've already wasted too much time talking. We have to find the evil cow before she has the opportunity to make her final kill.'

At which point she was interrupted by a series of heavy thuds from somewhere above their heads, which seemed to reverberate right through the rafters, followed by a hoarse strangled cry, which was abruptly cut off.

'Upstairs!' she exclaimed as she sprang back through the doorway into the corridor. 'We may already be too late!'

* * *

As usual, Hayden had a job keeping up with Kate as she raced off along the corridor and he stopped briefly to catch his breath as he watched her disappear up the staircase, taking the stairs two at a time. When he finally caught up with her it was to see her preparing to hurl herself against the door of the room allocated to Brewer and his girlfriend, which was obviously locked.

The heavy drumming sound of a tap turned full on accompanied by desperate choking, bubbling sounds coming from inside needed little explanation. Sweeping Kate out of the way with one arm, Hayden stepped back a couple of feet and did the demolition job for her, practically taking the door off its hinges.

The bathroom door was wide open and Adams was crouched over the overflowing bath, her hands tightly gripping Brewer's shoulders from behind as she tried to hold his head beneath the surface. But it was evident that with this potential victim she was not having it all her own way. Brewer was a big, powerful man, and he was struggling desperately against her, gasping and choking on the water flooding into his lungs, but fighting with all his strength to stay alive.

Adams must have heard the bedroom door burst open, but she seemed oblivious to the fact that she had company, so fixed was she on her intent to snuff out the life of the last target on her list.

Kate was unable to release the grip she had on Brewer's shoulders. It took Hayden's balled fist slamming into the side of her head to make her let go, which pitched her sprawling into the corner of the room, where she lay still, apparently insensible. The next instant Brewer erupted from the water, retching and hyperventilating, but for some reason he seemed to be incapable of pulling himself up into a sitting position. Furthermore, as Hayden bent over the bath to turn off the mixer tap and pull out the plug it became apparent that Brewer was completely naked. This was not in itself surprising, since to all intents and purposes he must have been taking a bath when he was attacked. But what was surprising was the fact that both his wrists were handcuffed behind his back and there was a narrow leather belt tightly buckled around his neck.

Releasing the belt, Hayden helped Brewer to sit up and supported him in the bath with one arm round his back as he leaned forward, still gasping and choking.

Brewer's eyes were rolling and his breathing was punctuated by rasping gasps, indicating his lungs had taken in a lot of water. But he was far too heavy even for Kate and Hayden together to pull him out of the bath and he seemed unable to fully comprehend what was going on.

Kate thrust her hand into the water behind him and shook the handcuffs.

'Key?' she shouted at him. 'Where is it?'

He turned his head towards her, drooling and with panic in his eyes, then the next moment seemed to cotton on and nodded towards the bedroom. 'Bed,' he wheezed.

Swinging back through the door she ran across the bedroom. She immediately spotted a strange-shaped key lying on one of the bedside cabinets, which she recognised as of an identical type to the key to the old hand-bolts she had been issued with earlier in her police service. But even as she snatched it up, she heard Hayden's warning yell issue from the bathroom. Spinning round she glimpsed the slim figure racing past her towards the bedroom door. Victoria Adams had upped and fled.

* * *

The mist cloaking Ghost Marsh was starting to thin as the police patrol car finally pulled off the hardcore track and swung through the rarely used gateway at the side of the Warneford Hall Hotel. As it did so, its headlights picked out the smouldering ruin of the outhouse on the far side of the building and the debris scattered around it. Griff Davies whistled as he pulled up in front of the hotel, the tyres spitting up surface water and gravel as the BMW came to an abrupt stop.

'Looks like it was hit by a missile,' he said. 'But at least we won't need to call out the fire brigade. There doesn't seem to be much left there to burn.'

To Charlie Woo's relief it had taken the farmer and his tractor a lot less time than they'd expected to free the police vehicle from the tight grip of the marsh and despite sticking to a low speed to avoid another mishap, they had covered the remaining distance to their objective relatively quickly considering the circumstances.

Now on site, the DI immediately felt that a great weight had been lifted off his shoulders. At least it wasn't the hotel itself that had caught fire, just an outhouse or shed of some sort, which meant the risk of casualties was going to be light, if non-existent. But he was surprised that there appeared to be no one outside looking at the mess. In his experience, fires, especially ones resulting in an explosion, tended to attract attention, and it was inconceivable that one right next door to the hotel could have escaped the notice of any staff or guests currently staying there.

'There's something wrong here,' he said, now feeling more than a little uneasy. 'An outbuilding next to a hotel bursts into flames, then blows apart. The lights are on in the hotel and the front door appears to be ajar, which suggests someone must be inside. Yet not a soul comes out to investigate. So where are they?'

'Want me to take a look, guv?' Jamie Foster asked, one hand on the door.

Woo shook his head. 'Better for a uniformed officer to do that,' he said. 'Sergeant Davies, you and PC Hooper see if you can get hold of someone inside. Jamie and I will take a look at the scene of this mysterious blaze.'

Grabbing a flashlight from beside the seat, Woo threw open his door and climbed out on to the flooded forecourt, wincing as cold water seeped into his Italian style shoes.

'What's that awful smell?' Foster asked as he followed his boss towards the gutted outhouse.

'Probably just the stink of the fire,' Woo replied.

Foster shook his head. 'No, it's something more than that. Like . . . like cooking meat.'

Woo grimaced. 'Maybe some poor animal was in there,' he suggested grimly, training his flashlight on the incinerated remains.

Foster stiffened instantly. 'What the hell's that?' he blurted. 'There. Look.'

Grabbing the top of the flashlight in Woo's hand, he physically guided it a little way to the left and held it there.

The blackened shape looked a lot like a long piece of burned carpet, but it wasn't.

'Good grief,' Woo breathed. 'It's a bloody body.'

'Yeah,' Foster agreed, 'and it looks as though there's another one right next to it!'

* * *

Kate made no effort to go after Adams. It would have been futile and in any event, Brewer was the main priority. He seemed to have survived his ordeal, just, and be reasonably compos mentis, but he had taken in a lot of water and they had no way of knowing the extent of his condition and whether some form of CPR might be required. That meant getting the cuffs off him as quickly as possible so that he could help himself to help them in getting him out of the bath.

It took Kate seconds to locate the tiny keyhole in the cuffs and to insert the key. Then as the ratchet jaws sprang open and she pulled the cuffs off, Brewer recovered sufficiently to appreciate what was required of him. With his arms free and with Kate and Hayden's support he was able to grip the edge of the bath and hoist himself out, still coughing and wheezing but no longer at risk of asphyxia.

Helped by Hayden into a dressing gown Kate snatched from a hook on the bathroom door, he was then led slowly across the bedroom and up on to the bed where he lay back against the pillows, breathing raggedly. For a moment he just sat, staring at them, white-faced, but plainly suffering more from shock than any physical injury.

'She-she tried to kill me,' he said suddenly through a fit of coughing and brought up some more water.

'You were her final target,' Kate said quietly. 'You're lucky to be alive.'

'But she-she was my girlfriend,' he croaked. 'She slept with me. Been living with me in my flat for two months.'

Hayden nodded. 'All part of the plan,' he said.

'She snared you as a way of getting into your old circle of uni housemates,' Kate added, 'and she needed you so she could set up this weekend. I suspect she's been planning it for a long time.'

He took a deep breath. 'But-but why?'

Kate shrugged. 'Somehow she's connected to Francis Templeton and she was determined to punish you all for his death. We suspect she put sleeping tablets into your drinks at night so she could slip out of the room without you knowing to kill each of your former housemates.'

He shook his head and closed his eyes for a few seconds.

'I've been a fool,' he said, a surprise admission from a man like Brewer. 'She obviously got hold of the email addresses of the others from my laptop, so she could send out those invites using a fake email address. Somehow she managed to use Cartwright's name for the one sent to me.'

'A very clever woman,' Hayden said.

Brewer looked straight at him. 'An evil conniving bitch,' he said.

'So how come you ended up handcuffed in the bath?' Kate asked pointedly.

His expression changed and he looked away from her. 'She tricked me,' he said.

'How did she do that then?' Kate asked innocently.

He hesitated, then scowled at her, but seemed at a loss for a reply.

'Sex game, was it?' she asked, determined to have her pound of flesh after his consistently bad attitude towards her over the last few days. 'Is that why you had the belt round your neck too? You know, sort of wet bondage?'

'Okay,' he snarled, now back to his normal aggressive self. 'So bloody what? She said she would get in the bath with me. Done it before, so I thought nothing of it. Then she came up behind me and tried to drown me. Satisfied now, are you?'

Kate smiled without humour, almost regretting saving his nasty overbearing skin and privately glad that he had at last got his comeuppance. But before she could ask any other questions she heard a voice calling loudly from somewhere along the corridor.

'This is the police. Hello? Anyone here?'

She almost collided with Hayden as they both abandoned Brewer and shot towards the door.

Two uniformed police officers were walking towards them from the direction of the staircase, peering at the rooms on either side as they passed by.

They looked up quickly when Kate and Hayden appeared.

'Sergeant Griff Davies, ma'am,' the taller one said. 'This is PC George Hooper. And you are?'

Kate smiled and introduced Hayden and herself, also producing her warrant card. Davies looked startled. 'DS?' he exclaimed. 'So you're the RO of the Mazda MK5 abandoned in the lane up there? We've been looking for you.'

'And am I glad you've finally found us.'

'So where is everyone and how did the shed outside catch fire?' Davies asked. 'We saw a lady running down the stairs when we walked in the front door just now . . .'

Kate stiffened at his words. 'A lady?' she queried.

He nodded. 'But when I called out to her she just ran back up again.'

'She would,' Hayden put in. 'You'd be the last people she'd want to see.'

'It's a long story,' Kate continued, seeing his puzzled frown. 'But I think I know where that "lady" will have gone. Who else is with you?'

'Er, a DI Woo from Highbridge CID and another CID bod. They're down at the burned-out shed.'

Kate's eyes lit up. 'Charlie Woo? Brilliant. Now listen. There's a guy in the room over there who's a vulnerable witness in a serious crime case. If George here could sit with him to make sure he comes to no harm, could you get hold of DI Woo and tell him you've found us?' She pointed along the corridor. 'We'll be up in the clocktower at the end of this corridor.'

'Doing what?'

'Hopefully nicking a mass murderer.'

CHAPTER 22

The door of the clocktower room was locked and when Kate tried her key, it met with an obstruction.

'Key's been left in on the inside,' she said to Hayden as he arrived on the heels of her brisk dash, puffing and panting.

'Reverse of the outhouse,' he wheezed, adding, 'do you have to run everywhere?'

He broke off when Kate held a finger up to her lips for quiet and pressed her ear against the door.

'Nothing,' she said softly. 'But she must be in there. It's the only place she could have gone.'

He nodded and bent over a little with his hands on his knees, trying to get his breath. 'Give me a moment,' he said.

But Kate was not about to waste any time and stepping back a couple of paces, she threw herself at the door — only to bounce right off again without making the slightest impression on it.

Hayden grinned as she stood there rubbing her shoulder.

'You're always going on about my weight,' he said. 'Well, sometimes weight has its advantages, old girl. Watch and learn.' Straightening up and sweeping her out of the way, he bunched his shoulder for the second time that night and directed a fifteen stone at the target. The door didn't stand a chance. As it flew open, keeling over on one hinge and slamming back against the inside wall, he went with it, finishing up crashing into the shrine occupying the table on the far side of the room and practically annihilating it.

Kate ran in straight after him, flicking on the light . . . Only to find that Victoria Adams was not there. The place was completely empty.

She swore angrily, her frustration boiling over. 'So where?' she exclaimed, practically glaring at Hayden. 'She had nowhere else to go.'

Hayden waved her to silence, then pointed upwards.

Frowning, she followed the direction of his outstretched hand and understood immediately. The trapdoor in the right-hand corner of the ceiling was slightly askew and there were traces of black dirt on the carpet in front of the ladder accessing it.

'Don't be a fool!' Hayden breathed through clenched teeth as she sprang towards the ladder, but she pushed him roughly aside when he stepped forward to try and stop her.

In seconds she was halfway up and carefully lifting the trapdoor a fraction to peer through the gap. Nothing moved on the roof above her head and she saw that the moon was just emerging from the dissipating clouds of mist.

'Come down now!' Hayden hissed. 'Wait for Charlie.'

Dismissing him with an irritable wave, she raised both hands to lift the trapdoor completely out of its frame and slide it to one side before starting up the remaining rungs of the ladder. She had only just stuck her head up through the hatch when she suddenly froze — acutely conscious of the sharp point pressed into her neck.

'Hi Kate,' a voice said from behind her head. 'I strongly advise you to stay perfectly still if you want to avoid ending up like Harold Hapgood, bless him.'

Understandably, Kate did exactly as she was told, her throat drying up as, not for the first time in her career, she cursed her reckless, impulsive nature.

'Now,' Victoria Adams said, 'I want you to climb through very slowly, but then stay on your knees and don't do anything silly.'

Kate had no option but to continue to comply and hoisting herself through the hatch on to the roof into the hazy moonlight, she stayed in a kneeling position, guessing from the feel of the weapon scraping against her skin as she moved that it was probably another of Daphne Parsons' extra-long roasting skewers.

'I was going to finish poor old Brewer off with this if he didn't drown quick enough,' Adams continued. 'In fact, as you turned up he was so adamantly refusing to die that I was losing patience with him and just about to use the skewer instead. Okay, is he?'

'He'll survive,' Kate replied without moving her head.

There was a sigh. 'Pity.' Adams promptly withdrew the skewer. 'You can stand up now,' she said. 'But no silliness please. I am very quick and even if this little beauty doesn't actually kill you, it will cut through you and cause quite a bit of tissue and organ damage wherever it strikes.'

Kate had been in many tight corners in her police service before. Unfortunately, because of her impulsive "go for it" attitude, she seemed to generate them. She knew that the worst thing she could do right now was to panic or make any sudden move. She was dealing with a mentally unstable woman who had already demonstrated that she had little compunction in killing people. Furthermore, after all the brutal murders she had so far carried out, she had nothing to lose by adding another one to the list. She would be going to Broadmoor or Rampton Hospital in the end, whatever she did.

'That's it, Kate,' Adams went on, clearly reading her mind as she climbed slowly to her feet. 'Play along with your captor. Don't antagonise them or give them any excuse to butcher you. Get them to talk and try to lull them into a false sense of security. That's what the psychologists would say, isn't it? So let's talk, shall we? Over here.'

Kate felt Adams nudge her in the back and walked ahead of her to the crenelated parapet wall looking out over the front of the hotel. Adams patted one of the crenels. 'Sit here, Detective Sergeant. Feel the breeze on your back. It'll make you feel alive. Especially on such a lovely night, with the mist practically gone and the moon out to greet us.'

Kate felt sick when she glanced over the wall as she was sitting down. The clocktower had been built over a steeply pitched, tiled roof. If she fell or was pushed through that gap she would slide all the way down those tiles with nothing to arrest her progress before she flew over the guttering into space and smashed into the forecourt far below.

'So,' Adams said, still in the same calm tones, as if she were conducting a relaxed interview on television, 'how did you discover I was your murderer?'

'You made a couple of blunders to start with,' Kate replied, equally calmly.

Adams leaned against the wall. 'Ah, it was when I said that bit about poor old Hapgood being dumped in the slurry pit with a skewer in his neck, wasn't it? I realised after I'd come out with that remark that I'd dropped myself in it, but I thought that perhaps it had gone unnoticed.'

'It did, until a short time ago when it dawned on me that you couldn't have known about Hapgood unless you were the one who had killed him.'

'Oh silly, old me, and the other blunder?'

'When we searched your room earlier and you joked that you hadn't hit anyone over the head with a blunt instrument lately. Neither my colleague nor I had told anyone that any of the victims had suffered a blow to the head and only the killer would have known what type of weapon was used anyway.'

'How very astute of you, Detective Sergeant. You are a credit to the force. Well, it was a piece of broken metal pipe actually. I finally dumped it in the wine cellar straight after clobbering Cartwright with it. The trouble was not all my targets succumbed to my little spray as easily as you did when we met on the landing. That meant I sometimes had to follow up my initial assault in a much cruder way. I found the pipe quite by accident, you see, lying by the lake with other bits of rubbish when I followed Caulfield out to the spot that first night. It must have been dumped there by Tom Parsons for later collection, but it proved to be very useful to me. Poor little Jimmy just wouldn't drown after he'd pitched into the lake, you see. A bit like dear old Ronnie. So he had to be given a tap to send him on his way.'

'What was in the spray, chloroform?'

'That plus a little additive of my own. Thing is, although I led Ronnie to believe I was working in a high-powered finance job like him, I was and still am in fact employed as a senior lab technician in a big international pharmaceutical company, and I have a first-class honours degree in chemistry. As a result, it wasn't difficult for me to put something together that should have done the trick. But theory doesn't always work in practice, does it?'

Kate could feel the cold biting into her back through her clothes, but she gritted her teeth and tried to ignore it.

Adams seemed unaware of her discomfort. 'I expect you're wondering why I killed all those people?' she said, as if she were explaining why she had taken a bus instead of a train ride somewhere.

'I know why,' Kate replied, trying to keep her voice steady and not think about the drop behind her. 'To punish them for Francis Templeton's death after they had spiked his drink all those years ago.'

'Very good,' the other acknowledged.

'What I don't know is your connection to Templeton. Boyfriend, was he?'

Adams laughed, but it was a hard, bitter sound. 'Good heavens no. He was my brother. Fact is, my real name is Victoria Templeton. I just made up the name Adams as a cover.'

'So how did you swing it with this hotel? Presumably Harold Hapgood knew who you were?'

She sniggered. 'Good old Harold. Yes, he knew. Couldn't fail to. Francis and I inherited the dump when our father died suddenly a while back. As manager, Harold was essential to my plans, enabling me to set everything up without the Parsonses suspecting a thing, and he believed me when I told him that the get-together was a sort of wake in Francis' memory.'

'Then you murdered him and dumped his body in the slurry pit to shut him up?'

''Fraid so. Necessary move under the circumstances, I think you will agree. Besides, he was no loss to anyone. Harold was a dirty old man. Kept a load of nasty mags in one of the barns . . .'

'I know, we found them.'

'Did you indeed? Well, he took a perverse shine to me and I must admit, I did lead him on to keep him sweet. But he then came on to me once too often, so in the end I stuck him like the pig he was.'

'And the hooded coat and Mawgana mask? What was the point there?'

Adams laughed. 'Oh, a touch of self-indulgence, Kate, that's all. I knew of the ghost story and just went along with it for a bit of fun. It was also helpful in concealing my identity just in case I was spotted by anyone, though the only person who did spot me, apart from those I killed, was you, of course.'

'Who you tried to influence by planting the fancy dress in Morrison's room with enough of the coat showing to ensure that I wouldn't miss it.'

'Just so, but it turned out to be wasted effort, didn't it?'

'In much the same way as your earlier attempt to convince everyone Abbey Granger had drowned in the bath after over-imbibing on whisky. Unfortunately she didn't even touch the stuff.'

'Another faux pas then, eh? But I thought it might buy me some time before the rest of them tumbled to the fact that they were all under threat.'

'They soon cottoned on when you nicked all the mobiles, then slashed everyone's car tyres. As a matter of interest, what did you do with those phones?'

A soft chuckle preceded Adams' answer. 'With that nice deep lake so close, it was the obvious place for them, wasn't it? Your underwater search team might get lucky and find them eventually, but somehow I don't think they will be in very good working order . . .'

Adams broke off as the trapdoor started to lift and she shouted, 'Anyone pokes their head through that hatch and little Miss Kate ends up on a slab. Got it?'

The trapdoor dropped back with a bang.

'Now where were we before that rude interruption?' she said. 'Oh yes, Francis . . .' There was a harsher note to her tone now. 'Poor naive Francis. He never did fit in anywhere. He was very bright, but not a mixer. He wouldn't have suspected his drink was spiked and when he foolishly tried to walk back to his lodgings half-drunk, his so-called friends just let him go.'

'And he fell in the river and drowned.'

Another hard laugh loaded with derision.

'Not quite that simple, Detective. He didn't just drown. Maybe it would have been better if he had. Instead, he was swept down the river over the weir but became entangled in some driftwood in the pool beneath. Otherwise, he would have ended up in the old mine workings. He was found there and pulled to safety by a railway worker on his way home who raised the alarm.'

She took a long trembling breath, now filling up with emotion.

'But he might as well have been dead. He had lapsed into a coma through lack of oxygen. The police found my telephone number in a notebook in his pocket and contacted me. He spent the next eighteen months in hospital, first under NHS care and then in a private hospital I paid for myself to prevent the life support systems that were keeping him alive being turned off.' She gulped. 'But he never regained consciousness and died anyway. Died because of a stupid prank by those who should have looked after him but didn't even bother to report that he was missing to the police or the university.'

'I'm sorry,' Kate said quietly, trying to hide the shake in her tone.

'Sorry?' Adams' voice broke into a snarl and she swung towards her, staring into her face from about six inches away. 'You're sorry? Have you any idea what it's like visiting someone in hospital who's dear to you nearly every single day and watching them gradually fade away until even the life support systems fail to keep them alive? Not to know whether they are aware that you are there? Not to be able to tell them how much you love them? Squeezing their cold hand and feeling no response? Sitting there listening to the machines clicking and hissing as they struggle against the inevitable?'

Kate made a point of saying nothing to avoid winding her up any further and after a few seconds Adams seemed to recover her self-control and straightened up again.

'As for the police,' she continued in a more level tone, 'apart from contacting me in the first instance, they did very little else. Oh, they approached the local pub and spoke to the landlord who told them Francis had been with a crowd, drinking heavily, but that was all. They just seemed to accept that my poor brother had brought everything on himself by trying to walk back to his digs along the river path when he was drunk. The only good thing the police did do was to find out the person responsible for renting Bridge House where the students all stayed, which turned out to be Ronnie Brewer. That's how I got hold of his name and address. But when they later interviewed him, he apparently came up with a plausible story about the incident, which had obviously been pre-agreed with the rest of the little shits, and he denied knowing how anyone could be contacted to confirm what he'd said. Then he kept the fact that he had been seen by the police to himself, so the others never knew about it. But *I* knew. As I also knew that Francis' drink had been spiked by them all after I had spoken to another member of the bar staff myself who had been serving them when it was done and was amenable to a little cash inducement . . .'

'Didn't you tell the police what he'd told you?' Kate asked, chancing her arm.

Adams shook her head. 'I thought about doing that but decided it would go nowhere, and it would be far more satisfying to mete out appropriate justice myself when the time came.'

'So once Francis had died you set up Brewer's seduction, moved in with him and planned everything even as you were sharing his bed?'

Kate could not entirely conceal the touch of contempt in her tone, but this time Adams didn't bite. Instead, she visibly shuddered, her thoughts seemingly centred on unpleasant memories. 'Can you imagine how hard it was to lie there letting that fat slob touch me,' she replied, 'while all the time I despised every inch of his vile, sweaty body and his groping hands? How I longed to slit open his belly with the sharpest object I could find and pull his guts out by the handful? But I knew I had to keep him sweet so that I could get hold of the names and addresses of his housemates for my grand event and ensure he not only attended as well, but remained at the hotel until his turn came.'

'The trick with the email invitations was quite clever.'

'Not really. I got advice from a friend in IT on setting up another account in a different name and filtered the replies on my own laptop as they came back. One reply, which was quite disappointing, came from a lad called George Lane, saying he would not be attending my little weekend party. I thought that was quite discourteous, so I made a point of visiting him instead and introduced him to the bottom of the lake where he was fishing. Gave me the chance of trying out my chloroform spray too, which worked exceptionally well that first time.'

'And Tammy Morrison, why her? She was against what they all did to Francis.'

'Oh yes,' Adams sneered, 'she was against it, but she still went along with it, didn't she? Anyway, I needed a scapegoat and she fitted the bill perfectly, even though in the final analysis it didn't work out as I'd planned. But I did sedate the pathetic little cow before suffocating her with the plastic bag, so she wouldn't have known much about it.'

'How kind of you.'

Adams chuckled again at the sarcasm. 'Well, I'm that sort of person, you see. All heart.' She pushed herself off the wall and faced Kate again, this time with the skewer held out in front of her. 'So there you have it all, Kate,' she said in a low, deliberate tone. 'And if you hadn't gate-crashed my weekend, I would have completed the task I had set myself, then disappeared without trace, and no one would have been any the wiser. As it is, the whole thing has been compromised, with the main culprit for Francis' death still alive and kicking. I've let poor Francis down. What should I do about that, do you think?'

Kate couldn't take her eyes off the glittering point of the long skewer. She was trapped. If she tried to get up, Adams could stab her even as she made her move. If she stayed where she was, she was completely at the ruthless killer's mercy, with nothing behind her but a sloping roof and a tumble to her death. She had been manoeuvred into a position where there was absolutely no escape.

Then as she futilely tried to think of a way out, the boom of the loudspeaker cut through everything. The public address system on the police car!

'Victoria Adams, this is the police. Release your hostage and give yourself up. Escape is impossible.'

'Sounds like the natives are getting restless, Kate,' Adams said with a heavy sigh. 'Nothing left for me to do then is there?'

Kate tensed for a last desperate attempt to try and over-power her, knowing in her heart of hearts that it was doomed to failure from the start. But just as her toes dug into the soles of her shoes and her hands pressed against the edges of the wall on each side for leverage, she was shocked to see Adams suddenly hurl the skewer over her head into the moonlight and heard it clatter away down the sloping roof. At first it seemed to Kate that Adams was going to comply with the instructions boomed out on the police p-a system and give herself up. But she could not have been more wrong.

The next second Adams stepped back a couple of paces and before Kate realised what she was about to do, she ran straight at the wall, leaping through the crenel in one bound. Kate shot to her feet, simultaneously jerking round to stare back over the wall, but Adams was already gone, a horrific fading scream accompanying her suicidal dive to the forecourt far below.

It was all over. A twisted multiple killer had finally paid the ultimate penalty for her sadistic crimes. In a perverse way justice had been served in the end, even if that meant both Broadmoor and Rampton had been cheated of yet another inmate for future psychological analysis . . .

AFTER THE FACT

Spring had come early in south-west Pembrokeshire. The hedgerows of the winding country lanes were ablaze with flowers and the patchwork of fields sloping down to an azure sea shimmered under a warm sun.

Fresh out of the shower, with a big, fluffy bath towel wrapped around her slim body and a hand towel wound around her wet hair, Kate leaned on the guard rail of the wooden decking and stared at the verdant green lawn falling away to a copse at the end of the half-acre boundary of the little cottage. Through the trees, the ocean, which formed part of the cottage's 'back garden', stirred gently in the heat haze, sending white-capped breakers marching into the shore below the cliffs in regimental lines as gulls wheeled noisily overhead. It was an idyllic scene and for a long time Kate just stood there, captivated by its magical beauty.

It was around eighteen months since the nightmare of Warneford Hall. The media feeding frenzy had finished long ago and life had moved on to other cases and traumas in the careers of both Kate and Hayden. Daphne and Tom Parsons had recovered from the effects of Adam's chloroform spray and, surprisingly, had agreed to carry on working at the hotel, which had been sold to a "brave" new entrepreneur. A new bridge had been erected over the river on the approach to the hotel to replace the temporary one the army had constructed at the time to enable the police investigators and forensic teams access to the crime scene, while the old barns and slurry pit had been removed and replaced with a smart tennis court and swimming pool. As for the police investigation itself, Kate and Hayden had played no further part in it, apart from attending the obligatory inquests, and the police case had finally been closed with the simple word: *Detected* printed on the front of the bulbous crime file now consigned to the archives. Together with other past murderous goings-on, legendary stories of spectral black dogs, witches and the hinky-punks, Warneford Hall and the ghost of Mawgana Keegan had become part of the dark history of the Somerset Levels. Something for crime buffs and historians alike to chew over and distort for their own ends in the future.

Once all the issues attached to the multiple murder case had been resolved, Kate and Hayden had made a momentous decision to take a twelve-month career break from the force on a much-needed sabbatical, to recharge their exhausted batteries and to devote their time to restoring a newly purchased holiday cottage in the little village of Freshwater East on the Pembrokeshire coast. It was a decision that had not been taken lightly. But the constant, unremitting stress of the job as a detective on Highbridge's busy CID; the pressure of delivering a successful result in each and every case, hampered by the petty bureaucracy of the system; the sleepless nights, bolted meals and intrusion on their private lives through long, unsocial hours and callouts: it had all finally taken its toll. They needed a rest and for Kate, exchanging the wilds of the Somerset Levels for those of south-west Pembrokeshire, albeit on a temporary basis, was a worthwhile trade-off. Receiving an assurance from Headquarters Personnel that, under police regulations, they would be able to return to their former roles in the force after their lengthy absence should they wish to do so, they had jumped at the opportunity.

Willow Cottage needed serious work on it to bring it up to an acceptable standard, but the lump sum they had received out of the blue in the will of one of Hayden's distant aunts had been like a dream come true, removing any financial constraints they might have faced. Kate had sold her Mazda MX5, which, after Warneford, had been on its last legs anyway, and they were now using just Hayden's beloved Mk II Jaguar. Their cottage in Burtle had been let out on a short-term lease, which meant they had not burned their boats and they now had time to consider what their long-term plans might be.

Kate was thinking about it all when Hayden suddenly joined her on the decking, having been out to purchase a newspaper for the crossword he loved to do.

'Heard about Ronnie Brewer?' he said.

She wheeled round to face him.

'Brewer? Now there's a blast from the past. What about him?'

He thrust his folded newspaper under her nose.

'Front page story in the *Telegraph*.'

She glanced curiously at the headline. It read: *SON OF TOP FINANCIER DIES IN FREAK YACHTING ACCIDENT.*

Snatching the newspaper from him, she scanned the first few paragraphs.

'His boat struck a rock near Jersey and sank yesterday evening,' Hayden recapped. 'No survivors apparently.'

She finished reading, then handed the newspaper back to him with a grim smile. 'So she got him in the end then,' she said.

He frowned. 'Who got who?'

'Victoria Adams — or Templeton, to use her real name.'

'I don't follow you. She's dead.'

Kate shook her hair free of the towel and began slowly drying it. 'So?'

He groaned and flicked his eyes at the blue sky. 'Oh come on, Kate, you're not suggesting she reached out for him from beyond the grave?'

'Stranger things have happened, you know,' she said. 'After all, he ended up drowning, didn't he? Just the way she wanted.'

'It was an accident.'

She smiled wanly. 'Of course it was, Hayd. An "accident" just waiting to happen. But for now, the sun is shining, the birds are singing. So let's forget the past and head down to the beach for a skinny dip.'

His jaw dropped with shock. 'A what? Good lord, no. We could be arrested.'

She shook her hair free of the hand towel, then released the towel wrapped around her body so that it dropped to the decking.

'Then let's live dangerously,' she said. 'What is there to lose?'

THE END

THE JOFFE BOOKS STORY

We began in 2014 when Jasper agreed to publish his mum's much-rejected romance novel and it became a bestseller.

Since then we've grown into the largest independent publisher in the UK. We're extremely proud to publish some of the very best writers in the world, including Joy Ellis, Faith Martin, Caro Ramsay, Helen Forrester, Simon Brett and Robert Goddard. Everyone at Joffe Books loves reading and we never forget that it all begins with the magic of an author telling a story.

We are proud to publish talented first-time authors, as well as established writers whose books we love introducing to a new generation of readers.

We have been shortlisted for Independent Publisher of the Year at the British Book Awards three times, in 2020, 2021 and 2022, and for the Diversity and Inclusivity Award at the Independent Publishing Awards in 2022.

We built this company with your help, and we love to hear from you, so please email us about absolutely anything bookish at feedback@joffebooks.com

If you want to receive free books every Friday and hear about all our new releases, join our mailing list: www.joffebooks.com/contact

And when you tell your friends about us, just remember: it's pronounced Joffe as in coffee or toffee!

9 781835 261491